Hell and High Water

A Maeve Malloy Legal Thriller

Keenan Powell

Three Hooligans Press

To Jane Does and John Does across the world and throughout time

"Continuing to build after a strong start, Powell turns her beady eye and compassionate heart towards the corrosive nature of old secrets and the dangers of reckoning with the truth at last. Maeve Molloy's third outing is atmospheric, gritty and completely satisfying."

-Catriona McPherson, multi-award-winning author of *Strangers at the Gate*

"*Hell and High Water* is part closed room mystery, part wilderness adventure, and part hard-boiled reluctant hero. World-weary Maeve Malloy must uncover a killer from a handful of suspects and avoid becoming a rampaging bear's next meal. Keenan Powell is at the top of her game!"

-Matt Coyle, author of the Anthony Award winning Rick Cahill series

"Nuanced characters and an edgy atmosphere in Hell and High Water will keep you up way past your bedtime. You'll want to add this book and the rest of the Maeve Malloy series tops on your to-be-read list."

-J.D. Allen Author of the Sin City Investigation Series

Contents

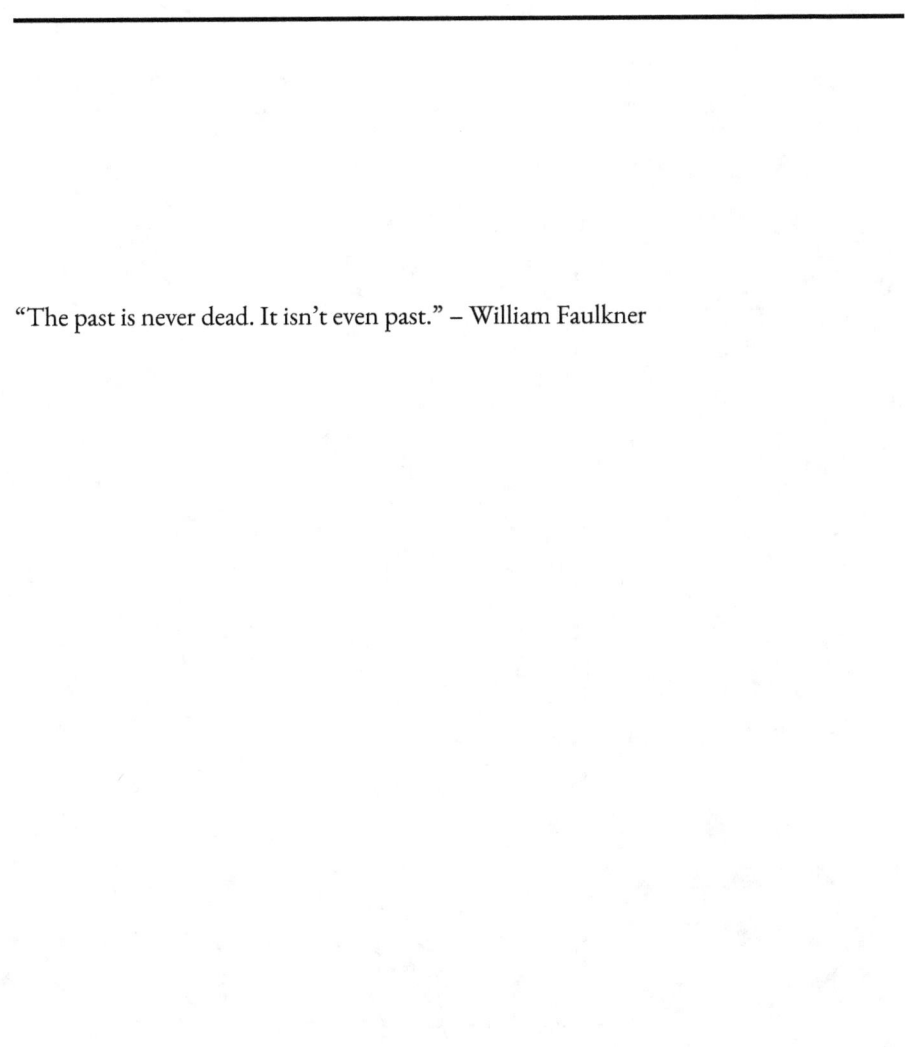

"The past is never dead. It isn't even past." – William Faulkner

Chapter One

A KILLER WHALE BREACHED. A full, flying-through-the air breach. Black bullet body, white spots and a black dorsal fin erupted. Sparkling droplets geysered from the roiling gash it had torn in the steel-gray surface. The monster hung in the air like a ballerina, and then rolled to one side, flopped, and sank out of sight.

From her booth in the glass-domed train, Maeve Malloy imagined hearing the mighty splash, a bubble of sound inside her mind drowning out the cacophony of excited tourists, cameras pointed in the direction where the whale had been.

This would have been Maeve's first vacation. She hadn't dared to take time off before. Ever. She worked weekends and evenings through college and law school, studying every morning before dawn. And then there were the sixty-hour weeks at the public defender's office: arraignments, bail reviews, motion hearings, trials, consulting with her client, interviewing witnesses, scouring through evidence, and drafting briefs when she wasn't either in court or asleep. And after going into private practice, she worked even harder and slept even less.

That didn't matter anymore.

The train rocked gently along the coastline, lulling her to let go, relax, unwind. Her hands felt heavy and warm. She rested her head on the seatback as the trees dwindled revealing choppy slate gray waters, Turnagain Arm, an offshoot of Cook Inlet, backed by the mountains of the Kenai Peninsula.

A long uneventful summer yawned before her. She had just quit the paralegal job created for her by her mentor, Arthur Nelson. Organizing files, doing legal research, all backroom stuff. It had been kind of him to find a place for her although she knew he had an ulterior motive. He wanted to ease her into an associate position when the suspension was over.

The back-office atmosphere at Nelson and Associates had been poisonous. Maeve had tried to talk to the other paralegals, although they were distant, distrusting, resentful.

They knew when Arthur had taken her in, some other new hire who needed the money to support her family didn't get a job. They knew her suspension would soon be over. They expected her to morph back into a lawyer again, the profession they served and despised. Right now, they called her "Maeve" but someday in the future, they would be forced to address her as "Ms. Malloy." No one would ever address one of them with an honorific. And, for all lawyers knew, paralegals didn't have a last name.

What they didn't know was that her three-month suspension had ended in May. She could have applied for readmission any time, yet she hadn't.

She'd fantasized about leaving law altogether. Do something fun. Work in a flower shop or a café or a cupcake van. Something where she interacted with people all day long. Simple problems she could fix by handing a bouquet, a cupcake, or even a latte over a gleaming counter. She would learn her regulars' names and ask about their families. They would like her and accept her. Just another ordinary working person.

A couple of weeks ago, she had been sitting alone in her Subaru during the lunch hour, picking at a plastic container of leftover dry baked salmon and rice, scrolling through a help-wanted site on her cell phone. The other paralegals and secretaries were having a birthday party for one of their own in the breakroom. She had not been invited so rather than hang around the office looking like the wallflower she was, she hid out in her car in the parking lot behind the building. If anyone she knew came by, she would start the engine and drive around the block, giving the appearance of attending to a lunch-time errand.

That's when she saw the Seward job advertised. Kitchen helper. It was perfect. Maybe she'd even learn how to bake. She called the lodge manager and got the job.

After lunch, she slipped into Arthur's over-sized corner office with floor-to-ceiling windows overlooking Cook Inlet, walked across the thick carpet so cushy each step seemed to launch her into the air, and stood tentatively at his desk, toying with a silver paperweight.

Arthur was in a crisp white shirt and dark blue silk tie. His blazer gone, probably hanging in a closet hidden in the paneling. He was leaning back in his chair, pushed away from his massive desk, legs crossed ankle on knee, reading a packet of papers. His silver hair was neatly combed.

Without looking up, he asked, "What's up, kid?"

"Think I'm out of here."

Arthur put his papers down. He tilted forward, waved her toward a chair.

She didn't move.

"I thought you were happy with us."

"It's not that," Maeve said. She looked around for an explanation. Beyond the windows, white fluffy clouds chased across the sky, the silver waters of Cook Inlet glittered.

"Just think I'd like to get out of town, catch the rest of the summer. When am I ever going to get a chance like this again?" she said, then looked at him. "You know?"

He frowned. "And go where?"

She took in a deep breath. "There's a job at a Fox Island Lodge. Sounds like fun."

"A summer job," he said flatly.

"Yeah, just a summer job."

"Can you get by on what they pay you?"

She was just barely making her mortgage as it was on the salary Arthur paid her. One or two late payments wouldn't matter. Besides, if she lost the condo, she could always live in the cupcake van. Maybe. She'd have to see if there were any health regulations that said someone couldn't live in a food truck.

"Sure," Maeve lied. "Thanks for asking."

She floated out of his office. A summer in Seward, Alaska, and then one step closer to rolling around Anchorage in a bright pink van. She could almost taste the buttercream frosting.

Her own law office was gone. She'd sold her furniture and equipment, her phone had been disconnected, her team, such as it was, disbanded. Mike Dimitri, the attorney across the hall, had moved his practice out of town. Tom Sinclair, her investigator, had gone fishing. He was crewing on a halibut charter like he'd threatened every time he got frustrated with her. She wondered if he liked cupcakes.

When she debarked the train, a boat would take her to Fox Island in Resurrection Bay made famous by the artist Rockwell Kent. There she would work at an eco-lodge. The glossy advertising materials showed guests hiking through wildflowers and kayaking amongst California gray whales as puffins bobbed in the water and sea lions sunned themselves on rocks. Fresh local produce. Crisp white bed linens. Recycled this and that. Dedicated to leaving a small footprint on Mother Earth.

The glass-roofed compartment was crammed with tourists. Overhead, a pale gray sky flickered in the tree canopy bathing the train in a soft light. Coffee, pancakes, and sausage being prepared in the kitchen below filled the air with a warm, slightly humid, pleasing smell.

An opera of different voices, different accents, and different languages filled the compartment as Maeve's fellow travelers pointed excitedly out of the window. She stood to see what had caught their attention. That's when she saw a second killer whale breach. And another. And another.

There was a great churning of water as the whales descended beneath the surface, forming a circle around their prey. A run of king salmon maybe. Or a perhaps a single beluga – one of those smiling white whales who seemed a little dim-witted.

Killer whales were the wolves of the sea. They weren't whales at all but giant dolphins with teeth. They hunted in packs, taking turns harassing the prey until it was too tired and injured to defend itself. Then they moved in for the kill, ripping chunks out of the victim, eating it alive.

Survival of the fittest, the great chain of life. This is Alaska, and, as Tom had so often said, it ain't no theme park.

A man leapt from his seat for a better view just as the train jostled, holding his beer bottle aloft. Droplets of beer splattered in Maeve's hair, on her face, and across her T-shirt.

"Sorry," he said, then turned his attention to the whales.

"No problem," Maeve said. The smell made her gag. She wiped the damp from her hair and face. Now her hands smelled like beer.

"How wonderous is our Lord's creation," said the nun sitting across the aisle. When she had first taken her seat, she introduced herself as Sister Mary Ignatius, "Sister Iggy" for short. Her fragile-appearing companion was Sister Clare.

Maeve had hoped for a leisurely ride, lost in reverie. Birds flying overhead. Moose, Dall sheep, and bear grazing alongside the train tracks. Mountains and lakes. And trees. Lots and lots of trees.

"Yes, Sister," Maeve said. It was an automatic reaction. She was surprised to hear the words come out of her mouth after all this time.

Maeve was trained to defer to nuns. She had been a charity student in a convent school where she received a rigorous course of studies that led to college scholarships and then to law school. After she left, she realized living in a convent school must be a lot like prison. So many rules and schedules. The nuns even called their rooms "cells."

These nuns were nothing like Mother Superior. They wore calf-length dove gray robes with fitted sleeves. No room to hide a ruler. Sister Iggy was square-faced with kind denim blue eyes, thick eyebrows that begged to be plucked, and the beginnings of a downy mustache. Fawn-colored hair streaked with white was pulled tightly underneath a white headband and short veil. Frown and laugh lines contoured her face in equal measure.

The younger one, Sister Clare, was small and thin with very pale skin and a smattering of large freckles which made her look younger than she probably was. She didn't speak when Sister Iggy introduced her and merely glanced at Maeve. Sister Iggy had guided Clare into the window seat where she spent the entire trip staring out.

When the whales sank back into the water, the tourists' voices petered out with disappointed muttering. Good thing, they didn't understand the slaughter that was taking place just beneath the water's surface. Good thing, the seeping blood couldn't be seen from this distance.

Maeve sipped her mocha from a paper cup. It had gone cold and tasted bitter. She excused herself to no one in particular and walked down the cramped aisle to the tiny bathroom. She washed her face, dried her hair with paper towels, and scrubbed her hands. Her T-shirt still reeked of beer, so she took it off, stuffed into her backpack, and zipped her hoody to her throat, catching a bite of skin. She unzipped it a modest one-half inch.

When she returned to her seat, the train had wound away from the inlet and into the forest. After a while, the tourists began chatting.

The waitress pushed up the aisle with a trolley laden with bottles of champagne and plastic cups. When she stopped at their row, she poured a cup of bubbly for each nun. Then as she turned to face Maeve, Maeve said. "None for me thanks."

"Can I get you anything else?" the waitress asked. By then, Maeve felt she had the full attention of Sister Iggy. Maeve was obviously of Irish descent. She didn't drink. There was bound to be an interesting explanation.

"Another mocha would be great, thanks."

After the waitress moved on to the next row, Sister Iggy gave Maeve a knowing smile. She probably had guessed Maeve was a recovering alcoholic. Just as well, no explanations were needed.

The man next to Maeve was engrossed in looking out his own window, camera held up, poised to take another photograph. Maeve thought she'd escaped social niceties when Sister Iggy reached across the aisle and touched her arm for attention. "Are you fortunate to live in this glorious state?"

Lying outright to a nun would have earned the ire of Mother Superior, not that she would find out from beyond the grave. Just in case there was an afterlife, Maeve didn't want to get called into the heavenly principal's office for breaking a commandment, much less involving a nun.

"Anchorage," said Maeve.

"How very lucky you are."

Maeve smiled politely. She didn't feel lucky.

She didn't miss the grueling drudgery of trial work. Eighteen-hour days, searching for that one witness who would break the case open, hypervigilant to the point of obsessiveness, reviewing the files over and over again, long hours of brief writing, court all day with no time for a real meal, eating stale crackers and cookies from vending machines, waking up in the middle of the night screaming "Objection!"

She was tired of being the hero of someone's story and, at the very same time, the villain to others. If she was her client's hero, defending him from the crushing prosecutorial machine, she was a villain to the prosecutor and cops who wanted to put that guy away. Other times, when a client didn't like what she'd told him, he'd accuse her of being in bed with the prosecutor, not true, and still the prosecutor wanted to squash her like a bug. Win-lose and lose-lose. And that was before the judge and jury weighed in.

If she was honest, she missed the big wins. Like most attorneys, she was a glory hound. Tom always said, if you own the wins, you got to own the losses too. She didn't want to own the losses. She was tired of making decisions that impacted other people forever, sometimes destroying lives.

She was so very tired, far more tired than a twenty-nine-year-old should be.

Right now, she just wanted to be like everyone else, see what it was like not to be judged because she was a lawyer, assessed by people as either hero or villain, reviled or glorified accordingly. An ordinary human being. Maybe even make some friends like normal people do. Sitting on this train surrounded by strangers could be an opportunity to practice small talk. After that, she'd never see the nuns again for the rest of her life.

"Actually," Maeve said. "I'm going to work at a lodge in Seward for the rest of the summer."

"What lodge is that?"

"Fox Island."

"What a coincidence!" Iggy said with an easy smile. "That's where we're going, too!"

Oh, hell.

Chapter Two

GRACE ENTERED THE LITTLE box of an office that was hers. She paused at the threshold, as she always did, lifted her right hand, and lightly touched the photograph on the wall next to the door. It was his first-grade school picture. He had been so excited that morning. He came out of his room wearing his favorite caped crusader t-shirt.

"Is that what you're going to wear, Danny?" she asked. She was sitting at the kitchen table with a cup of coffee in front of her, feeling like she had been electrocuted.

"My name is Dan the Destroyer," he said. "When I grow up, I'm going to kill all the bad guys and take care of you, Mom." He grabbed milk from the fridge, cereal out of a cabinet, found a bowl and spoon, and made himself breakfast.

She couldn't remember what she had said back to him; she had been that hungover.

The photo was hung so that the only person who could see it would be her. He was her son and no one else's. The desk took up most of the room of the cell-like office, leaving space only for a file cabinet and one visitor chair. No windows and just the one door facing out into the rest of the world. Her chair backed to the wall, her favorite spot in a room, just like old Wild Bill Hickock, so no one could sneak up behind her.

She scooted around the desk and sat down, remembering the times when he visited her in prison, and how the sight of his face, even on the other side of a window, was both salve and poison. She had drunk up the nearness of him, imagined his little-boy played-hard-outside smell, his tiny body curled up on her lap, his silky hair brushing against her cheek. As he looked through the grimy window at her, there was terror in his eyes. How much it must have scared her little boy being marched through cold cement hallways by big, unsmiling jailers, the jangling keys, the heavy steel doors banging near and far.

She'd hoped he couldn't remember the string of men coming and going from their dingy apartment at all hours, her drunks, hangovers, rages, the mornings he tried to wake her, shaking her shoulder, whispering "Mommy, Mommy" so she would take him to school. She would roll over to get away from him and later yell at him because he let her oversleep. Could he have forgotten the times she disappeared into her bedroom for hours with some guy while he sat in front of the television with a bowl of cold cereal, sodden with chocolate milk because she couldn't be bothered to go to the store.

He was better off without her. She had no one to blame but herself. And she couldn't make it up to him now.

She fingered the tattoo on her left arm, the arm nearest to her heart, a band of forget-me-nots. Perfect. Forget-me-not. She never would.

She pictured the revolver in the bottom desk drawer. It was the same thought her mind always traveled to after the jailhouse memory, having filled herself with as much guilt and shame as she could conjure.

Fresh air gushed into the room. Someone must have opened the lodge's big front door. A shadow crossed the reception desk, then a large figure of a man drifted into view.

She skirted around the desk and out of the office. The lower leg prosthesis wobbled as she took the two steps towards the reception counter. Most of the time she could walk on that thing without thinking about it. But sometimes she had to focus, place it exactly where her weight would slide into the boot without torqueing her knee.

"Can I help you?" Grace said to the man who stood across from her, the man she had been waiting for.

Tall, sandy-haired with strong regular features, some would have thought him handsome when he was younger. Age had added flesh to the jawline. He wore a plaid flannel shirt and one of those many-pocketed vests birdwatchers liked, all crisp and clean. His jeans had a crease ironed down the middle. Who ironed their jeans? No one. Someone did it for them.

He pulled himself to his full height and looked down his nose at her, clearly expecting bowing and scraping. She'd be damned if she gave him the satisfaction. She still lived by the code of the biker chick. Suck up to no one.

He paused before he answered, giving Grace an extended opportunity to worship. When she didn't, he spoke in a deep voice, reserved with the slightest hint that he could be charming if he so chose. "Greetings. I believe I'm expected. Francis Nolan."

Pompous ass. He might as well hold out his ring for the kissing.

"Have the guests arrived?" he asked. "On my walk up from the pier, I took a little detour up the path into the woods. There is a beautiful display just outside your door.

Chocolate lilies, bog rosemary, columbine, wild roses. We could take an early morning hike right after breakfast."

"That's right!" Grace snapped her fingers. "You're the flower guy!"

An angry light flickered in his eyes. Bull's eye!

She said, "There wasn't as much interest as we'd hoped, but to answer your question, everyone who signed up is here. The meet and greet is after dinner, in the conference room." She nodded in the direction of a door just off the lobby.

"I'll order from room service so could someone give me a call when dinner is over? I'd like to check my slide show, make sure it's working correctly. You know how computers can be."

Like that was going to happen. "Dinner is buffet, Frank. You're welcome to fix a plate for yourself and take it back to your room."

Just like everyone else.

Nolan smiled, looking like a wolf baring its teeth. He scanned her face like he was memorizing it for later when he would want to repay her rudeness. "My name is Francis Nolan." His eyes then dropped to the forget-me-not tattoo partially covered by her t-shirt sleeve. His shaggy eyebrows lifted briefly, came together, wiggled and then settled back down. They looked like caterpillars trying to escape.

When he raised his eyes again, they returned to her face without slowing across her chest. Before dinner, she'd dig out that low-cut T-shirt that showed boobs and tats galore. He'll love the dragon.

He said, "I would like to thank the lodge owners for inviting me to this event, if they're around. Resurrection Bay is a unique ecosystem. By the way, do you know how it came by that name?"

In Alaska, there was no shortage of strange place names and stories to go along with them. It didn't take much of an imagination to figure out how a town got named Chicken or Coldfoot or Dead Horse.

Point in fact, Grace was a recent transplant to the Last Frontier. It might as well be a foreign land, so different from the America she knew. In Alaska, everything was classified as "Alaskan" or "not-Alaskan." Long-time Alaskans could tell by looking at someone if they were new. Maybe it was the clothes. Maybe it was the suntans.

Grace had been here longer than Francis Nolan, even if it had only been a few months. He had just arrived this morning by jet, so he shouldn't be lecturing her on Alaska. While she thought about her come back, how snarky she could make it, she lost her rhythm. He started talking again.

"It was named by a Russian ship captain who sought harbor here during a storm. The storm passed on Easter Sunday and so he named the bay 'Resurrection.'"

"Lucky sea captain," Grace said. "Not everyone gets a second chance, Frank."

That fire in Nolan's eyes went out. And Grace was pleased.

"Are the owners about?" Nolan asked.

About? She snorted. "Sure, they're somewhere. You're bound to run into them at dinner. Bernie and Lester. She's our chef. You'll know her by the apron. Lester does the handyman stuff. He's usually carrying a hammer."

She slid the room key in his direction. The lodge still used real door keys, not having the money for fancy electronic locks. When guests asked about it, Bernie passed off the old-fashioned keys as vintage and a nod to the lodge's history.

As Nolan drug his carry-all towards the guest rooms, Bernie rounded the corner wiping her hands on her apron. She'd spent the morning in the kitchen prepping tonight's dinner, stressing over having enough food for so many guests. Not that the lodge was full, but there were more folks than they had before. Grace stuck her head in a few times that morning to top off her coffee, only to get barked at.

When Bernie caught an eyeful of Nolan, she froze in her spot. The long beaded earrings dangling from her droopy holes swayed back and forth from her sudden loss of momentum.

She watched as he rolled his suitcase down the hall. After he disappeared, she practically hopped to Grace's side. "What's he doing here?" Bernie hissed. She was so close, Grace could smell the stink of last night's booze.

Bernie's hair was pulled back into a sloppy braid, dark pouches sagged over her cheeks, and the web of blood vessels in her nose shone. She was suffering with an especially-nasty hangover this morning.

"He can't hear you. He's gone," Grace said, just a little louder than needed to be heard. Bernie winced.

Bull's eye! Two in one morning. It was going to be a good day.

"He's our flower guy. For the weekend event. You remember, don't you? I told you about it a bunch of times. And, guess what! He wants to take a hike up the path into the woods. First thing in the morning."

"Oh, dear God," Bernie said. "Grace McNair, what have you done?"

***

MAEVE STEPPED OFF THE train and squinted as dazzling light stabbed her eyes. A few thin clouds were useless for shielding the sun. Light shimmered across the harbor waters, flashed off the masts, and gleamed on boat hulls. She dug in her backpack, past the beer-soaked T-shirt, found her sunglasses and put them on.

She checked her phone and found no voicemails and no texts, not that she was expecting any. It was hard to get out of the habit of checking, hard to relinquish the gnawing feeling someone somewhere needed her. It seemed the world was getting along quite well without Maeve Artemis Malloy.

It'd been over a week since she had heard from Tom. He had sounded remote, distracted. He was beginning a new life with new people that didn't include her.

The nuns climbed down from the train and joined her. Screaming seagulls wheeled overhead. Sister Clare threw up a defensive arm and cowered. Sister Iggy smiled knowingly at Maeve – yes, there's something wrong with that girl, try to overlook it. "Nothing like the sea air," Iggy said. All Maeve smelled was rotting fish. "Nothing like," she agreed.

Maeve glanced at the time on her phone. They had an hour before the boat left for Fox Island and she was hungry. She wanted to ditch the nuns already. Four hours on the train of small talk had been exhausting, and she was beginning to resent the intrusion on the grand sulk she had planned.

But this was day one of her new life as a normal person, a man amongst men, a woman amongst women, just another blade of grass in the meadow. What would normal people do after having just met someone going in the same direction? Suggest they walked together, she supposed.

"Would you two like to grab a bite to eat?" Maeve asked.

"We would," Sister Iggy said, speaking both for herself and Sister Clare.

Maeve shouldered her backpack and started down the boardwalk with the nuns lugging their old-fashioned suitcases. As they drew closer to the tourist shops, the fishy odor gave way to something hot and fried. Maeve stopped in front of a food cart and read the menu: reindeer hotdogs, smoked salmon hotdogs, and for the timid, all beef hotdogs.

"Ladies?" asked a short, bullish man with long gray hair wearing a greasy apron.

"Reindeer, spicy," Maeve said.

"Good choice," he said and reached into his icebox.

"Are they really made from reindeer?" Sister Iggy asked.

"Yes, ma'am."

The nuns conferred quietly, then Iggy said, "Two beef, please."

As the cook put sausages on the grill, Maeve felt a presence sidle up to her and the crisp blue uniform of an Alaska State Trooper filled her peripheral vision. At her eye level was a name plate inscribed "P. E. Kelly." The man was huge, even taller than Tom not that Tom would admit it.

Maeve and Tom had met Patrick Edward "King Kong" Kelly on a fishing rights case a few years ago in Ketchikan. The trooper had grown up in Southeast Alaska, a member of a large Tlingit family who had lived on, hunted and fished that area since the beginning of time. After he hit his growth spurt and it didn't seem it was going to stop, the other kids started calling him King Kong. The name stuck.

Tom had taken an immediate liking to King, bonding over the art of fishing. The two disappeared for a week every summer just when the first run of red salmon arrived.

"Howdy, Counselor." Trooper Kelly said as he touched the brim of his hat.

"Good to see you, King." She tried to sound like she meant it.

It was the line she'd practiced for bumping into people from her recent past. She'd found it useful. If she said, "how are you?" the other person would respond "how are you" and she would either need to lie or obfuscate, not wanting to talk about it. Instead if she said, "good to see you," the other person responded in kind and then she could direct the conversation to the weather.

"Had you going there for a minute, didn't I? Maybe got some unpaid parking tickets?" King's expression was friendly. "Looking pretty guilty to me."

"I was raised Catholic," Maeve gave her stock answer. "We're imbued with free-floating guilt. It keeps us in line."

Sister Iggy cleared her throat.

"Sorry, sister," Maeve said. *And there you have it*, Maeve thought, *I'm apologizing for feeling guilty.*

Standing on the boardwalk of Seward Harbor, thousands of miles from parochial school, and the church she'd taken her First Holy Communion and Confirmation, it suddenly struck Maeve as odd that she'd have a stock answer to the question "Why do you look guilty?"

Is that normal?

"Sisters," Maeve said, "this is Trooper Kelly. Trooper, this is Sister Ignatius and Sister Clare. We met on the train."

"Ladies," King said, touching a finger to his hat brim. She'd bet he'd seen that move on a TV show.

"Nice to meet you, Trooper Kelly," Sister Iggy said. "Sister Clare is very interested in your local history. Would you mind if she asked you a few questions."

"Here to serve, ma'am. Go right ahead."

Sister Clare had fished a tourist guide out of her habit and was thumbing through it. "Can you tell us where the Indian villages are?" Her voice was so quiet, they all had leaned in to hear her.

Maeve felt her shoulder muscles tighten. In Alaska, the indigenous peoples are known as Alaska Natives, a term that is more respectful than "Indian" or "Eskimo."

King gave no hint that he was offended. "Yes, ma'am. You can't see it from here but there was a Chenega village further up the bay, but it's gone now. The '64 earthquake swept a third of the people out to sea. So the ones left upped and moved over to Prince William sound." He looked down at the little nun, waiting for another question.

The color drained from her face. She put her book away and wiped her eyes.

"We had no idea," Iggy said.

"It's one of those historical footnotes you hear about," King said. He took in a deep breath, hooked his thumbs in his belt and looked around. "Tom with you?"

"Halibut fishing in Homer," Maeve said.

"I should give him a call."

"So you should." The conversation died out. They stood awkwardly side by side, King looking down at her. He knew. He'd heard the story. She could tell.

"Order's ready, ladies," the cook said.

Maeve doctored her hotdog with mustard, onions and a dash of Tabasco, just in case the hotdog wasn't hot enough.

"Where're you headed?" King asked.

"Fox Island Lodge."

"Nice place. Taking some time off for yourself, or something?"

"Something like that," Maeve answered.

King waited for an explanation. Maeve took a big bite of her hotdog.

"Then I'll be seeing you around, Counselor," he said. He touched his hat brim again and said to the nuns, "Have a safe trip, ladies." He walked down the boardwalk, picked up a hot dog wrapper the breeze was pushing toward the water, and threw it in a garbage can.

The nuns turned to each other. Whispering ensued. When they broke apart, Sister Clare smiled up at Maeve, her cheeks warmed with some emotion. "Is Tom your boyfriend?"

"Tom?" Maeve laughed, a little too loud. "Sh...I mean, shoot, no. Tom and me? No way."

The nuns looked at her with conspiratorial smiles.

"He was just someone I worked with," Maeve lied again. To a nun, no less. Sure enough, she was going to burn in hell.

***

BERNIE STOOD IN THE kitchen doorway, wiping her hands on her apron, staring into the forest. From where she stood, she could see the path where there was a dark shape uphill deep in the woods. It was her log cabin, the one she shared with Lester.

They had fixed up the old cabin, so they could have some privacy after a day of mothering tourists. Or so they'd planned when they first bought the place.

Lester ambled down the path, his loose limbs gliding as if he knew every tree root, every rock, every divot. A shotgun was broken across his arm. As long as she'd known him, he always had something in his hands. A hammer, a screwdriver, a shotgun, a joint.

"Lester!"

He looked up, saw Bernie standing in the door and adjusted his course in her direction. He slowed and said, "yep?"

She motioned him closer.

When he was in front of her, she said. "Grace invited Francis Nolan for the weekend."

"What the..."

"And he's here."

"But..."

"But he *is* the flower guy she's been talking about. And he wants to take a hike in the woods, take everyone up the hill to see the flowers. First thing in the morning."

"No shit?"

"No shit. So, you know, do whatever you got to do."

Chapter Three

TOM SINCLAIR SAT IN a window-side booth and watched a charcoal-colored smudge on the horizon churning in his direction.

He took a long drag off a cigarette wedged between two fingers then reached for the coffee mug. His right hand, big and boney, came into view. It was red and chapped with cuts he didn't remember getting. He turned the hand over, examined the palm. Yellow calluses lined the rim. More cuts. He pulled the left hand into view. It was the same.

These were the hands of a man who worked for a living, not the soft white hands of the private investigator he had been. Before, he had been paid, and paid well, for his services at the Public Defender's office. But taking the money felt dirty.

He wasn't smarter than anyone else. He didn't have a college degree. There was no good reason why he became a private investigator. He just fell into it. He had a knack for talking people up. It wasn't talking so much as listening, looking interested, and remembering their names. People like that.

His knack had come in handy gambling. In between boat crew jobs, he'd make ends meet with poker. One night, in an after-hours club, he'd met some lawyer a stripper on each arm. That lawyer liked to hang in the underworld fringe late at night, as if no one knew he led a double life. The joke was on him. All the other lawyers knew, and all the players sure as hell knew, because his little partying buddies talked. They talked to anyone who'd listen once they got busted, hoping to trade juicy information for a better deal. He got disbarred a few years later for stealing money from a client to support his coke habit.

That lawyer figured out Tom could get information from real people, the people who didn't talk to lawyers, even sleazy lawyers, and he hired Tom to find a witness. The next thing Tom knew, he had a cushy job with benefits and paychecks every week of the year at the Public Defender's office.

And soft, white hands.

A tree branch scratched the window like it was trying to get inside, away from the incoming storm. At the docks across the street, boats bobbed at their lines. Eagles that usually flocked on the shore were nowhere to be seen.

Maeve should be tucked up safe and sound in that lodge. A big lodge like that would have a generator and lots of food and water stored. It would be built like a Sherman tank, sound enough to withstand even a hurricane. And it was a hurricane that was coming, to be sure, although the weather service didn't call it that.

Instead, they called it the "pineapple express." They usually didn't hit until fall or winter but last he checked, tropical storms didn't keep a calendar. One hundred mile an hour winds and torrential rain speeding towards Alaska from the tropics. If that wasn't a hurricane, Tom didn't know what was. Maybe he should call Maeve, just to make sure she was okay.

He took another drag of the cigarette, stubbed the end in the ashtray, folded it once, and crushed it out. The warmth of the dying ember seeped through his calluses. He was reaching for the cell phone in his pocket when a skinny arm extended in front of him. The waitress, that little blonde Tom had been flirting with, poured coffee, her tits in his face. Her T-shirt was so tight, he could see the lace pattern of her bra.

"Hey, stranger," she said.

He struggled to remember her name. It was the same as a month, January, February ....no, April.

He pulled back. Come to think of it, she wasn't cute at all. She wasn't ugly either, just plain. Ragged ends of blonde hair hung past her shoulders. Her skin was flaking. She had brown eyes under shapeless eyebrows. He hadn't noticed the rest of her face before because he was hypnotized by her lips, plump and full and slathered with bright pink lip gloss, and parted. The darkness of her open mouth invited fantasy.

He resisted the urge to adjust his pants.

People would say that she was too young for him. He didn't care. He was used to women hitting on him, young, old, and in-between. Not that he was pretty, he knew that. There were scars on his cheekbones and in his eyebrows from fighting. His nose was lopsided, broke too many times. Someone had said girls liked the size of his hands.

He grabbed three bags from sugar bowl, tore the ends off in one move, and poured the sugar into his cup. She watched his hands as he lifted a spoon from the table and stirred. Then he slowly, gently laid it facedown. The spoon's shell glistened as liquid dripped off.

The pink tip of her tongue ran along her upper lip.

"Hey, yourself," Tom said. He unbuttoned his sleeve cuffs and turned them up. The Rolex on his left wrist glittered. He had won it in a card game. It reminded him that no matter what happened, he could make his own fortune. Besides, girls like bling.

She glanced at the watch. "Not fishing today?"

"Weather rolling in," Tom nodded at the window, focused on her mouth. It hung a little bit open even when she was done talking.

"I get off at two." She rolled her shoulders back one at a time, making the bulging bra wave at him just at eye level. "Want some company while you wait out the storm?"

At least a C-cup, Tom figured. "Come to think of it," he said, "I sure would."

***

AFTER A CHOPPY RIDE across the bay, Maeve sat in the boat, still gripping the bench, while the skipper helped the nuns onto the floating dock. He followed them, carrying their bags towards the beach as Maeve hauled herself out of the boat. Water rushed across the slick mildew underfoot as the dock rolled with each swell. Her leg slid out and she fell. Blackness surrounded her. There was a buzzing in her ears.

"You okay?" the boatman called.

Her hip had taken the brunt of the fall. It felt numb. "Nothing injured but my pride," she answered. The blackness faded and her vision sharpened. She rolled over, carefully placed her feet, and pushed to a stand.

"You sure?" He put the suitcases down and started towards her.

She held up a hand. "No, please, I'm fine. Just embarrassed." Maeve slipped both arms through her backpack to balance the weight.

The nuns and boatman walked up the rocky beach to the big log-constructed lodge. It was grand in appearance, two stories high, with picture windows facing the waterfront and large, heavy wooden doors. Even from this distance, Maeve could see a giant set of moose antlers mounted over the front door. Very Alaskany. Several yards away lay a pile of split firewood with an ax planted in a nearby tree stump.

The boatman set the nuns' suitcases on the porch, then passed Maeve on his way back to the boat. She stood loose-limbed on the pier, rocking with the lapping waters, and watched him hop into his boat. For a moment, she thought she saw Tom instead, her mind playing tricks on her. She waved. The boatman jerked his head upward, just as Tom would have done. He untied the mooring, pushed away from the dock, and jerked on the starter chord.

The motor revved. The boat turned in a wide arc, heading back across the bay. The man faced forward, body angled as he rested one hand on the rudder. He looked as if he and the boat and the bay were perfectly-fitted pieces of their own little cosmos. Like he belonged. *What would that feel like?*

Standing in a courtroom was the closest Maeve had come to that feeling. Most of the time, she felt like she played dress-up pretending to be the fierce criminal defense attorney, but sometimes she instinctually knew what she should do. Now she didn't even have that.

The dock rolled again pitching Maeve off-balance. She slid to the edge, half her foot going over. If she went into the water with that backpack, it'd carry her to the bottom before she could pull out of it. Maeve righted herself and loosened the shoulder straps, better for dropping the load fast.

The nuns waited for her on the porch. As she walked up the beach, she passed dark pancakes deposited on the pebbles. Bear droppings with bits of fur just visible. Just as she was about to join them, a tan woman with bleached blonde hair came around the corner of the building and stopped abruptly. She wore tangerine-colored running shorts, a yellow sleeveless t-shirt, and lime running shoes. She blew out a lung-full of smoke. "I didn't know anyone was here."

"We just arrived," Sister Iggy said, then smiled, waiting for a response.

The woman blinked rapidly. Her eyes were so bright blue, they had to be contacts. "You won't tell my husband that I was smoking, will you? He thinks I went out for a jog."

How did she cover up the odor? Or did she and her husband have one of those little marital conspiracies where one partner lies and the other pretends to believe it, too tired to fight anymore?

The tableau froze. The woman appeared to wait for a promise. Iggy seemed caught between dishonesty and interpersonal conflict.

Maeve couldn't get past this cluster to go inside. Her hip was starting to ache and she wanted to lay down. "Won't say a word." She hitched up the backpack, hoping the gesture would inspire the nuns to move forward.

A gunshot cracked the silence and echoed. It was not too far away by the sound of it. Lime Shoes jerked. Clare took a step closer to Iggy.

"Hunters?" Iggy asked Maeve.

It was way too soon for moose season. "Maybe," Maeve said.

***

To the parents of Danny Johnson,

I'm sorry that you were unable to attend parent-teachers conference, and hope you are feeling better. It was a delight having Danny in my first-grade class this year. He was an attentive student, got along well with his classmates, always cooperative, thoughtful and kind. I look forward to watching his progress at St. Francis.

Yours Truly,

Miss Granger

Chapter Four

GRACE HEARD A GUNSHOT. A few minutes later, the lodge's heavy front door opened and the two nuns she had been expecting entered. Behind them were Sheila in her ridiculous jogging outfit and a fourth woman with wild auburn hair. The new kitchen helper, Grace supposed.

"Sisters!" Grace said. She pulled out the hotel registry, about to sign them in, when she heard the backdoor bang closed and heavy boot stomping towards them. Lester strode into the lobby, rifle broken over his lanky arm, looking like a hillbilly: tall, skinny, sun-bronzed, baggy clothes, greasy light brown hair hanging to his shoulders, scraggly beard, dirt-smudged face covered in stubble.

"Damned bear," he said before he noticed the nuns. "Sorry, sisters."

"Same one?" Grace asked.

"Yup. It took down a cow moose between here and the cabin, right on the path. I took a shot at it before it got away." He noticed Sheila dressed in her bright jogging clothes. "Better not wander too far from the house, 'less I'm with you."

Keeping everyone afraid of the bear and inside the lodge worked perfectly into Grace's plan. *Good job, Lester, you finally did something right.*

"Pfft," Sheila said. "Bear, shmear."

"You won't think that when he tears your head off," Grace said.

Grace pointed in the direction of the brochure display. A sign hung over it: a picture of a brown bear and the word "Beware!" in red. "There's a flyer, tells you what to look for, what to do if you're attacked."

Sheila snorted. "Attacked?"

"Especially this time of year, bears come down to the water looking for fish. I'd sure as hell be hungry if I hadn't eaten in six months. Pissy too. You really don't want to get between a mama bear and her cubs. And you especially don't want to get near a bear kill, so don't go up the way towards the cabin."

"You're putting me on, right?" Sheila asked.

"Last year, a couple of joggers got separated," Grace began. "Husband took off ahead of the wife. When she came down the trail, she ran right between a mama bear and two cubs. The bear dragged her off the trail and all the time, she's playing dead. Husband had no idea what was going on. He was long gone."

"She lived?" Sheila asked, her breathing shallow.

Grace nodded. "Mama bear led her cubs back into the woods. The lady waited until she knew the bear was gone and walked herself back to their vehicle. Found her husband there playing on his cell phone."

"You don't have cars on this island."

"Wasn't here. This all happened up in Anchorage."

"Got any bear bells?" Grace asked.

"Bear---bells?" Sheila repeated the phrase slowly, apparently unsure of what she had heard.

"You know, like jingle bells. You can wear them on your wrist. Some folks attach them to their belt loops." Using his lips, Lester pulled a hank of mustache into his mouth and began sucking on it.

Sheila's face contorted. "Like Santa Claus?"

"Warns the bears you're coming," Grace said. "They don't want a confrontation any more than you do."

Lester spit out the mustache, the hairs of which glistened with spit. "You know what bear scat looks like?"

"Scat?"

"Bear sh—"

"Droppings," Grace interrupted. "Bear droppings."

Sheila looked from one to the other, then puffed herself up. "You're putting me on. Very funny, ha, ha. I'm not going to tell you what I think." She spun around and stalked down the corridor. A guest room door opened and slammed shut.

Grace watched Sheila disappear. It was a mistake inviting her. It hadn't been Grace's idea. That was Bernie's doing. Sheila was a wild card. There was no telling what she might do or say.

The newcomer was standing behind the nuns. She'd dropped her backpack on the floor and was paying close attention.

Grace spun the hotel registry around to face the guests. "Sisters," she said, "would you care to sign in?"

"Sister Ignatius and Sister Clare," the older nun said as she signed the registry for both of them. "Please call me Sister Iggy. Everyone does."

"Sure thing, Sister Iggy," Grace said as she placed two room keys on the desk, one for each nun. "You'll be sharing room 103. If there is anything you need, anything at all, please feel free to stop by the desk."

Sister Iggy thanked Grace, picked up the keys and her suitcase. Sister Clare didn't say anything. She seemed transfixed on a point in space, like a cat watching dust particles. "Sister?" Iggy said, to get her attention. The little nun snapped back to reality. She picked up her own suitcase and followed Iggy down the corridor to the guest rooms.

Something was definitely wrong with that girl. Nice for the convent to take her in. She wouldn't survive in this big, bad world on her own.

Grace turned to the newcomer. "You the new kitchen helper?"

"That I am!"

Grace had been expecting a college kid. "Kind of old for a summer job, aren't you?"

"Not as old as you."

Grace laughed out loud. "Touché! Maeve Malloy, right?"

"Right."

"Hey, Lester. Show Maeve around, would you?"

Lester had been standing to the side, watching the drama with Sheila, then studying the nuns. He shot Grace a dirty look. She knew how he hated Grace telling him what to do, as if he was the handyman. He owned this place, he and Bernie that is, and Grace worked for them. Or so she let them think.

"Grab your gear," he said to Maeve.

***

MAEVE PICKED UP HER backpack and fell in behind the handyman as he sauntered through the lodge. The decorating was very Alaskany. Bare logs for walls. Stone fireplace flanked by a leather couch and chairs. Bear skin mounted on the chimney. More antler racks hanging on the walls: moose, caribou, deer. Small pelts dangled from a hook as if the hunter had just come inside and hung them. The window overlooked the bay and the pier where Maeve had landed, the rocks, water, and trees on the far shore washed of color by ceiling of dark clouds.

"Are those yours?" Maeve asked, gesturing to the hides.

"Nah," Lester said. "Picked them up at a flea market in Anchorage. I don't hunt for sport. Don't believe in it. But, you know, that's what the tourists expect to see so that's what we got."

As she followed him, she noticed a spicy, green smell in his wake. Marijuana. She remembered it from her law school days. She had indeed inhaled.

Maeve held her breath. But she didn't want a contact high, not sure if she'd have to change her sobriety date if she accidentally got stoned. She didn't want to give up the sober time she had worked so hard for. That and the contents in her backpack was all she had.

The lobby opened onto a dining room with another picture window. The view was filled with a tree-covered slope. A footpath from the lodge disappeared into the trees.

"Is that where you saw the bear?" Maeve asked.

Lester stopped in the window. He pulled the lank of mustache into his mouth, sucking on it as he peered up the incline. "You can't see it from here. It's a ways up that path there." He seemed stuck, mesmerized by his thoughts, for a moment. He snapped out of it and slowly rotated his head around, spotting Maeve. "Oh, yeah," he said with a slow smile, apparently amused by himself.

Oh, yeah, he was high.

Lester pushed through a swing door and Maeve followed.

In the kitchen, a sink was set beneath the window overlooking the path into the woods. In the back corner was a door going outside. In the middle of the room was a butcher block counter-high table, a few stools shoved underneath, and a hippy-looking middle-aged woman chopping onions with a vengeance. Her long beaded earrings swung and shimmered with each whack.

"Bernie," Lester said. "Here's your new helper."

Whack.

"Bernie!"

Bernie dropped the knife, startled. "What?"

"This here's your new kitchen helper," Lester said.

"Maeve Malloy," Maeve said, stepping forward to offering her hand. Bernie looked at it as though she didn't know what it was for. This whole blending with real people wasn't working out so far. Maybe it'd help of Maeve didn't act like she was introducing herself in a business meeting.

Bernie was solidly-built, as tall as Maeve, with crinkly salt-and-pepper hair pulled back loosely, jeans, and a T-shirt with the image of a screaming eagle painted in a New Age style. She wiped her hands and accepted the offered handshake. It was then Maeve detected the odor of wine. The cook had all the signs: the ruddy nose and cheeks, baggy pouches, and yellowed eyes. This lady was a chronic boozer and her husband a pothead.

Bernie took a look at Lester with the gun broken over his arm. "I heard a shot."

"Bear." Lester jerked his head in the direction of the pathway. "Took down a cow moose up the hill."

"No shit?" Bernie asked.

"No shit."

"Did you get him?"

"Nope, ran off."

"He'll be back."

"Yup, he'll be back. Best keep everyone away from that path until he's done with that cow."

Bernie looked lost in thought. "Guess we can't go on that hike up the hill tomorrow morning."

"Guess not," Lester said.

While those two were talking, Maeve took in the rest of the room. No dead animals tacked the walls here, only shiny industrial surfaces. Beyond the butcher block table was a walk-in fridge. Along the remaining walls were cabinets and counters and an impressively large wine collection, the bottles racked, tipped downwards. There had to be thirty bottles at least. "Do you have something for me to do?"

"I got dinner under control," Bernie said. "Lester can show you to your room. Take a load off. Buffet's set up at five. Get your dinner and when you're done, help me clean up."

"Yes, ma'am."

"Bernie," Bernie said.

"Yes, Bernie."

"Off with you both," Bernie said. She had picked up the knife and was waiving it at them. "You're underfoot."

Lester turned and led Maeve back out through the dining room, the lobby, and then to a corridor to the guest rooms. Along the way, he pointed at stairs going to the second floor. "There's more rooms up there but no one's in them, except me and Bernie stay up there sometimes. Probably will tonight, 'cause of the bear. Grace has the first room on the left here on the first floor. See there? It says 'manager' on the door. So if you need anything, try her first before you come looking for us. We got some guests across the hall from her." They passed another pair of guest rooms facing each other. When they approached the third set of rooms, he said, "Here's the gym on the left. And this is your room on the right," he said pointing to the last door. At the end of the hall was a large door with an "exit" sign overhead. It wasn't a fire door usually seen in the backs of commercial buildings, but just a regular house door. Lester grabbed the knob and gave it a jerk. The latch clicked into place.

"Sometimes it drifts open," he said. "You might want to give it a tug when you come by. We don't want that bear wandering inside."

He said it like he wasn't joking, then he pushed open her room door. "Lock's broke on this one. Been meaning to get to it, but the generator's kept me busy. We never had a problem with stealing or anything around here, so your stuff should be safe enough."

"Is there another room, maybe on the second floor? I don't mind the stairs."

"Haven't finished remodeling all of them. This is all we got," he said without looking at her. It was a typical hotel room with twin beds, a couple of nightstands, a desk and chair, a dresser, and a small television. A couple of Alaska scene photographs hung on the wall, one over each bed. One of the aurora borealis, the other a dog team mushing through snow. "We don't have cable or anything," he said. "We got a bunch of videotapes if you want to watch something."

"I brought some reading." In the bottom of her backpack were several mystery paperbacks she'd picked up at the used bookstore.

A window looked out onto the rocky beach. Dark clouds were churning in the distance. Downward shreds from those clouds meant it was raining somewhere. "Looks crappy out there," Lester said.

She wanted Lester gone so she could check her cell phone for messages. He didn't look like he was in a hurry. He was chewing on his mustache again. "How's the cell reception out here?"

"Good as any place, I suppose." Then Lester looked around as if he had forgotten why he was there, then said, "I'd better get back to work. See you around."

She waited for Lester to leave the room, then pulled out the phone and checked. Plenty of bars but no calls and no texts.

Did Tom ever think about her?

***

AT HOME, MAEVE HADN'T appreciated how meditative dishwashing was. Pick up a pot from the counter, dunk it in soapy water, run a brush across it, rinse, inspect, then set it on the drain board. Glistening water streams away leaving behind a shiny, clean pot. It was a Zen thing.

Dinner had been awkward.

"It's overcooked," the tourist Lime Shoes had said. She had paused at the head of the buffet, stopping the guests' progression while she stared at the food platters, her plate empty except for a couple lettuce leaves.

Maeve was at the end of the line, loading her plate with salad greens, insurance against too many carbohydrates finding room on her plate, when she overheard the tourist complaining. Which wasn't hard to do.

Lime Shoes was picking at the three-foot long salmon fillet with a serving fork held in a diamond-encrusted hand. She had changed into shorts and a sleeveless t-shirt, the lean muscles of her arms apparent under tanned skin. Probably from playing tennis. Or a whole lot of time on a treadmill and in a tanning bed.

No reason to be snarky. The woman takes care of herself. Maeve sucked in her gut. Maybe she'd check out the gym after dinner.

"It isn't lox, dear," a tall balding man with black horn rim glasses said quietly. Trim as well, he was dressed in shorts and a polo shirt. "Perhaps they make fish differently in Alaska."

"Still—" Lime Shoes let the word hang in the air.

Maeve's stomach ached for food and the smell of salmon roasted with garlic and rosemary tortured her. She bent across the table, inventoried the dishes, and made her decisions while she waited for the line to get moving.

The nuns entered the room and fell in behind Maeve. Instantly Maeve regressed to a first grader, sitting upright at her desk wearing an itchy plaid wool uniform, hands folded, both feet squarely on the floor, eyes straight ahead. She could even hear heavy black shoes prowling the aisle behind her, the nun's rosary beads clacking inside the folds of her black robes.

Maeve looked at the shoes of the nun behind her in line. Lace-up leather affairs, just like the nuns of yore. Gray shoes, not black. Crepe soles had replaced Cuban heels. Quieter. All the better for sneaking up on school children.

Maeve stepped out of line. "Would you two like to go ahead of me?" she asked Sister Iggy.

"Are you sure?"

"Please," Maeve said. "I'm not that hungry."

As the nuns passed her, she hoped they couldn't hear her stomach growling.

Lime Shoes dished up a thin portion from the middle of the fish and moved toward a selection of sauces, marinated fern fronds, sourdough bread, small red potatoes, steamed vegetables, and the desserts. She topped her greens from a small pitcher designated as "lo-cal vinaigrette" and walked past the blueberry pie, ice cream with assorted toppings, chocolate suicide cake, and fruit compotes.

It's a vacation after all. Lots of hiking, maybe some time in the gym. A little splurge couldn't hurt.

The procession finally began moving. Maeve found an unoccupied table and was soon joined by the nuns who had been delayed by filling their teacups. *They can tell by looking at me, I was raised Catholic.* Her auburn Maid Marian curls had turned even more red in the sun. She had acquired a sprinkling of freckles underneath her green eyes walking from Arthur's office to court to file papers. Mother Superior used to say if you connected the dots on Maeve's face, they'd spell "Erin Go Bragh." *When was the last time I went to Mass?* Someone's bound to ask, sooner or later. She would need an answer, an honest one. "I can't remember" would make them scowl.

Maeve was slipping the second forkful of salad into her mouth when the nuns closed their eyes, bent their heads, and folded their hands to say grace. *Dammit, busted already. Would the rules be different if I wasn't Catholic? Maybe I'll tell them I converted to Buddhism. No, they'd offer to pray for my soul.*

Truth was, Maeve prayed plenty for her own soul. Every morning she prayed to be restored to sanity, to have her defects of character removed, to be relieved of the bondage of self. As the day wore on, she prayed for serenity sometimes ten or twenty times a day. She was white-knuckling her way through life one prayer at a time.

The nuns finished grace with slow large signs of the cross, touching each shoulder, their foreheads, their hearts. When they looked up, their eyes met Maeve's wide stare. She smiled. They smiled back.

Maeve tried to slide the food down her throat inconspicuously, choked, took a sip of water, and asked, "So, Sisters, what brings you to Alaska?"

Chapter Five

THE DINNER SCENE FADED from Maeve's mind as she reached for the next pot. Bernie was stacking cups and saucers on a trolley where she'd already placed a coffee urn. She took a step back and inspected her work. "Done."

She reached for the half-filled goblet of red wine she'd been working on ever since dinner. She wasn't gruff anymore. She seemed to be dancing to music that she could only hear, her head tilting right and left to the beat, a smile crossing her lips from time to time, light in her steps. Bernie had a buzz on.

Maeve remembered that glow. Towards the end of her drinking, she needed the first drink just to feel normal and only caught the glow after the second. Then she'd spend the rest of the night chasing that fleeting moment of all-was-right-with-the-world and finish up with her arms wrapped around the toilet, puking, and thinking about suicide.

Bernie's beaded earrings swayed as she knocked back the remaining wine. "Catch the door, will you?"

Maeve held the door while Bernie pushed the cart through. When they entered the meeting room, several people were seated around a long table. Maeve flashed on the bar association conference room where she sat the previous winter as she was being judged by a roomful of suits.

This room was different, she reminded herself. There was a screen and a projector with a laptop attached. The nuns were seated quietly at a table, their hands folded in front of them.

Lime Shoes had positioned herself next to the head of the table. The bespectacled man with her at dinner, he must have been her husband, was sitting next to her, curled away. At the front of a room, a large man in his sixties sat with one hip on the table as he chatted with her. He must have been the weekend speaker.

Grace was seated next to her husband and the nuns were opposite.

"Do we expect more participants?" The large man asked Bernie.

"That's the lot. And Maeve, here." Bernie jerked her thumb in Maeve's direction.

Bernie took a seat in the back of the room, leaving only one spot open. Next to Sister Iggy. Sister Iggy tapped her finger on the table in front of the empty chair, indicating to Maeve she should sit. Everyone turned to Maeve. Their attention made her itch all over. She wanted them to quit looking at her, so she did as she was told.

"Well, then, let's get started, shall we?" The man asked. "I'm Francis Nolan and I've spent a lifetime studying botany. My interest is in wildflowers. The organizers of this event kindly asked me to lead you good people on a series of hikes where we'll have the opportunity to glory in the wonderful abundance and diversity of Resurrection Bay's flora. I recently published a book about the wildflowers of the Pacific Northwest." He held a book in the air. "And I have several copies for sale." He patted a stack of books on the table.

"And who do we have here?" he motioned towards Lime Shoes. "Please tell us a little bit about yourself and what brought you to us."

"Sheila and Roger Wadsworth," Lime Shoes said with a little dance in her chair. Her speech loose, she played with the glass of red wine she held with both hands. "I'm an engineer in California and my husband works on the slope. You know, the north slope where they drill all the oil. I've never been to Alaska, so we decided to take a cruise during his two weeks off. We just got off a cruise ship and we always try to get some hiking in wherever we go. I don't know much about flowers, but the pictures in the brochure were so pretty, we thought we'd sign up." Her left hand fluttered in the air, her clunky diamond ring flopping on her finger.

Sheila's tanned skin was leathery and flushed. Her dark roots needed touching up. Her bright blue eyes looked odd against her complexion. She blinked frequently as if contacts bothered her. Although her husband didn't look her way, he was in tune to her every word, evident when he widened his eyes or barely nodded after each of her declarations. Nolan watched him, maybe to see if Roger had anything to say. Roger took a sip of his beer, noticed the attention upon him. He adjusted his hornrims, waved a hand in the air, and curled up again. Nolan turned to Grace.

"Grace," she said. "Remember me, Frank? We met when you registered."

Nolan's face tightened. If he had been a prospective juror and reacted to Maeve that way, she would have found a way to get him off the panel. He clearly didn't like Grace.

She had changed her shirt since the last time Maeve had seen her. Now she was wearing a low-cut T-shirt revealing a tattoo, a Chinese dragon, that seemed to crawl up from one breast. Nolan's eyes stuck on the tat. His face reddened. Grace smiled.

Lester stepped into the room and poured himself a cup of coffee. He leaned against the wall, one working boot crossed over the other. Nolan gave him a nod. Lester hoisted the cup in return salutation.

"Grace. That's right. You're the desk clerk," Nolan said, then to Bernie. "And you?"

"Bernie Parker." She jerked a thumb in Lester's direction. "This here is my husband, Lester. He and I own the place." Her speech was loose now, not quite slurring. She must have been nipping away all afternoon in the kitchen, drinking on the sly, which was why she had refused Maeve's offer of help.

"Good to meet you, Bernie and Lester Parker," Nolan said softly, looking at her like he was trying to remember something. Then he turned to the nuns. "And you, Sisters?"

"This is Sister Clare and I'm Sister Ignatius," Iggy said. Clare took a pinch her habit and began twisting it. Iggy rested her hand on Clare's, stilling her. "We're from the Chicago area."

Nolan choked and then started coughing. His face reddened as he covered his mouth with a fist. The coughs grew more ragged, more desperate. Grace stood, poured a glass of water from a pitcher that had been set in the middle of the table, leaned across Roger and Sheila, and offered it to Nolan. From where Maeve sat, it was apparent that Grace's top had fallen away. She held the glass directly in front of her chest so when Nolan took it from her, he had to look down her shirt. He held up a hand, refusing the offer. His color deepened and he struggled to control the fit.

"Take it, Frank," Grace said. "Before you have a heart attack."

He had turned away from her, then glanced back quickly, and snatched the glass from her hand, water spilling across the table. Sheila hissed, pushing herself away from the table. Nolan stepped back and sipped the water, staring at the wall, until the coughing died off.

Grace remained where she was, like a lion ready to pounce, crowding Roger into Sheila, who shoved him back into Grace. "Knock it off, will you?" Sheila said to Grace.

Maeve wondered what she had just witnessed. Grace had tormented Nolan with her sexuality. Did they know each other before today? Had they been lovers? The biker chick and the old botany guy? Or was Grace mentally unbalanced, the way she dominated the gathering, flaunted herself, and practically crawled across two people she'd only just met. As an example of the hospitality industry, she was not the finest.

Maeve stole a look at Bernie to gauge her reaction. Bernie rolled her eyes at Lester. In return, he raised his eyebrows. His lower lip rolled over the top, pulling a hank of mustache into this mouth.

Nolan cleared his throat and put the glass down on the table. "Thank you, Miss Miller."

Grace was still on her feet. Bernie sucked on a tooth. Grace shot her a look, then sat down.

"Let's get back on track, shall we?" Nolan said. He looked at Maeve, "Can you tell us a little bit about yourself?"

"Maeve Malloy." She gave the group a little wave, like Roger had done. Of course, she'd find the only obviously introverted alcoholic to imitate. Next time, she'd find someone else more normal to copy. She surveyed the room. One narcissistic tourist with an inebriated husband, a couple of nuns, a crazy old biker chick, a New Age woman, also drunk, her pot-smoking husband, and an awkward botanist. No one normal. Just her luck.

"Welcome to all of you," Nolan said.

"Thank you," said Sister Iggy.

"Thank you," Maeve said. Better imitating Iggy. At least the nun had some social skills.

"Anyone for coffee?" Bernie asked, pointing to the cart. Those who acknowledged the question shook their heads.

Nolan drug heavy drapes cross the windows, darkening the room. The laptop hummed as he adjusted the screen. A shaft of light projected a photograph onto it, a flowered-filled valley set in front of snow-capped mountains. The image flickered, then died.

"Dammit," Bernie said. She pulled herself out of the chair and toggled the light switch on the wall. Nothing happened. "Must be the generator again." She looked accusingly at Lester.

"On it," he said as he rolled out the door. Bernie followed him.

The stillness in the room felt heavy. Grace got up, poured herself a cup of coffee and sat back down. Maeve stood next and poured coffee for herself. On second thought she said, "Sister, would either of you care for some coffee?"

"You've found my weakness," Iggy said. "But Sister Clare won't be having any."

Maeve placed the cup in front of the nun and asked, "Anyone else?" No one responded, so Maeve filled a cup for herself and sat down.

A few patters of rain struck the window as the group sat in silence. Sheila finished off her wine. Sister Clare fiddled with her habit. Maeve sipped her coffee. Grace knocked hers back like a frat boy, then got up and fixed herself a second cup. Roger produced a book from his pocket and began reading.

The temperature cooled. Maeve felt exposed, like in one of those dreams where she was in court and suddenly noticed that she was naked and everyone was staring at her. She wished she had the hoody she had left it in her room.

Bernie returned. "Lester's working on it. Says it'll take a couple of hours. Sorry, folks."

Nolan slipped his laptop into its carrier. "We'll meet right after breakfast then. Lester has assured me he can take all of us in his boat across the water to a spot far away from this bear. And he will escort us, just in case. Say eight o'clock?"

"No one asked me but won't we get wet?" Sheila asked.

"If you don't have gear, I can outfit you," Bernie said.

Sheila grimaced. She appeared to doubt Bernie had raingear in her size, much less her color.

Sister Iggy stood, then Sister Clare stood as well. "We're early risers, so we will say good-night. We're looking forward to tomorrow," Iggy said.

Francis Nolan was busy wrapping the laptop cord. ""Thank you for coming, sisters. Good night."

Nolan and the Wadsworths followed the nuns out of the conference room leaving Maeve with Bernie and Grace.

"You go on," Bernie said to Maeve. "I can handle this by myself."

Maeve glanced at her cell phone. She'd put it on silent before dinner, so if anyone had called, she would have missed it. Dammit, no calls. No texts. Maeve felt that drifting sensation again, like when the boat had just been tethered to the dock and she was waiting for the boatman to help the nuns climb onto the pier.

The time on the cell said just after eight o'clock. She could hit the gym, pound the treadmill, work out the kinks in her hip and burn off that chocolate cake. A good, hard sweat would make her feel better. Maybe.

Chapter Six

GRACE STOOD, ARMS FOLDED, at the head of the butcher block prep table, imagining what it would feel like to hear those words come from his mouth: "I did it. I molested your son. I used him. I polluted his body. His mind. His soul. I made sure he would never fall in love and that every time he wanted a girl, he would think of me and how I hurt him. I destroyed his self-esteem. I destroyed his ability to trust. I betrayed him. I lied. I never cared about him because I am a lecherous, depraved, predatory sociopath whose only care in the world is getting my rocks off. I ruined your baby boy."

It would feel like vindication. Everyone would see that she had every right in the world to exact revenge. And then she would kill him. No one needed to know that ahead of time. They needed to think she was acting within the law, so that they would help her.

Grace had all the players present and accounted-for in the lodge. She never thought it would go this far. Expecting it would all fall apart long before now, she had never planned past this point. There was no plan for afterwards after it was done. She didn't care what happened then.

Right now, she needed to get everyone on board, to understand what their roles were, to remember their lines. Especially Sheila. "Where the hell is she?"

Bernie said, "She'll be along." She was sitting next to Iggy on bar stools pulled up to the table, each with a cup of tea. The hippie and the nun side by side. Life was a costume party.

"I don't want that new dishwasher catching us together."

Iggy said, "Maeve was headed to the gym a few minutes ago with headphones on." It was weird hearing Iggy talk like a normal person all dressed up in those medieval robes.

A gust of wind shook the window. A smattering of fat raindrops hit the glass and streamed across it at an angle. The three turned their heads to look outside. Spruce trees swayed with the wind. Whitecaps skittered across the bay.

The door swung open, and Sheila came in wearing her rich tourist costume, the fashionista in running shoes, banging her hip into a counter as she zig-zagged her way to the table. "No one told me. Why are we all here anyway?"

Three sheets to the wind already. If Sheila wasn't given something to drink, she'd leave in search of booze before the meeting was finished. That wouldn't do.

Bernie's private bottle was stashed in a corner of the counter, the foil long gone, a red-stained cork reinserted only part way. She wouldn't mind if Grace popped the cork. She was only waiting for everyone to leave so she could finish it anyway and there was plenty more where that came from.

Grace grabbed the bottle by the neck. "Wine?"

Sheila frowned. She looked confused, like she was trying to work out if Grace was going to pick on her for being drunk. "What?"

Grace slid a glass out of a rack. "Would you like some wine?"

"Sure, fill 'er up."

Iggy and Bernie sipped their tea. Even before she joined the convent, Iggy never was much of a drinker. Bernie, on the other hand, was a lush and had been since high school. Right now, she was pretending she didn't want any. It was only an act. Grace could smell wine on her breath; she must have snuck a drink sometime after dinner. She wanted people to think she was just a social drinker, like everyone else didn't know better. They knew. They'd always played along. It was easier that way.

That was the problem with this family. Pretending was easier. No wonder they didn't know what was real anymore.

Sheila tapped her diamond ring on the butcher block while she watched Grace fill her glass, stopping halfway. "What, you're my mother now?"

Grace filled the glass to the brim. Sheila bent over and slurped without taking it from the counter, just like she used to do when she was a kid drinking pop. After siphoning off a half-inch, she picked the glass up and leaned against a counter. Sheila wagged a finger in Iggy's direction. "Like your outfit. Is it new?"

Iggy gave her an indulgent smile.

"Isn't that the Monaghan girl with you?" Sheila asked Iggy. "Her mom worked at the school, Bernie. You remember, right?"

"Your age?" Bernie asked. "Barely remember her. Quiet kid, as I recall. Kind of strange."

"She's actually quite intelligent," Iggy said. "She joined the convent after graduating college cum laude. She's been through a lot and worked hard to overcome her unfortunate start in life. I thought she'd enjoy the trip."

"Enough of this chit-chat," Grace said. "We're wasting time."

Sheila ignored her. "And what's *he* doing here? No one told me." She had directed the question to Bernie, the oldest sister and the one who had raised Sheila after their parents died. It was only natural for Sheila to treat Bernie like she was in charge, still Grace resented it. Anyone paying attention could see Bernie was lost inside some maze inside her own mind.

"Don't ask me," Bernie said, staring at the bottle Grace had put on the counter just beyond Bernie's reach. She was sobering up from her last nip and it showed. Sagging jowls. Sunken eyes. Curtains of skin draping over her eyelids. Tiny red veins in her nose more obvious. She had to be hurting. Did Bernie want a drink bad enough to get off her bar stool for it or would she sit there watching Sheila drain the bottle? After everyone left, she would just grab another bottle from storage instead of the wine rack and, she thought, no would know. She'd always been so self-righteous about being the responsible one.

It's a family disease. Alcoholism. Denial. Enabling.

Sheila took another big slurp from her glass and rounded on Grace. "You did this?"

Grace had enough. She banged her fist on the butcher block, startling Sheila. "I'm calling this meeting to order. There's news." Grace paused for dramatic effect. "The statute of limitations has been repealed."

Grace let that sink in. Bernie fidgeted, her eyes on the bottle just out of reach. Iggy took a sip of tea, her eyes on Grace were sharp, the dogged police nun.

Sheila gave Grace that steely-eyed stare of hers. She was angry about something, like always. Anger had been her drug of choice. That and red wine. "So what?"

"So we can get a conviction now. He can go to jail where he belongs."

"He doesn't belong in jail," Bernie said. "Jail's too good for him. If it were up to me, I'd shoot him like the dog he is." No one reacted. They were used to Bernie running her mouth off.

Patsy, thy name is Bernadette. Grace suppressed a smile. Bernie never did any of the drastic things she said, but she could be trusted to shout them from the rooftops. Grace hadn't thought about a getaway plan before and here was Bernie handing her an escape. When the cops came, everyone would tell them how Bernie vowed she'd wanted him dead. Sadly, Grace would be forced into admitting that she, too, had heard Bernie threaten Nolan's life. After Bernie's arrest, Grace would go free. It just might work.

Iggy set her teacup down slowly. "So, you brought him here to get a confession."

"You got it, Sarge," Grace said.

"And you want him to confess because there is no one to testify against him anymore since Danny's gone."

"We don't need a confession," Bernie interjected. Her forehead was beginning to glisten with sweat. "We know what happened. He deserves to die after what he's done."

Keep it up, Bernie. Grace will be on a plane out of state while before Bernie was even arraigned. Iggy must have sensed Grace's thoughts. She shot Bernie a look, the cop "stop you in your tracks" look she'd perfected back when she was on the police force. "I didn't hear that."

Doesn't matter if Iggy denied hearing it, Grace heard it. Sheila had too.

"Leave him alone," Sheila said as she pulled herself away from the counter, weaving in the air. "He didn't do anything to me. He was nice."

"He gave you candy," Bernie said.

"You don't get it, Babycakes," Grace said.

"Get what?"

"He was grooming you."

"Then why didn't he try something with me if he was this monster you think he is?"

"Maybe he did. Maybe you suppressed it."

"Bullshit!"

The blood had drained from Sheila's face. Did Nolan get to her too? Maybe that repression thing was real.

Sheila's lower lip began to tremble. "What I think never mattered."

True enough. Growing up, no one had listened to Sheila. She'd always been the baby, one of those late-in-life surprises to their parents when the other girls were in their teens. They had ignored her babbling since she was in a highchair. As the years went on, every once in a while, Grace would pay attention to Sheila, just to see if she said something smart. She didn't. It didn't matter she'd gone to college; she was an idiot. "Lower your voice."

"Like who cares? Lester's stoned out of his mind by now. Roger's reading. He doesn't care what I do."

"Nolan could wander in any minute," Bernie said.

Grace said, "I don't think so. I took him fresh towels this afternoon and saw a bottle of sleeping pills in his bathroom." What she didn't say is that she took four of the pills, just enough not to be noticed, wrapped them in tissue, and stuck them in her pocket. They might come in handy later. "What about Iggy's little friend?"

Iggy said, "Sister Clare went to bed. She was sleeping when I left."

Bernie finally broke down. She got up from her stool, grabbed a wine glass, filled it, and sat down again. The night was wearing on too long for her. Grace knew what she was thinking: as long as she was one drink behind everyone else, they couldn't accuse her of drinking too much.

Bernie took a long pull from her glass and closed her eyes as if she was meditating. All the women had stopped what they were doing. They were watching her. It had become one of the family rituals, marking the moment when Bernie took the first drink that got her drunk with a communal silence. Eyes still closed, she swung her loose hair back a la Cher. When her eyes flicked open, they were glassy but had a new light shining deep inside them. "So, Grace, what's the plan?"

"The plan is to rain hell down on that miserable bastard Francis Nolan. We'll get him alone tomorrow morning when he does his slide show. Bernie, can you send Lester to town with the new kitchen helper, get them out of the way? Tell them we need some supplies before dinner."

"Sure, if the storm dies down. What about the hike?"

Thunder rolled in the distance and another wave of rain splattered against the window.

"In this weather?" Grace said. "Even if it quits raining, it'll be too muddy to go walking. We'll get Nolan into the conference room. There's only one door. He can't get out if we block his way."

"And then what?" Sheila asked. "You think he's just going to confess? Like you all say, we got you surrounded. The jig is up." Sheila gestured around the room with her glass. "You three? A drunk, a nun, an ex-con? For chrissake, I'm the only normal one here. It was Danny's word against his. None of you knew what Danny was really like. He was mean and a liar and he did stuff all the time and blamed me for it."

Grace saw her hand sailing through the air and felt the smack in her palm even before she registered the impulse. Her hand went numb, then began to warm. Dead silence followed. She'd put up with Sheila's crap for a long, long time but Grace would be damned if she listened to Sheila badmouth her baby boy.

Sheila staggered back, over dramatically for how hard she was hit. Wine splashed onto the floor. One hand flew up, covering her reddening cheek, but you had to give her credit, she never dropped the glass. "Bitch!"

"Stop it!" Iggy said. "Both of you."

Grace wheeled around slowly. Ever since Iggy announced that she had found Nolan, she'd been trying to control things. The kangaroo court had been Grace's idea and Iggy played along. Now she was showing her true colors. Iggy had let Grace pull this whole thing together and now she was going to step in and take over. Because she was the good sister.

"There's a better way," Iggy said, addressing Grace as if they were alone in the room. Sheila whimpered loudly for attention.

"Will you shut up?" Grace grabbed the bottleneck, topped off Sheila's glass, then slammed it down.

Bernie knocked back her wine. "What better way?"

"She wants to do a therapy session." Grace barked a laugh. "You know, we all sit around the table and take turns telling him how he's injured each of us. And he'll feel bad and apologize. And then what, Iggy? A big group hug?"

"It's called 'restorative justice.' I'm only thinking of you."

"I got a better idea," Grace said. "He confesses. He goes to jail. And then he can apologize." Grace slapped her head in a mock-realization. "At his sentencing! When he speaks to the court? You know the part when the judge tells the prisoner he can say anything he wants right before he passes sentence? Then, you'll get your apology. I promise you. Tears rolling down his face, he'll be real sorry. Sorry he's going to jail, that is."

Iggy laid one hand on top of Grace's, wrapping it around hers, squeezing gently. Grace felt the warmth of Iggy's hand seep into her own. "You are in so much pain, macushla. Revenge is never the answer. Let him atone for his sins. It will bring you peace. I promise. It's what Danny would have wanted."

Grace jerked her hand away. "Don't talk to me about what Danny would have wanted. He was my boy."

Grace felt something inside her crumble. She tried to get her determination back. She focused hard on the images of her son, the newborn in her arms, the little boy playing on a tire swing, watching cartoons on Saturday morning sitting on the floor. It wasn't working. Iggy had worked her good-person magic and all Grace could feel was sad. Deeply, darkly sad.

Sheila crashed into the worktop, unable to stand up straight anymore, then gripped the counter with both hands to steady herself. "Well, this is a major bummer. We all feel for your loss, Grace. But you know what? No one's asked me what I think. And I'm the only one who was there and no one asked me what I think. And I'm not going to tell you what I think. 'Cause no one asked me."

She grabbed the bottle by the neck. "I'm warning him. That's what I'm going to do. Because what you guys have cooked up isn't fair. You trapped him. And none of you were there so none of you get it. You don't get it. And I'm not explaining it to you, 'cause no one asked me."

Sheila spun around and headed towards the swinging door with bottle in hand. She hit the wall instead, grunted, then took a couple of steps to the side, and pushed her way through the door.

"Baby's going to sleep hard tonight," Grace said.

Iggy laughed. She pulled off her veil and headband and scratched her scalp with both hands. "Where can a girl get a drink?"

"Now, you're talking," Bernie said. She slipped off her stool, went over to the wine rack, pulled two bottles, and held them in the air. "Red or white?"

Chapter Seven

SHEILA OPENED THE DOOR to the crappy room she shared with Roger. What a dump. It reeked of wood, the exterior wall made out of logs. Hanging over the beds were cheap photos of northern lights. The bedspreads were thin polyester affairs with folksy moose print.

Grace had given them twin beds, her twisted idea of a joke, not knowing she'd hit a sore spot. Roger had not made love to Sheila in over a year. She was beginning to wonder why she was still married to him.

Every night when he was home from the north slope, it was the same. Dinner, television, then Roger reading in bed. The only thing he would have said the entire evening was, "nice dinner." It didn't matter what she served him. It could have been frozen pizza or beef bourguignon. "Nice dinner."

Then, she'd follow him into the bedroom, wash her face, and brush her teeth in their master bathroom, change into an elegant nightgown, take a seat at the vanity, brush her hair the requisite one hundred strokes, and slip into bed at which time he would pull of his glasses, place them carefully on the night stand, turn out the light, roll away from her, and mutter a good-night.

"I hate this place," she said.

Roger didn't answer. He was stretched out in bed, reading a book.

"I want to go home." She wasn't sure why she said that. Home wasn't any better than here. She just wanted something to change. Any change.

He didn't respond again. Sheila poured the wine dregs into a water glass. She hated the dregs, the mealy and slimy texture slithering across her tongue. It almost made her gag, but she would drink it anyway. She dropped the bottle into a little wastepaper can and then sat on the twin bed beside him. He scooted over to get away from her without lifting his eyes.

She put the glass on the floor, rolled over on her back and stared at the ceiling. There was a water stain on the sheet rock right over her. She wondered how long it would be before the rain made its way through the roof, seeped across the ceiling, and began dripping on the bed. Outside the storm noise was relentless, waves and waves of water. She had nearly tuned it out.

Just when she thought Roger was going to ignore her all night, he asked, "Did you have a nice visit with your sisters?"

Sheila laughed. She rolled over and picked the glass up off the floor. "What do you think? It's the ninth circle of hell. Treachery."

She waited for him to follow up with a question or a comment, but he just went on reading his book. She didn't know how to get through to him anymore. If he noticed her at all, it was only for a moment in time. She poured the slimy dregs down her throat and coughed.

The television on the dresser played a travel video of Alaska. "Is that the only thing on?"

"They don't have cable," Roger said. He turned a page. "I told you that."

Sheila took a deep pained sigh. She got out of bed and peeled off her top. She was feeling kind of sexy. A good fight always did that to her. She knew she looked good. When she was swimming in the cruise ship pool in her yellow bikini, all the men watched her. Her muscles were toned. Not an inch of fat anywhere. She was tan and healthy.

"Can you help me with this?" Sheila turned her back to Roger so he could undo her bra.

"Not now, Sheila, okay? I'm tired," Roger said, his eyes fixed on his book.

"You're always tired. You've been tired for a year."

He must have a girlfriend. A mistress. Or maybe he went to whores. No, Roger was a germ freak, he'd never go to prostitutes. Definitely a girlfriend. Probably someone from work, some girl at the oil rig. That's the only reason he could have lost interest in her. Because she was dynamite.

She worked out hard in the gym every day, went to Pilates class, cycling class, lifted weights. Her hair stylist was the best colorist in southern California. Every week, she had a mani and a pedi. The skin on her feet was as smooth as a baby's butt. She had monthly facials and every three months, a little refresher: shots, electrical zapping, peel. Men looked at her. For chrissake, women looked at her.

But Roger never looked at her.

She pulled her top back on. Pressure was building in her face and her eyes started to burn. She was going to start crying, right here, right now, in front of him, the bastard. And he didn't give a shit. She could set herself on fire, and he wouldn't give a shit.

"Do you want a divorce?"

"Not this again." Roger closed his book, pulled off his glasses, and laid both on the end table. He turned off the light and scooched down into bed. "Sheila, it's late. Try to get some sleep."

No, he didn't want a divorce. She was the real breadwinner. He'd have to make his own payments on that little sports car he bought last year. The sports car! That was it! He said he'd bought it for her, but he must have wanted it to impress some bimbo.

"Screw you." Sheila went into the bathroom, slammed the door, flipped the toilet seat cover down, and sat on the cold plastic. She fished through her make-up kit, found the travel-size bottle of gin, and leaned against the tank. The cool porcelain felt good on her back.

She drank the gin in one go and tossed the bottle toward the trash can. It missed and clattered to the floor. Screw it. Grace could pick it up when she cleaned the room.

It'd been so long since Roger touched her, she couldn't exactly remember what it was like but she knew it wasn't fireworks. She might have bitched him out. Was that when he got a girlfriend? Or was he already seeing her? He had been acting different for a long time.

She dug in her make-up kit again, found her cigarettes and a lighter, got up, and pulled the door open slowly. The room was dark. Roger was pretending to be asleep. She could always tell. He didn't realize his breathing changed when he really fell asleep, and she never let on she could tell. It was one of her little secrets that might come in handy someday.

She tip-toed into the hall. She didn't want to get caught, having had enough of family life for one night.

It had been years since she'd seen any of them. Not since she and Roger moved to L.A. No one came out to visit. She'd asked Bernie, who always said they were too broke to travel. And then when they got money, too busy. She didn't bother asking Iggy, who never had time for her anyway, or Grace who was in prison. Like she'd invite Grace into her home.

So when Bernie had first called to invite Sheila and Roger for a long weekend, she thought Bernie really wanted to see her. Bernie and Lester had bought the Alaska lodge, a dream come true, she had said. Grace got paroled, had come to work at the lodge, and everything was going well, she said. Grace was clean and sober and walking the straight and narrow.

But Bernie never said Iggy was going to be here. It was a big surprise when she saw Iggy walking up the beach with her little nun friend in tow. Why was it nuns traveled in pairs anyway? That's when Sheila realized Bernie was up to something. No, not Bernie. It had to have been Grace. Grace was the manipulative one. And Bernie would fall for anything Grace told her because Bernie wanted to believe so much that Grace had been rehabilitated.

And when Sheila saw Francis Nolan, she knew.

They had invited her here to use her, not because she was family and they missed her. Because they wanted something from her. Whatever it was, she wasn't giving it to them.

She walked to the next room and knocked on his door.

***

FRANCIS NOLAN LAID IN bed, staring at the white ceiling, waiting for the sleeping pills to take effect. His pajamas weren't warm enough, even with a bathrobe, so he had pulled on a sweatshirt and his raincoat over that and two pairs of socks. Alaska was infernally cold. When it started to rain, the room got even colder. He had looked for a thermostat. When he found none, he searched the floors and the walls for heating vents and found none of those either. They certainly hadn't mentioned that on the website.

This is not what he imagined for his middle years, and not what his grandmother, the harridan, wanted. He'd visions of a tidy sitting room, a cup of tea, and a housekeeper scurrying around quietly doing whatever women do. His grandmother had visions of a grand home, the kind bishops live in, and himself the bishop. Oh, how she wanted a bishop at her birthday party, when her friends only managed to have a priest or just a nun. Good thing she was dead.

The shouting next door had finally subsided. It had been going on for twenty or thirty minutes. The flashy woman, Sheila, and her meek husband. Nolan heard their door close. A moment later, there was a knock on his door.

He wasn't sure he heard it. Why would anyone come to his door at this time of night?

Then the knock again, louder, persistent.

Nolan threw off the covers, slipped his double-socked feet into a pair of slippers, and shuffled to the door. The pills had made him drowsy. It was all the energy he could muster to drag himself across the room.

When he opened the door, he left the chain in place.

Sheila Wadsworth stood inches from him, head bobbing and staring blearily at his chest. He pulled his raincoat closed.

"May I help you?" Nolan asked.

"Can I come in?"

Holy Mother of God, what did this woman want from him? Had he given her reason to think he desired her?

Back when he was a priest, women showed interest, sexual interest, in him all of the time. It was beyond belief. Married woman. Spinsters. He'd been warned by other priests not to be taken in. There was something enticing about the forbidden, about seducing a man who had taken a vow of celibacy. These women were not in love. If there was a scandal, he would be moved across the country to hush it up. Affairs were a constant headache to the bishops.

His grandmother had ambitions for him and he didn't want to disappoint her. He was so naïve that he thought only good priests got promoted to bishop. Nolan had been a good priest. He'd rejected those Jezebels. And when he was scapegoated like some burnt offering to the gods of political correctness, they no longer pursued him. It was just as well. They hadn't interested him.

"It's late," Nolan said. "I've already gone to bed. Perhaps tomorrow?"

She shook her head so wildly, he thought she was going to fall over. "Tonight! It has to be tonight. I know something very import...something impor...something you need to know."

"Sorry?"

"Im-por-tant!" She staggered a couple of steps while she spoke. She seemed to have only had enough focus to stand or speak. She couldn't do both at the same time.

There was no way Francis Nolan was letting this drunk woman into his room. Nothing good could come of it. What if she peeled off her clothes and fell onto his bed? How would he get her out of there? How would he explain it? Would he go complain to the manager? Or spend the night on a couch in the lobby?

"Got a light?" Sheila Wadsworth had pulled a cigarette out of her pocket.

He had an idea.

"There's no smoking in the building."

She twisted and pointed toward the exit door. "Outside. Around the corner."

"What about the bear?"

"Bear, shmear."

"I'll get my cigarettes and lighter and meet you outside," he said.

"Okey, dokey," Sheila said, then she started down the hall.

Nolan pulled the door shut, turned the lock, crawled back into bed, and pulled the covers up to his chin. Just as he was drifting off, he thought he heard another door close.

***

SHEILA WANTED THAT CIGARETTE. She'd have it when Francis Nolan came outside with his lighter. And then she would tell him.

How would she start? They're plotting against you. Or, flat out tell him, Grace wants your hide. Or be coy about it, *they're* in it together. What plot, he would ask. Who is they? And see, she would be right, she knew something he needed to know.

Danny was such a piece of shit. You couldn't believe anything he said. Not that he ever said anything about Father Nolan. Not to her. Not to anyone. She would have known if he had. When they were little, they were like twins. They did everything together. Shooting hoops in the driveway. Playing hide-and-go-seek with their friends after dinner.

She remembered the day everything changed. They must have been twelve or thirteen years old. It was a Saturday. He'd been gone all day on some church thing and she was bored. At breakfast, he was all excited about the trip, swimming at some lake and a cook-out with hot dogs, and she was moody because she couldn't go along. It was a boy thing, he said. No girls allowed. Bernie promised to spend the day with her to make her feel better, but what that meant is that she could help Bernie with cleaning and laundry. No, thank you very much.

Just before he left, he walked past her chair at the kitchen table and gave her a shove. "When I get home, we'll go outside, find some kids and hang out. OK, Squirt?"

"Don't call me 'Squirt'," she had said, slapping at him, although she secretly loved it when he did. It was his pet name for her. He didn't use it for anyone else and she'd give any other kid a black eye if they tried to call her by that name.

There was nothing good on TV all day. She was flopped on her belly on the itchy living room rug trying to read *Black Beauty* for the umpteenth time. It was hard to follow the story when she was listening for a car to pull up. She never did. Instead, she heard the front door slam. She pushed herself to a sit, waiting for him. He shuffled into the room. He never looked at her, didn't say hello, didn't say anything. The book was splayed open in the middle of the floor and he gave it a vicious kick, sending it flying across the room. She heard the spine crack and pages tear when his tennis shoe made contact.

She was on her feet. She grabbed his shirt and spun him around. "Hey! That's mine!"

He had a look so evil that she had never seen it before or since on anyone. His face was dark, literally dark. His eyes glinted. He pushed her so hard, she fell. "Grow up, will you? You're not a little kid anymore. Stop whining like a baby."

She would have fought him. They had pushing matches before and she had given as good as she got but this time he scared her. He stomped off to his room and slammed the door. She found Bernie bent over a toilet with a scrub brush and told her the story in between sobs.

All Bernie could say was, "Boys will be boys. Leave him alone. He'll outgrow it."

He didn't. He only got worse. He wouldn't eat with the family anymore. He spent all of his time in his room. When she knocked on the door, he didn't answer. "Just like his mother," the grown-ups said later when they thought she wasn't listening.

The guestroom hallway was long, dark, and cold. She walked carefully, step by step, like when she was a kid playing Cowboys and Indians. She was the Indian warrior in the woods sneaking up on her enemy.

Light shone under the gym door. Someone pounding away on the treadmill as she snuck by.

When she pushed the exit door open, it caught in the wind. She struggled to keep it from slamming against the wall. She went outside and pushed it closed, then scooted around the corner, finding a spot against the wall where the wind didn't reach. The rain was dying off now, just a drizzle. She pulled out the cigarette. And oh, funny, look here, she had a lighter in her pocket the whole time! She lit it.

She took a long deep drag from the cigarette. As smoke filled her lungs, a zing ran through her body, lit up her brain. How did Roger get her to hide her smoking from him? What did he care? Every time she snuck a cigarette, she felt guilty. Here he was screwing some other woman, and he didn't feel guilty about that, but he made her feel guilty about one of the few pleasures she had in her life. It wasn't right.

Before she knew it, the cigarette was finished. She threw the butt on the ground, stubbed it out with her shoe, and lit another. Sure was taking Nolan a long time to come outside. Maybe she shouldn't tell him. Maybe it was a mistake to interfere. What would happen if she ruined Grace's plan? They'd all be mad at her, for sure. Well, not Iggy. Iggy would forgive her. But they wouldn't tell her secrets anymore. Finally, just when she had a chance to be included, to be treated like an adult, and it was slipping away from her.

If Nolan didn't come out before she finished this cigarette, it'd be a sign that she shouldn't warn him. She'd go back inside and tell the others in the morning she'd changed her mind.

A gust of wind blew water off the roof, splattering her head and shoulders. The cigarette was drenched, dammit. She tossed it to the ground and came around the corner to go back inside.

Someone was hiding in the shadow of the building. The bear? Maybe Lester hadn't lied. Bear, shmear. It was a person. Francis Nolan had come out to hear her story. Another sign. She had to tell him. It was the right thing to do.

Lightening ripped through the sky, revealing the person before her for a flickering instant.

"Oh, it's you," Sheila said and laughed. "You scared me."

Chapter Eight

MAEVE WASN'T SO SURE there would be hiking tomorrow anywhere tomorrow. Not close to the lodge with the bear hanging around. And nowhere else with the rain coming in waves, heavy, then light, then heavy again.

The gym was a small room, rank and stuffy with the smell of male sweat. She had left the door ajar and cracked a window to clear out the odor. She had just jumped on the treadmill when she heard a woman's angry voice. Maeve went into the hallway just in time to hear, "Do you want a divorce?" It sounded like the tourist, Sheila, and the voice came from the direction of her room. A rumble of a man's voice followed. Maeve stepped back into the gym and pulled the door closed.

The air in the room was cleared out by then and chilly with the incoming storm, so she pulled the window shut too.

Then she put on her headphones and jumped back on the treadmill. She ran for a while, switched to the weight machine and then back to the treadmill. Alternating the work-out broke up the monotony, and with any luck at all, she might be in better shape by the end of the summer. Besides, changing the exercise every few minutes made her focus and kept her mind from wandering to the past.

On the last day she was a lawyer, she had gone to a bonfire with Tom. It had been thirty days since Esther Fancyboy died. Her family was burning her clothes, a Yup'ik tradition. Maeve was a friend of Esther's mother, Cora. A few days after Esther disappeared, Cora asked Maeve to find her. The police had said she'd come home when she was done partying, but Cora and Maeve knew better. Esther was a chief financial officer and a single mother. She didn't wander off to go partying. Something bad had happened to her.

As it turned out she had died the night she'd disappeared. Then, a witness was murdered before Maeve's eyes and Evan, Esther's son, was kidnapped. Maeve and Tom rescued Evan and found the murderer.

While all that was going on, an ethics complaint had been filed against Maeve. The certified letter came in the mail on the day of the bonfire. Maeve knew what was inside the thin envelope without opening it. She didn't want to read it because until she read the letter, she was still a lawyer. She wanted to hold on as long as she could.

She gave the letter to Tom at the bonfire. He read it, wrapped his arms around her in a bear hug, and kissed the top of her head. His boney sternum and ribs poked at her. It was real now. She had been suspended from practice. She couldn't hold back the tears. The night, the people, the bonfire swirled around her. She would have fallen if Tom wasn't holding her up.

Voices down the hall distracted her again. It sounded like Sheila in the hallway. "Im-por-tant!"

Then a man's voice, too quiet to make out, and a muffled back and forth between the two.

The trouble had started for Maeve with Filippo Mataafa, a guy she got acquitted on an armed robbery charge. After the acquittal, he killed an innocent bystander in a drug-deal-gone-wrong. One thing led to another. The bar complaint was about how she handled the trial. She had missed evidence that Mataafa's alibi was a lie. And because she didn't know he and his alibi witness were lying, she put them on the stand, and convinced the jury that Mataafa was innocent. She won.

Why did people think it was funny to pronounce "lawyers" as "liars", then look at the attorney they just insulted, smirking? Do they think they're being clever and are laughing at their own jokes, or are they hiding behind a smile, embarrassed by their own effrontery? Whatever it was, it hurt to be called a liar to your face. Maeve didn't like being a socially-sanctioned punching bag.

Did people really think lawyers sit around jail cells cooking up ridiculous stories with our clients? The truth was an attorney was stuck with the story his client told because it was the client who was on trial. It was his story and his life.

Being a good advocate wasn't good enough. It mattered to her clients, getting them what they wanted, but not to the bar association. Nothing tastier to a bunch of backroom paper-pushers than to take down a trial lawyer. The bar gave her a three-month suspension that started just as the snow melted.

Maybe she wasn't cut out for this bullshit after all. She could always be a librarian somewhere. Ghost-like with no social interaction above a whisper. She would be a nice librarian, walking the readers to the stacks they were looking for. And they would like her just because she did something as simple as finding a book for them. She'd probably have to go back to school and get a degree in library science. Owning a cupcake van sounded like more fun.

Tom would be fine without her. Maybe she could go visit him in Homer. Maybe he'd come to wherever she was in the winter to visit her. She couldn't see it. What would they do? Go to a movie? Get a pizza? If they weren't talking about cases and clients, what did they have to talk about?

After replaying the train wreck that was the past year of her life again, Maeve slowed the treadmill, stepped off, and paced the room, catching her breath. Then she finished up with three sets of ten crunches. Her cell phone said it was almost eleven o'clock. She closed the window and turned out the lights.

When she stepped into the hall, Maeve noticed the back door was ajar. A trail of water led from the door onto the rubber mat where it petered out. She pulled the door closed until she heard it latch, then went back to her room for a hot shower before she crashed for the night.

***

APRIL WANTED TO CUDDLE. Tom did not. He wasn't the cuddling type.

He rolled away from her, flicked on the lamp, and reached for his Rolex on the bedside table. It was going on ten o'clock. Rain hammered on the motel's roof. The room, moldy already, was damp and cold.

He patted a pack of cigarettes next to the Rolex. Four left, by the feel of it. A couple for tonight and a couple for the morning.

He swung his feet to the floor. April rolled away and pulled the blanket over her shoulder with a snort.

If he was subtle about it, she'd leave and come back another night. If he wasn't subtle, she wouldn't come back. Not that it mattered that much too him, there was always another girl.

Used to be, when he was investigating, he'd tell her, whoever she was, that he had to go on a stake-out, then he'd get up, and start a pot of coffee. There never was a stake-out. And they always came back.

Right now, he was stuck for an excuse. He was a fisherman in a fishing town socked in with weather. All the other fishermen were drunk in some room with some girl. Tom didn't drink anymore and spending a few days locked up in a room with some woman he barely knew, sober, would be boring, even if the sex is convenient. Much less a girl half his age whose universe was full of celebrities he never heard of.

She might want to talk, God help him.

He pulled on his underwear, jeans and a t-shirt, grabbed the cigarettes and lighter, walked around the bed, and opened a window. Who cared about a non-smoking sign scarred with cigarette burns from prior guests? There was no way he was going outside in all that rain. Little known secret, Tom Sinclair didn't like getting wet. He could swim only if he had to. He took the shortest showers he could. On the boat, he was covered from neck down with slickers so only his face got wet.

According to the weather report, the storm would first move over Homer and then hit Seward. Maeve would be socked in, too. He imagined her complaining how the humidity making her hair frizz. He laughed. Her hair was always frizzy.

"What's so funny?" April asked.

"Nothing. Go back to sleep."

He lit a cigarette and leaned out, blowing the smoke into the night.

April pulled the covers up to her chin. "It's cold out there."

Tom pretended he didn't hear.

The night was inky-black. No stars, no moon, no streetlights. Only black and the sound of rushing water.

"You're letting all the cold air in." She rolled away from him, her fine blonde hair fanning across the pillow.

Once he had watched Maeve sleep. Her curly hair didn't fan out so much as it jumbled like ropes dropped on the ground. She was passed out on a couch in her condo. He was sitting in a chair watching over her in case she vomited. He didn't want her choking to death in her sleep. If she started puking, he'd flip her over and put his hand down her throat to clear the passageway. It hadn't come to that.

Smoking cigarettes and drinking coffee to stay awake, he had wondered how she didn't smother herself with all that hair. Just as he was wondering that, Maeve pushed the jumble out of her face, without waking.

It was her last drunk and the night the Mataafa verdict came in. Maeve had just found out that Addison Royce, their boss, had gotten married. She had a thing going with him, and everyone in the office was in on the secret. She drank that night like she had a death wish. She must have thought it was true love.

They were in the Fourth Avenue Bar, the hangout of assistant public defenders. People were buying her drinks as fast as she could pour them down her throat. Long Island ice teas, shots of tequila, beer. The PD crowd pretended they were celebrating the acquittal she'd gotten that day when they were really consoling her without letting on they knew she'd been dumped.

Just as she got sloppy-drunk, that little prick Ryan Shaw moved in. He was so cheap, he didn't even buy her a drink. He waited until she could hardly hold her head up, then he slid into the booth next to her.

Shaw was another assistant public defender, a scrawny little wannabe. A brownnoser, if there ever was one. He wasn't as smart or as tough as he thought he was. Just the kind of guy who'd do well in the old boys' club, catching bones thrown to him by the big dogs. Maeve Malloy wasn't a bone to be fought over.

She was an alcoholic. Even when she was drunk, Tom felt his chest swell when he thought of her compassion, her fierceness, her realness. She never lied to you, never pretended. Her green eyes flared when she was mad. Her cheeks turned pink when she was embarrassed. Her right hand flew up, finger stabbing the air, when she was angry. Her disease didn't make her any less in his eyes.

When Shaw slipped his hand between Maeve's legs, Tom clamped down on his shoulder. And squeezed. Hard.

Shaw slunk away. Tom grabbed Maeve's purse and pulled her out of her chair, half-carrying, half-guiding her to his truck, all the time with her purse slung over his shoulder. She nearly passed out on the sidewalk. He caught her before she fell.

By the time they got back to her condo, she was out. He carried her inside, laid her on the couch, found a blanket in her bedroom, tucked her in, and sat up all night.

He made a fresh pot of coffee when she came to later that morning. When she was on her second cup, he started telling his story.

"I used to drink," Tom said.

Maeve squinted at him. The sunlight must have been hurting her eyes.

"Used to use a lot of drugs, too."

"Hmm," was all she could say. Her head was bent and shaking hands were wrapped around the half-filled coffee cup he'd given her. Her entire body twitched now and then.

"Got busted a few times. Usual stuff. Disorderly conduct. Assault. Drunk driving. Came to in a jail cell more times than I can count."

She raised an eyebrow.

"The convictions are so old they don't show up on my record, so the public defender didn't find them in the background check before they hired me. It was in the days before computers. Small shit, anyway. Never got caught for the big shit."

"Like?" She was shaking so violently, she was about to spill the coffee all over herself. He took the cup out of her hands.

"Stealing mostly. Rolling drunks. Ripping off drug dealers. Bank robbery." He laughed. "There was this one time when I'd robbed a bank and they'd given me a pack of money with a dye-bomb inside. When I opened the pack, blue dust blew up in my face and I had to live in the woods for three weeks, waiting for the shit to come off.

She pushed deep into the couch and braced her head in her hands. Looked like she was nodding off. The twitching stopped. She came to again and ran a palm across her face and wiped it on her pants leg, the same pants she had slept in and had worn to court, leaving a long, wet streak.

"One day, I woke up in another jail cell and I knew I'd had enough."

Her head dropped even lower and she raked her hair over her face. She was nearly doubled over when the body shaking began, tiny rhythmic moves at first, then big rolls and shudders.

He stopped talking when she ran bent-over to the bathroom. He could hear her hit the floor, dry-heaving. When the gagging noise stopped, he poured a glass of water, not cold, not hot, from the kitchen tap and took it to her. She was sitting on the floor by the toilet, head lolled back, eyes closed. Her face was red, bloated, and streaked with mascara.

He put the glass on the bathroom counter. She opened her eyes. In that mess of a face, her eyes were calm and clear. She had enough, too. He could see it.

That evening, she was on a plane for Seattle, pale and shaky, going to rehab. A month later, she got off the plane looking five years younger, thinner, relaxed, yet unsure of herself. Getting through that first plane ride without a drink is a big deal for an alcoholic. She had done it. When he was standing at the gate and she stepped into view, he could see that she got it. She got how to live sober.

There was a light coming from her face. That light shone ever since. A miracle had happened, and he was there to see it. You don't get to see a lot of miracles in your life.

Tom blew another lungful of smoke out the window. With a thumb, he wiped rain-water from his face. "Fresh air's good for your lungs," he said to the blonde, what was her name again? April, right.

"You say that as you suck on a cancer-stick."

Tom took a long inhale of the cigarette, burning almost a quarter of it. He allowed a thin stream of blue smoke leak from his mouth, curling upward as the motel room's warm air poured out into the night. There was only so long he could make this cigarette last and April wasn't moving. She was still laying there, waiting for him to act right. The room seemed to shrink. Darkness swirled in the corners, spreading like a fog.

Maybe he'd grab the Louis L'Amour paperback he'd left on the desk, the page marked with a matchbook, turn on all the lights, and settle into the armchair, waiting her out.

Nah, he wanted the bed to himself. Now.

"I always sleep with the window open," Tom said. He could feel her thinking about it. The sheets rustled as her body tensed. It looked like she was about to get up, yell some profanity, get dressed, and leave. He didn't mind getting cussed out. He was being kind of a bastard.

That's when the door busted open.

It wasn't a man with a gun. It was a man with a vodka bottle. And he looked pissed.

Tom threw his cigarette out the window and crossed the room in two steps. He shoved the guy into the wall and raised his left arm for a block. The guy ducked and nailed Tom in the spleen. That was going to hurt.

Tom nailed him with a right uppercut. The guy's head snapped back and hit the wall, but he was still moving. Tom was winding up for a haymaker when the guy tackled him.

They flew onto the bed. April's bony legs scrambled under Tom. She screamed. Not a horror-movie scream, more of pissed-off girl shriek. "Anton, you asshole!"

Anton? Who the hell was Anton?

The guy was rearing up, loading a right jab when Tom kneed him in the groin. The drunk grabbed his crouch and hit the floor.

"Stay down!" Tom didn't want to hurt this guy, but he might have to.

The drunk was rolling around on the floor, groaning.

April was on her feet, jeans on already. She was pulling her sweatshirt over her naked body.

So this is how lacy bras get left behind.

The guy on the ground rolled around, groaning. He looked like he was going to nod off. The booze that finally had hit him.

"Who's Anton?" Tom asked.

April squatted beside the man on the floor. "My boyfriend."

Boyfriend. Figures.

Chapter Nine

SHORTLY BEFORE 5 A.M. Maeve found Bernie in the kitchen, her crinkly salt-and-pepper hair pulled back with a rubber band, a clean apron on, slicing cantaloupe. Fresh-baked blueberry muffins were cooling on the counter. A pot of coffee was half gone. Maeve poured herself a cup, dropped an apron over her head, and tied the ends behind her back. A bucket of potatoes stood next to the sink. She grabbed a vegetable scrubber, started the water, and began scrubbing.

Outside, rain streaked the window over the sink. Across the ground, rivers poured towards the bay. The skies were nearly as dark as they had been the night before, low heavy clouds unleashing sheets of water. Downpour billowed like curtains across the earth, the trees beyond, the pier, and the bay. Whoosh after whoosh accompanied gusting winds and new torrents.

Bernie wasn't talking this morning. Maeve had only known her for one day. She didn't have enough information to form an opinion and Bernie hadn't been especially gregarious the day before yet this morning she seemed even more absorbed in her own thoughts. Or really hungover.

The exit door opened and Lester stepped into the kitchen. He stomped his feet on a rubber mat, peeled an anorak off, water streaming from the coat, and hung it on a peg. He wiped his face with his thumb, the same way Tom did when he got wet.

"Lester, did you take my knife?" Bernie asked. She had to raise her voice to be heard over the storm.

Lester yelled back at her, louder than was needed. "What are you talking about?"

"My knife is missing. It's the same one you always grab when you're cleaning fish. The eight-inch chef's knife."

"I wasn't cleaning fish last night. You know that. I was working on the generator."

The lights flickered.

"The generator you fixed?"

"For the time being, but I got to run to town and pick up some parts."

"Oh, yeah, okay. How about taking Maeve along? With Sheila here, we're running out of wine faster than I expected."

Maeve pointed out the window. "You sure?"

"You'll be fine," Bernie said. "Lester's got some extra slickers. Be sure to layer up."

This would be a good day for ghost stories, hot chocolate and s'mores. Maeve wondered if nuns told ghost stories, or if they only told saint stories. Unexplained ghostly activity, saintly post-mortem miracles. Kind of the same thing, Maeve thought, except for the good versus evil thing. If Tom was here, she would have said that out loud and he would have laughed.

Roger came into the kitchen, rubbing his glasses with the hem of his T-shirt and looked around. "Has anyone seen Sheila?"

"Did you look in the gym?" Bernie asked.

"She's not there."

"The sauna?"

"She's not there."

Bernie dried her hands on her apron.

"You look outside? Maybe she went out for a cigarette."

"Not there."

The image of the back door standing open the night before flashed in Maeve's mind.

"Last night, I found the door open," Maeve said. "When I was leaving the gym."

"Oh, Jesus," Bernie whispered.

Maeve jogged out of the kitchen, down the hallway to the exit door, grabbed a slicker hanging on a nearby hook, and held it over her head. When she stepped outside, she was pelted with warm water. It felt like rocks being thrown at her, hard. She scanned the complex, got her bearings, and pulled the hood low over her face.

Maeve slid on mud as she climbed up the incline, trudging two steps up and sliding one step down. Gullies of water rushed past her. Her feet sank ankle deep in some places. She stepped off the path into the brush, looking for where the plants had soaked up the water and she could get better footing.

The surge of rain abated and the sound replaced with crashing in the woods. Something big and heavy was moving through the brush. She froze.

The bear was dragging something. Something she hoped wasn't Sheila Wadsworth.

***

To the parents of Danny Johnson,

We have noticed lately that Danny seems to have trouble concentrating in third grade and often forgets to bring his homework. He has also been absent or tardy quite a bit this year. Absenteeism is beginning to impact his grades. Also, he often tells us that he has forgotten his lunch. We are only happy to provide Danny with nutritious meals both for lunch and breakfast. If you could bring him to school an hour before the bell rings, we would be happy to accommodate him.

Yours Truly,

Sister Michael

P.S. Please make sure Danny is dressed appropriately for the weather.

***

THE MUZZLE FLASH BLINDED Maeve. She clenched her eyes, then opened them just enough so she could watch her footing. Two more blasts percussed in Maeve's ears. Sound was blotted out by the roar of white noise in her head. All she could hear was the thumping of her heart and the wash of air drawn in and pushed out by her lungs.

Rain and wind slashed at Maeve, Bernie, and Lester as they stood around the body. When Maeve looked at it, her stomach lurched. Bernie's head was bent over the shotgun she held at shoulder-height. She jerked her head at Lester, catching his attention, and mouthed the word "tarp", then jerked her head again, this time toward the lodge.

As Lester trotted back to the building, Maeve spotted the bear pacing in the under-growth. She waved for Bernie's attention and pointed.

Sound came back to Maeve. The relentless drizzle. Trees groaning in the wind. The bear crashing through devil's club.

The backdoor slammed. Bernie dropped the muzzle, turned to look. The bear launched.

Maeve leapt towards the bear, waving her arms overhead, whipping the poncho in the wind. "Go away, bear! Go away!" It sounded stupid. She had been told that if charged, she should yell at the bear, but no one had said what words worked best.

Bernie spun around, leveled the shotgun, blasted.

Lester and Grace appeared at their sides with a tarp.

"That should keep him away for a while," Bernie shouted into the wind, pumping the gun. "Hurry it up. She might still be alive."

From what little Maeve had seen of the body when she had dared to look, she was sure Sheila Wadsworth was dead. There wasn't much of a face left.

Lester unfurled the tarp. The wind whipped it back into his face. Maeve grabbed an end, knelt in the mud, and helped him lay it out flat. Grace anchored the corners with rocks while Bernie stood guard.

Lester positioned himself at the head. Grace took one foot. Maeve took the other. The leg, like the rest of the body, was drenched. It was true what they said about dead weight, it felt so much heavier. Maeve's hands slipped when she gripped the ankle. She grabbed a pants leg and twisted it around her fist. She zoomed in on Lester, watched him for cues.

More crashing noise in the brush. Bernie shot again, pumped again.

Lester lifted his end. Grace and Maeve lifted the legs. The body barely cleared the ground as they sidled over to the tarp. Maeve lost her grip on the rain-soaked pants and the body fell into the mud. "Sorry," she said.

Maeve wiped her hands on her jeans and grabbed the leg again, higher up this time. Grace did the same on the other side. They lifted.

Bernie was standing behind Lester. She aimed the gun and shot. The crack exploded in Maeve's ear. She shot again. Maeve was sure she'd be deaf when this was all over. Bernie waved furiously at them to get moving.

They positioned the body on the tarp. Grace went to the front and helped Lester drag it to the exit door. Bernie moved around to the tail end of the procession, walking backwards with the rifle at her shoulder pointed at the woods. Maeve walked alongside her, feeling useless.

She stumbled. An electric pain shot up her leg to the hip she had fallen on the day before. She looked around to see what she'd tripped on. A few feet away, something was out of place, something man-made and shiny. She stooped and picked up the missing chef's knife.

Behind Maeve, the bear roared and charged through the underbrush. Bernie fired again. Light flashed across Lester's face. Maeve had never seen terror before. The boom of the shotgun followed, and Grace dropped the tarp. A second explosion sent sparks arcing overhead as the generator blew up. The bear must have gotten between the generator and the lodge when Bernie shot at it.

Lester tugged on the tarp. Grace grabbed the end she had dropped and fell in beside him.

Maeve held the door open while Lester and Grace hauled the tarp and its load inside. Bernie grabbed the door and jerked her head at Maeve gesturing to go in. After Maeve stepped into the hallway, Bernie followed and slammed the door shut.

***

"What boyfriend?" Tom asked April.

"Anton Zakharov. My ex," she said. "Won't leave me alone."

"Bitch," Anton muttered as he tried to push himself off the floor.

Tom pointed at him again. "Stay down, dammit."

Anton collapsed. Tom wasn't sure if it was from the warning or if the booze had finally gotten to him.

She found her bra on the floor, picked it up, seemed to argue with herself about whether she should peel off her T-shirt in front of both Anton and Tom. "Close the door, will you?" April said to Tom. He did.

She seemed to change her mind and had stepped over Anton to get to the bathroom for some privacy when someone pounded on the shut door.

"Anymore boyfriends?" Tom asked.

"Fuck you," April said. She stuffed the bra into the bed and threw the covers over it.

More banging at the door, this time with a man shouting, "Police! Open up!"

Tom swung the door open. It was Larson, a friend of Tom's from A.A., in his Homer Police Department uniform, a big, blonde man with a soft layer of fat over solid muscle. Behind him, rain pelted down like machine-gun fire.

"What's up, Tom?"

"Not much, Larson. You?"

"Had a call. Mind if I come in?"

Tom looked behind him. April's arms were folded across her chest. Anton was still, eyes closed, mouth hanging open. "Sure," Tom said. "Why not?"

Larson stepped into the room, sidestepping Anton.

"Hey, April," Larson said.

"Hey, Larson."

Larson cocked his head while he looked at the man snoring on the floor. "Crazy Tony?" he asked April.

"Yup."

"Heard you two broke up."

"You heard right."

Larson surveyed the room with a lecherous eye.

"Screw you," Tom said. "The lady and I were spending a quiet evening when this joker busted in."

"That joker's got a split lip and those mitts of yours are all busted up."

Tom examined his hands. True enough, the knuckles were skinned. He flexed each of them in turn to see if they worked okay. The left was fine, the right, not so much. A pain jabbed his knuckles. Probably busted. Wouldn't be the first time.

"Problem is, Tom, we got a complaint about a disturbance. You know how it is. I can't take sides. So, how's about you and April and Crazy Tony come down to the station and we'll get this all sorted out? Help me load this guy in the back of my cruiser and April and you can drive your own truck, meet me down there. That work for you?"

There wasn't much Tom could say. Larson would have to arrest him if he didn't go willingly and it would be unfair to put that off on him. It wasn't Larson's fault. This clusterfuck wouldn't have happened if Tom hadn't picked up a girl he barely knew just because he was bored. Next time, he'd ask about any jealous boyfriends first before he took a girl home. Not having checked was a rookie mistake. "Sure, buddy," Tom said.

"You don't think he's going to puke?" Larson asked. "I don't want him messing up the back of my cruiser. It's not like Anchorage where you got some kid who cleans the car every night. I got to take care of it..."

Just then, Anton rolled over to one side and vomited all over Larson's shoes.

Larson scowled. "....myself."

***

THE COPPERY SMELL OF blood made Maeve gag. She remembered the knife in her hand and looked for a place to put it. That was when she noticed she was covered in blood.

"I heard a bang, it sounded like...."

It was Roger speaking. He had been standing in front of his room when they drug the tarp in. Maeve had forgotten about him.

He was standing behind Lester and Grace. He looked confused. From where he stood, he wouldn't have seen clearly what was on the tarp.

"What's going on?" Roger asked.

The sudden warmth of the room caused steam to rise from the bodies, all the bodies except the one on the tarp. Maeve looked at the others. They were all staring at the corpse. Upon hearing Roger, they looked at each other. No one, it seemed, wanted to tell him what they had found. Lester and Grace stepped aside, allowing Roger to see the body.

"No," Roger whispered. His knees buckled, and he fell. "Oh my God."

Grace turned on Bernie. "What the hell was that?"

"A bear, that's what the hell was that."

"You get him?"

"Maybe winged him. He ran off."

"Like that's what we need, a pissed off bear hanging around."

The nuns room door open. Sister Iggy came out, Sister Clare following behind her. "Ladies, what is...?" Iggy asked. Her eyes were drawn to the mauled remains of Sheila Wadsworth, the head and face reduced to raw meat, a large blood stain blossomed across her shirt.

Grace and Bernie squared off, their faces flushed, eyes wild. Maeve expected one of them to lunge at the other. They stood like that, frozen in anger.

"She went outside," Grace said. "The bear got her."

Iggy and Clare crossed themselves and began praying.

"Oh, Jesus," Bernie sobbed loudly, her anger suddenly gone. "What was she doing out there?"

Roger was sobbing. He touched Sheila's hand tenuously, like a child trying to wake his sleeping mother.

Another room door opened and Francis Nolan stuck his head out. "I thought I heard something, a big bang like..." He searched from face to face, then followed the line of their gazes to the floor. "Our dear Father in heaven," Nolan said as he crossed himself.

Lightening flashed. Another gush of water poured over the window. The rumble of distant thunder could barely be heard over the rain.

"Hey, that's my knife," Bernie said, noticing it in Maeve's hand. "Where'd you find it?"

"It was on the ground, just outside the back door," Maeve said.

"I thought you took it down to the dock," Bernie accused Lester.

"I told you there wasn't no fish. I didn't take it." He jerked his head toward the walk-in refrigerator. "Go look for yourself."

Bernie said, "That's not the point. Why was my good knife laying around in the dirt?"

Lester peered at Sheila's body. "Doesn't look right. That blood isn't from a bear attack. Look, there's no slash marks."

Iggy took a knee and studied the injuries. "You're right." She pointed to one in particular. "That's a stab wound."

Maeve's guts rolled. Cold shimmered up her body. Stars floated in front of her eyes. It was the adrenalin wearing off, she knew, yet she didn't want the others to think she was a wimp, or worse, demanding attention. She leaned against the wall for support before she realized no one was aware anymore that she was there.

"Oh, baby, I'm sorry," Roger whispered.

Nolan's hands were clasped as he whispered prayers to himself in Latin. He lifted his head and said, "she should have the Last Rites."

Grace wheeled on him. "Not from you, she won't."

Nolan looked stunned. He surveyed the people in the room. Roger on the floor patting Sheila's hand. Bernie, Grace, and Lester staring at him stony-faced. Iggy and Clare kneeling beside the body.

"Sister Ignatius will handle it," Bernie said.

"Very well. If you need me, I will be in my room." He pulled his head back inside and his door closes soundlessly.

"It's all my fault," Roger said. He was rocking back and forth on his haunches, his arms wrapped around his ribcage.

A long moment drew out, the only sound was water rushing outside and Roger's whimpering.

"Someone killed Sheila," Grace said.

"Fuck me," said Lester.

Chapter Ten

How MANY YEARS AGO was it when Iggy realized police work wasn't the solution?

It was when a case file was spread out on her desk in the detective's bullpen. Men and women were tapping away on the keyboards, talking on the phone, coming and going. Right up until then, she had been one of them.

And then it was like a fog lifting, a fog she hadn't known was there. Suddenly the room shone with light, everything and everyone glowing. Her metal desk blazed so brightly it hurt her eyes. Her hands were lean, the fingers slightly arched, artistically formed, a revelation of the complexity and beauty of creation, poised on the keyboard. And she realized that the task she was working on was futile.

The criminal justice system didn't save anyone. It was punitive. The cops found a bad guy, put him in jail, where he met more bad guys and learned more ways to be bad.

Prison was a university for criminals. Very few of them were rehabilitated, not because of what they learned or saw in prison, not because they were afraid of going back when they got out, instead because a miracle had occurred in their lives, a quickening of their souls. They were like the renaissance paintings where a dove flew over the saint's head signifying that the holy spirit had descended upon them.

Who got the redemption and who didn't was between each soul and God. But if Iggy could improve the chances that more souls connected with the divine, not by filling out another incident report, but by reaching young people before they became hardened criminals, showing them the beauty of a spiritual life, and praying for them, she would answer the call. To do that, she needed to get out of the police station and go where she was needed. It was all so clear.

On her morning coffee break, she called Mother Superior and made an appointment. That afternoon, she gave notice to her captain.

And now, right before her, laid the remains of her murdered sister. Iggy had missed something, a warning, that someone was in so much pain they would take Sheila's life. She should have seen it coming. She could have stopped it.

She made the sign of the cross and prayed.

"Eternal Father, I offer Thee the Most Precious Blood of Thy Divine Son, Jesus, in union with the masses said throughout the world today, for all the holy souls in purgatory, for sinners everywhere, for sinners in the universal church, those in my own home and within my family. Amen."

Sister Iggy made a deep sign of the cross, then lifted her head. "Prayer of St. Gertrude."

"Oh, yeah, sure, I knew that," Grace said.

Iggy returned to praying silently. This time she asked for the serenity to accept things she could not change, the courage to change the things she could, and the wisdom to know the difference. When she was finished, she crossed herself again. The other women followed suit.

When she looked up, Bernie was hyperventilating. Her gray hair was glued to her head by rain. Lester stared into space, appearing helpless, water dripping from his scraggly beard. Roger's glasses were askew on his nose and he was still rocking, his eyes closed, his arms wrapped around his ribs. Grace's face was frozen in a defiant mask Iggy recognized in her even before she had joined the force. Later as a cop, she saw that look on suspects sitting behind an interview table. The only person not related to this family was that troubled young woman, Maeve Malloy. She looked deeply sad.

"We need to call the police." Iggy pushed herself to a stand. "Lester, would you take Roger back to his room?"

Iggy squeezed Roger's arm. "You go along with Lester now. We'll let you know what the police say."

***

MAEVE HOVERED AT THE threshold of the manager's office, the knife still in her hand. The handle felt grainy in her hand from dirt glued to congealed blood. Grace was behind the desk, on the phone. Bernie and Iggy were crammed in beside her. They had left Sister Clare behind in the kitchen praying over the body.

"He wants to talk to you," Grace said with a frown and handed the phone to Maeve. She took it with her free hand, conscious of the weapon she held.

"Why does he want to talk to her?" Bernie whispered. Grace hissed in response and shook her head.

Maeve stepped inside the room and took the phone. "King?"

"What the hell is going on there?" King Kelly asked.

Maeve reiterated what Grace had just told him, that Sheila Wadsworth was dead.

"When was she killed?"

"Some time before ten thirty last night is my best guess.That's when I found the back door open. There was a lot of water on the floor like someone had come in from the rain."

"Are you free to talk?"

Bernie tapped Maeve on the back. "Why does he want to talk to you?"

"Hold on a minute, King." Maeve covered the mouthpiece. To Bernie, she said, "Excuse me, I need to talk with him privately."

"Why you?" Bernie's voice was louder.

"Because she's a lawyer," Sister Iggy said.

Bernie and Grace stared at Iggy. Maeve hadn't told Iggy her secret. She'd like to know how she figured it out.

"I'll explain it to you later," Iggy said to Bernie.

"What's going on?' King's voice sounded small on the receiver.

"How quick can they get here?" Bernie asked. "I mean, she's just there in the middle of the hallway."

"King, the body is in the hallway. How quick can you get here?"

"Is that where she was found?"

"No, we found her outside."'

"And you moved the body?" His voice squeaked.

"We weren't sure she was dead, King. We saw a bear dragging her into the woods and we tried to save her. We didn't know for sure until we got her inside." That wasn't exactly what happened. Maeve figured a little bit of consideration for Bernie's feelings couldn't hurt. She'd tell King the truth later, that it was obvious Sheila was dead and that Bernie's hoping otherwise had been unrealistic. And even though it was clear she was already dead, the right thing was to protect the body for the family. If he continued to argue, she'd point out that there would be scant evidence if the bear had its way.

"You think the bear got her?" King asked.

"No, she'd been murdered first and the bear found her."

"How could you tell?"

"She had a knife wound."

"You got the knife?"

Her hand grasped the knife tightly in reaction to his question. Pebbles glued to it dug into her palm.

"Found it in the mud."

"And she's exactly where now?"

"In the guest room corridor. On a tarp."

"This is the problem, Maeve. We got a pineapple express rolling in. It's going to rain hard for days. Rain, wind, thunder, lightning, the works. The streets in Seward are flooded already. No boats in or out of the harbor. I can't get across the bay. The mayor called the governor early this morning and got her to declare Seward a disaster area. So, you're on your own, Counselor. I need you to bag the weapon and find a cold place to store the body. Wrap it up as best you can and try not to touch anything. Got it?"

Maeve turned to the women watching her. "He can't get here right now. No boats in or out of the harbor. We need to bag the knife and we can move her. Do you have somewhere out of the way, somewhere cold?"

"Like the walk-in fridge?" Bernie asked.

"That'll work," King said, having overheard the conversation.

"I'll let them know. Hold on." Maeve covered the mouthpiece again. "King says the walk-in fridge will work."

"We'll take care of it," Iggy said, then herded Bernie and Grace out of the office.

When the door was closed and Maeve was alone, the sound of pounding rain subsided yet she could hear it from King's end of the call.

"I can talk now," she said.

"Who killed her?"

"No idea."

"What do you know about the victim?"

"She was a tourist from California visiting with her husband. He works on the slope, two weeks on, two weeks off. She'd never been to Alaska before so on his two weeks off, they took a cruise up and stayed a couple of extra days for a wildflower hike that was scheduled."

"Well, look, you're stuck there with a body and a murderer until I can get over. It could be a day or two. Get them separated and tie down their stories. Names, why they came to the lodge, where they're from, how they know the victim, alibi, you know the drill."

"I'm not a cop, King. I am, I was, a defense attorney."

"You're the only person I know and trust on that island, Maeve. If what you say is true, there is a killer on the loose. You don't want to be the next victim."

"I don't know these people, why would someone want to kill me?"

"Not a Shakespeare fan?"

"What?"

"Never mind."

There it was again. Lawyer bashing. No one says stuff like that to a cupcake lady.

"Was that supposed to be funny?" Maeve asked.

"Sorry, you're right," King said, with a note of genuine remorse. And she felt regret for having rebuked him. It made her feel like they had both revealed a little bit of vulnerability to each other. Maybe this was what making friends was about. King went on, "I'm worried about you. You got to keep your eyes open, Counselor. You don't want someone getting killed on your watch, do you?"

Right. Just like that they were at arm's length again. King was talking about how Mataafa killed Manny Reyes because Maeve had dropped the ball. Of course, King knew about it. Everyone did. It's a big deal when an attorney gets suspended from the bar association, a juicy bit of gossip. The courthouses would have been full of tittering for weeks after the Supreme Court published the notice in the Anchorage newspaper.

"Okay, fine," Maeve said. "What do you know about the lodge owners?"

"They just bought that place a couple of years ago. Before that, it'd been abandoned for decades. They fixed it up themselves and opened for business a year or two ago. They're not from around here. Rumor has it they came into some money and decided to move into the woods." King added, "It's just like a damned reality show."

"What about Grace?"

"Who's that?"

"The manager. Do you know anything about her?"

"Never heard of her. Get me a last name and I'll run it. Get all their names, full names, aliases, dates of birth, and I'll run them, get back to you." King asked for Maeve's cell number so they could call each other privately. After she gave it to him, he said, "Oh, yeah, Maeve?"

"Yes, King?"

"Watch your back."

***

BEFORE SISTER IGGY HERDED Grace and Bernie out of the manager's office, she took a last look at Maeve Malloy standing behind the desk, the phone to her ear, watching the women file out. Not just watching them but appraising each. Iggy could almost hear the cogs turning in Maeve's mind as she sorted what she knew from what she didn't know, all framed under the ultimate question, which one of them was capable of murder.

Maeve looked comfortable for the first time since Iggy had met her. She might doubt her calling as an attorney now, yet it was obvious to Iggy that she was capable and intelligent. And she would put the puzzle together before anyone else, and probably long before the police arrived.

As soon as the manager office door was closed, Bernie wheeled around to Iggy. "How did you know she was a lawyer?"

Iggy walked on. She found Sister Clare, sitting on the floor next to Sheila, her hands folded in her lap, chewing her lip. "Thank you, Sister. You can go back to our room now. I'll be along in a few minutes."

It took a while for Clare to react. She was lost again somewhere in that mind of hers until real life seeped in and got her attention if only briefly.

Clare stood and Iggy showed her to their shared guest room.

"How did you know?" Bernie asked again.

Iggy opened her eyes wide. "You never heard of the internet?"

"What made you think to look?"

"When we were in Seward, a state trooper who she clearly knew addressed her as 'counselor'. It struck me as strange that a lawyer is claiming she was a dishwasher, so I looked her up."

Honestly, how these people made it through life at all was astonishing, Iggy thought. They stood over Sheila's ravaged body, Bernie trying hard not to look and Grace arms crossed, staring at her. At least Grace was sober. For a little bit last night, Iggy had seen beneath Grace's shell, the vulnerable mother whose guilt tortured her. Now that defiant look, the hardened criminal mask, was in place again. How much anger could one heart hold?

Bernie's face was red and bloated, from a hangover and from crying. She had meant well. After all her years laboring to support and raise children she had not borne, she had a dreams of her own. She'd often spoken of her desire to live in a log cabin deep in the wilderness. When the opportunity to buy this lodge arose, she spun a fantasy where nothing could go wrong and where the tourism industry would subsidize her Utopian retirement. Now all she had left to show was their little sister dead on the floor, murdered.

Bernie peeled wet hair off her face. "You don't think she's undercover, do you?"

"Worried she's going to find out about your pot grow?" Grace laughed.

"Shut up."

"It's not all about you," Grace said. "Someone killed Sheila."

"Like you were ever that close. I was the one who raised her when the two of you took off."

Iggy had enough. She picked up the foot of the tarp and began dragging.

Grace took one corner of the tarp from Iggy.

"What should I do?" Bernie asked.

"Make sure she doesn't roll of the tarp."

"How do I do that?"

"You could pick up the other end," Iggy said. She and Grace exchanged looks. Bernie was helpful only when she had a very clear understanding of what was expected of her but otherwise, she couldn't be expected to take initiative.

"Catch the door." Iggy said to Grace.

Grace held the door while Iggy dragged the body inside the walk-in fridge. Iggy said another quick prayer for the salvation of Sheila's soul.

Bernie was standing by the window when Iggy came out. "You sure she's dead?" she called over her shoulder.

"I'm sure," Iggy said.

"Now what?" Bernie asked Iggy.

"You're both soaked and filthy. You should both take a shower and get into something dry."

"Not that. Sheila. You're the cop. You know this stuff. What's going to happen next?"

"Right now, the trooper is telling Maeve to separate us and get our stories before we have time to cook something up."

Bernie untied her apron and wadded it up. "Cook what up?"

"A cover story, you idiot," Grace said, tugging at the wet sweatshirt stuck to her body. "Alibis."

Iggy tsked. "You might want to consider telling the truth."

Grace laughed.

"What truth?" Bernie asked.

"Honest to God, are you as stupid as you sound?" Grace asked. "Or is it an act?"

"What are you talking about?"

"You're the one who wanted Nolan dead. Sheila threatened she was going to warn him." Grace jabbed Bernie in the arm. "You're the first one they're going to look at."

"You think I killed her?"

"Well did you?" Grace asked.

"Stop it," Iggy said. "Bernie didn't kill Sheila. She couldn't have." There were other more likely suspect. Grace. Roger. Cops always looked at the husband first. Nine times out of ten, women were murdered by the man in their lives.

"Lester sure didn't have a reason to kill her," Bernie said. "He hardly knew her. And if Roger was going to do it, you'd think he'd have planned it out better. He's an engineer for chrissake!"

Iggy let the blasphemy go without comment. She didn't want to get sidetracked as she silently listed suspects to herself. Grace, Roger, Lester, Francis Nolan. Even Bernie until she was ruled out, although Iggy wouldn't admit that out loud. It would be unkind. Even if she had killed Sheila, Bernie was grieving. Besides, there was a little bit of Iggy the cop that whispered she should keep her thoughts to herself.

Grace slapped Iggy on the arm with the back of her hand. "You suspect Nolan did it."

"I'm not sure. What I do know is that we all need to think about our alibis. I'm not saying you should make something up. I'm saying you need to be clear on where you were and what you did last night before you make a statement because if you later remember something or correct yourself, it will look suspicious."

"Well, we know where you were last night, Sister," Grace said. "Locked up in your room with that crazy little Clare. I've been meaning to ask, why did you bring her along anyway?"

"I thought the trip might do her good."

"Lester and I sacked out right after we all talked," Bernie said. "He can vouch for me."

Grace looked at Bernie. "What are you talking about?"

"My alibi," Bernie said. "I was with Lester all night."

"You forget," Grace said. "Lester and you sacked out after we played cards until two a.m. in your room."

Bernie frowned at Grace. Grace stared back.

Grace might not be the killer, Iggy thought. She might think she needs to cook up an alibi because she was alone all night and as soon as they find out about her past, she's the first person they're going to look at. On the other hand, Grace was working really hard to make Bernie feel like she would be the most likely suspect. Why would she do that unless she had something to hide?

"Oh, yeah," Bernie said. "The card game. That's right. I forgot. We played cards until when?"

"Two a.m."

"Is that when Maeve found the back door open?"

"Long after. She found the back door open around ten-thirty, closed it, and then went to bed."

Bernie appeared to be working it out. "Two a.m. That's right. We played cards until two a.m. in our room and then you left."

"Two a.m.," Grace said. "Don't forget."

"Two a.m. Got it. So, how much are we going to tell her?"

The door swung open, and Maeve entered the room. The knife was still in her hand. "We need to talk, but first I have to put this away." She pulled open a drawer with her free hand, pulled out a plastic bag, and slipped the knife inside. She headed into the walk-in refrigerator and then came out again without the weapon.

Grace mouthed her response to Bernie's last question, "Later."

Chapter Eleven

KING KELLY PAWED AROUND his desk drawer, found Tom Sinclair's business card and punched the numbers into his desk phone. King had known Maeve and Tom for years since that fishing case down in southeast. From time to time since then, he would see them in court together. When he was in Anchorage, he'd give Tom a call and they'd grab a cup of coffee. He always felt comfortable around Tom. Maeve was another matter.

She had a good reputation with the cops and the prosecutors, for a defense attorney. Everyone knew that she believed what she said. You couldn't ask much more, considering the kind of people she represented. She couldn't help it if her clients lied to her.

Lying clients and lying witnesses were a risk that everyone on both sides of the law faced, prosecutors and cops, defense attorneys and investigators. Everyone knew that Maeve Malloy would never knowingly spread a falsehood and that she cared about justice for everyone, for the witnesses and the victims as well as the defendants.

King had taken an instant liking to Tom. He was straight-up, the kind of guy you could count on. The kind of guy who would pull over if he saw your car broken down beside the road. Last summer, Tom had come down to Seward and King had gotten a day off, so they could go fishing. The entire time Tom was checking his phone to see if Maeve had called or texted. Man, he had it bad. Tom Sinclair was in love. Not that he ever admitted it.

It was strange to see Maeve without him on the boardwalk yesterday. King chalked it up to the problems she'd been having with the bar association. She had gotten suspended. If she wasn't practicing law, she didn't need an investigator hanging around. So, no Tom.

King wondered how Tom was handling the separation. He would want to know that Maeve was trapped in a lodge with a dead body and a murderer. And Tom would expect King to call him as soon as he could. There would be hell to pay if he didn't let Tom know.

"Hello?" a man's voice answered. It didn't sound like Tom.

"Is this Tom Sinclair's phone?"

"It is. Who's calling?"

"Trooper Patrick Kelly. Who am I talking to?"

"Homer Police Department, Officer Smith at your service. Your Tom Sinclair is our guest."

"You arrested him? For what?"

"Assault. He got into a fight over a local girl. You know the story. Bad weather. Bored fishermen. Booze."

Tom was a little too old for fighting over a girl, King thought. Apparently, he wasn't handling the separation from Maeve well. And when did he start drinking again? During their day-long fishing trip, Tom had told him about being a recovering alcoholic, how he'd had more than ten years clean, how recovery had saved his life. "You're telling me Tom Sinclair was drinking alcohol?"

"I wasn't here when they brought him in, Trooper. Only telling you I heard that a drunk fisherman got into a fight over some girl."

"I need to talk to Sinclair. Right now."

"Sorry, Trooper, he's over at the courthouse waiting to see the magistrate."

"Magistrate Kelly?"

"Yeah, that's funny. You got the same name."

King smiled. "Yeah, right. Funny."

***

MAEVE FOUND THE WOMEN in the kitchen. The noise of the storm seemed louder here than in Grace's office. The generator must be fixed. Ceiling light fixtures burned brightly, making the dark outside seem blacker. Beyond the window, tree line was gone, and sheets of rain poured almost sidewise from the sky.

Maeve went into the walk in and found the body was laying on the floor, wrapped loosely in the tarp. Maeve's skin turned cold. If she stood in there any longer, an old case of frostbite was going to make her toes burn. Maeve lifted the corner of the tarp and placed the bagged knife on top of the body. She nodded, then came out.

"Where's Lester?" Maeve asked. She found herself speaking louder than she would have normally to overcome the storm's howling.

"Still with Roger." Bernie answered. She sniffed. Her eyes were red from crying. "You're a lawyer."

"I'm not practicing currently."

Grace spoke, "You didn't mention it on the phone when I asked about your work history."

Maeve never liked the "you didn't ask" defense. Snarky witnesses flourished it, suggesting that they were smarter than the attorney for not having asked the question sooner. Thing was, the question did get asked. So, the witness wasn't that smart after all. Just obnoxious.

"You're right," Maeve said. "And I apologize for that. I'm taking some time off."

"I thought lawyers were rich," Grace said.

Here Maeve would have said, "I thought lawyers were rich too!" and everyone would laugh. But with a dead body in the fridge, it wasn't the time to joke.

This was a time for truth. Honesty was more likely to induce honest responses. "It's a brutal business," Maeve said. "I'm not sure I have the intestinal fortitude for it."

Bernie pulled several glasses from the dishwasher. "I need a drink. Who's with me?" She waived the glasses at Maeve. Right about now, Maeve would love a drink. Used to be she would loll away a rainy day with a fifth of whiskey. No one in Anchorage would ever know. Even Tom wouldn't find out.

Still, as sure as the sun rises, Maeve knew what would happen if she took a drink. One drink would lead to more drinks would lead to passing out, then coming to and drinking more.

She had a job to do. She needed to figure out who killed Sheila Wadsworth. Just for this moment, she wouldn't drink. "No, thanks."

Iggy held up one hand in refusal. Grace stared at the whiskey bottle from which Bernie was pouring herself two fingers. Bernie waved the fifth at Grace, inviting her to take a drink. Iggy tsked.

Bernie shot Iggy a defiant look. "Let her decide."

Grace's body was tense. Maeve knew an alcoholic when she saw one. Every cell in Grace's body felt drawn to the bottle Bernie was shoving at her but her mind was telling her to think, think, think instead. The first drink gets your drunk. One day at a time. One minute at a time.

Grace asked, "Got any coffee?"

Maeve silently cheered her resolve. Maybe there would be a chance later to talk privately about their common crosses they bore. And why Bernie would try to undermine it. It was clear from the interaction between the three of them that Bernie knew of Grace's addiction and Iggy was trying to protect her. What was it to Iggy anyway? And how did she know Grace was an alcoholic?

"Didn't get around to making it," Bernie said.

"Water's fine. I'll get it myself," Grace said. She took one of the glasses Bernie had set on the counter and filled it from the tap.

Maeve washed her hands in the sink under steaming hot water. "Here's the drill. Trooper Kelly wants everyone to go to their rooms and remain there until I can finish collecting statements."

"Then what?" Bernie asked.

"Then we wait for the police to come."

Bernie took a slug from her glass. "And what will they do?"

"They will transport all of us back to the station for formal statements. A medical examiner will come and transport the body to the local hospital. And they'll search the lodge and everything around it."

"Body?" Bernie said. "The body had a name. Sheila. Sheila Wadsworth." Bernie turned to face the sink again. Iggy stroke her back lightly.

"Of course," Maeve said. "Sorry I offended you. I didn't mean anything by it."

"Will they arrest someone?" Bernie asked.

"If they know who did it."

"Do they?"

Maeve looked at Bernie. How would King know who did it unless Maeve already knew and told him just now? Was Bernie implying that Maeve should have enough information already to identify the killer?

Bernie spoke. "You're the lawyer. I got a question. What if they find other stuff? What will they do?"

Maeve frowned. "What other stuff?"

"She means evidence of criminal activity not related to the murder," Iggy said.

If evidence of other criminal conduct was discovered, they could prosecute. "That's a mighty big 'if'," Maeve said. "I really can't answer that. I was a defense lawyer, not a prosecutor, so I'm not entirely sure of what goes on behind the scenes in an investigation before charges are made."

Bernie exchanged a meaningful look with Grace. Whatever crimes Bernie was worried about, Grace was in the know. The pot, Maeve figured. As much as Lester reeked of it, there had to be a grow operation nearby. Maybe upstairs in an unused guest room Lester was adamant Maeve couldn't use. Maybe in the cellar.

Maeve said, "I'd like you, Sister Iggy, and you, Grace, to go back to your rooms. After I've gotten all the statements, you'll be free to access the lodge as you please. I'd advise you not to leave the building, but with the storm outside you can't anyway. If anyone does try to sneak away, please let me know as soon as possible."

"Who are you to tell us what to do and what not to do?" Grace asked.

"You are absolutely right. I have no authority whatsoever. But I do have the ability to tell Trooper Kelly what happened and who did it."

"Couldn't you make a citizen's arrest?" Bernie asked.

Right, the citizen's arrest thing. People watch entirely too much television. "It depends on the circumstances, whether a person is justified to make a citizen's arrest. As a rule, it's a stupid thing to do. Someone could get hurt. Besides, we're on an island. If someone tried to leave the lodge, where could they hide?"

Maeve's statement was met with a long silence. Clearly there was something the three of these women knew that Maeve didn't. Something she would have to dig out.

"You mind if I wait in my office?" Grace asked. "I have some work to do."

"Sure, that'll be fine."

"What about me?" Bernie said.

"I'd like to talk to you first, if you don't mind."

"I need to get something out for breakfast." Bernie glanced at the clock on the wall. "Brunch, now." She pulled a bottle of kitchen disinfectant from under the sink and began wiping down the counters.

"I'll help," Maeve said.

Bernie held up a hand. "That's okay, I got this."

And just like that, the transformation was complete. Maeve went from one of the gang, albeit the dishwasher, to an outcast, the lawyer. She had first felt it in the manager's office the instant when King asked to speak to her. When Iggy outed her for being a lawyer, it seemed like everyone took one step back. Maybe they didn't, maybe it was in her head. Even so, it felt like they had. And now, here she was the interrogator, someone to be distrusted, someone to be lied to and tricked.

"We'll be waiting," Iggy said, then she touched Grace's elbow and they both walked out the swinging door.

***

MAEVE SWUNG BY HER room, changed into dry clothes, and grabbed a yellow legal pad and a pen from her backpack. That last night in her condo when she had packed for the trip, she saw the pad on an end table, one of several she'd strewn about the condo out of habit from when she was a trial lawyer. She had stood over it for a long time wondering why she'd need it. Maybe she'd write Tom a letter. Nah, she'd text him if she had anything to say. In the end, she decided she didn't feel right without paper and a pen handy.

Back in the kitchen, she found Bernie alone, sitting on a stool, drinking. She had changed into dry jeans and another New Age t-shirt, this with the image of a Native American mounted on a horse overlooking a valley.

Maeve opened the audio recording app on her telephone, set it on the butcher block table and then put pen to paper, ready to take notes. Bernie returned to the cantaloupe she'd abandoned on the counter when they first noticed Sheila was missing and finished slicing the melon she had been working on.

"Can I get your full legal name and date of birth?"

"Mary Bernadette Parker. December 7, 1960."

"Maiden name?"

"McNair," Bernie said absentmindedly. Then she lifted her hands in the air and looked around the room as if she had lost track of what she was doing.

"I'd be happy to help," Maeve said.

"Not necessary." Bernie pulled a platter out of a cupboard and arranged the slices.

"And your husband?"

"Lester Alvin Parker, January 23, 1982."

Bernie looked older than Lester but Maeve was surprised by how much. Twelve years was more than she'd expected – they jelled like an old married couple.

"How long have you lived in Alaska?"

"Three and a half years."

"What brought you?"

Bernie didn't answer right away. She retrieved a bowl of grapes from another counter and dumped them in a colander. She ran water over them while she went to the muffins still in their pans and carefully turned them out, then arranged those on another platter. She stepped back, admiring her work and noticed Maeve watching. "Did you say something?"

"What brought you to Alaska?"

"We always wanted to come up. Live off the land, be close to nature, you know. So when we retired, we figured it was now or never."

"So you bought this lodge?"

Bernie retrieved her whiskey. Maeve watched as she lifted the tumbler to her lips. The surface of the amber liquid maintained level while the glass around it tilted. That had always fascinated Maeve. It was like magic. Bernie drained a considerable amount of the contents down her throat and put the glass down exactly in the spot that she had lifted it from.

"Sure you don't want something?" Bernie asked.

"I'm sure," Maeve said. A truth and a lie. She could feel the whiskey burn in her throat and tasted a phantom peat flavor on her tongue. Did that mean she wanted it? Was it her mind or her body that craved alcohol?

No one would ever know. She could take a drink and get away with it. Her stomach lurched, promising to vomit if she gave in.

Maeve looked at her legal pad. "Tell me about buying the lodge."

"We cashed out our investments, sold everything, and came up here."

"What happened to living off the land?"

"We're doing that too. I have a garden. Lester fishes and hunts. We just thought it might be a good idea to hedge our bets. Everyone was coming to Alaska for vacations. There were ads on television all the time. So when we saw this lodge for sale in the back of a magazine, we thought we could pick up a few extra bucks from having guests, especially since we're right here in Seward where all the cruise ships drop off their passengers." Grace took a slug from her whiskey. "And now, this! We'll never get any business if people hear there was a murder."

"Not turning out like you planned?"

"Lester was way over his head with fixing this place up. You know how men are, say they can do anything. He'd worked in construction. But when something got complicated, he'd have to call someone in to help. Drained all our extra money. And then there's all this stuff that didn't get finished." She waved her glass around. "The busted up old generator. The leaking roof. Our cabin up the hill is a dump."

"Trooper Kelly said the lodge had been abandoned for years before you took it over. It must have been a lot of work to get it in shape."

"You were talking to him about us?"

"Is there some reason why I shouldn't?"

"What you should be doing is finding out who killed Sheila. She didn't deserve it. She didn't do anything wrong. And I don't want to wake up in the middle of the night with some lunatic standing over me with a knife."

"That's what I'm trying to do. Any information you can give me would be helpful. Is there something in particular you're worried about?"

"Why should I be worried. I didn't kill her."

"You seemed concerned about evidence from another crime being found."

"Just curious," Bernie said. She filled her glass with four fingers of whiskey. "I don't know what I can tell you. She and her husband showed up here the day before you. I'm betting it was him. They fought like cats and dogs. Isn't it usually the husband? Is that what you're thinking, Roger did it?"

"What I think doesn't matter."

"Sure it does. The cops trust you. That's why they asked you for help."

"I'm just collecting information, Bernie. I'm not making any judgments. Trooper Kelly doesn't make the call either. It's up to the District Attorney to decide who will be charged."

"Are all murderers caught?"

"By no means. Even if they have a suspect, they need evidence to prosecute. So anything you can tell me would be helpful."

"All I know is Roger and Sheila argued last night."

"I heard them. But I couldn't make out what they were saying."

"You know as much as I do, then. I was upstairs in my room with Lester and Grace, playing five card stud. Usually we spend the nights up at the cabin but with that bear prowling around out there, it'd be stupid to make the trip. So we stayed here. I couldn't make out what they were saying, just kind of muffled voices. Angry, though you know?"

***

To THE PARENTS OF *Danny Johnson,*

Please be advised that Danny is suspended from school for a two week period following the discovery of marijuana in his school locker.

Yours Truly,

Principal Quigley

Chapter Twelve

SISTER IGGY FOLLOWED GRACE into the manager's office. Grace flopped down in the chair behind her desk. Iggy took the visitor chair.

"Aren't you supposed to go back to your room?" Grace asked.

"In a minute," Iggy said. "First, I wanted to talk to you alone. How are you doing? Are you okay?"

Grace slapped the desktop. "It wasn't supposed to happen this way."

"What are you talking about?"

"This wasn't part of the plan. No one was supposed to get hurt. Well no one besides Nolan, that is."

"Do you still want to go through with it? Maybe we should reconsider."

"Hell yes, I still want to go through with it." Grace pulled the bottom desk drawer out, stared inside, and closed it again.

From where Iggy was sitting, she couldn't see what Grace was looking at. "What's that?"

"Never you mind. It's just that there's things going on I don't understand. That bothers me. Like that lawyer showing up out of the blue."

Grace's attempt to distract Iggy from the secret contents of the drawer hadn't worked. She would find out what was in there, later. It must have been important for Grace to be looking for it at the same time she was talking about Sheila's death.

"You're overreacting," Iggy said.

"Bullshit, I am. What lawyer takes a job washing dishes? Don't you think that's weird? What you want to bet she's undercover, working for the feds? They're going to bust Lester's pot grow."

Although Alaska had legalized the pot industry, Iggy knew growing and selling marijuana was illegal under federal law. There was nothing stopping the feds from prosecuting, especially if they thought someone was smuggling pot across state lines. But the possibility that they'd enlist a disgraced criminal defense attorney was laughable. "That's ridiculous," Iggy said.

"How do you know she didn't get into trouble with the feds, like maybe she was sneaking drugs into prison, and she went undercover to get a good deal, or to get off altogether."

"Not seeing it," Iggy said. "People who become defense attorneys don't gravitate to becoming informants for the government. And the government wouldn't trust them anyway. Prosecutors think defense attorneys are lying scum. Besides, what I found on the internet said she lost her license because of a case. She only got a short suspension. She could have gone back to practicing by now. I believe her. I think she doesn't know what she wants or where she fits in."

"Well she's falling into the cop role pretty easy."

Iggy thought about it. Maeve was falling back into law easily and it suited her. Even if she didn't know where she fit in, she clearly had a gift for the law.

"Maeve's will be done talking to Bernie soon," Iggy said, standing. "I need to get back to my room."

"So you should, Sarge."

"Before I go, I wonder what you have in mind for Francis Nolan."

"Tonight. After Maeve Malloy goes to bed."

Iggy heard the sound of the swinging kitchen door thump open.

"I'll explain it to you later," Grace said quietly.

Iggy scooted out of the office, skirted the reception desk and headed down the hall, listening to footfalls behind her. She had just slipped into her room and closed the door when she heard Francis Nolan's voice in the hallway.

**

TOM WAS SITTING IN the jury gallery handcuffed to Anton Zakharov, the man who'd attacked him in the motel room that morning. Tom's lip was swollen and tender. He poked at it with the tip of his tongue from time to time, tasting blood when he did.

Anton was slumped against him and Tom tried to adjust his weight so the man didn't fall into his lap. As soon as they sat down, Anton had passed out, head on chest, snoring, and drooling into his long, sparse blonde beard. Every time he exhaled, the sweet stink of last night's beer filled the air around him. Anton's nose was splattered all over his face. By the looks of it, not for the first time. Maybe Tom helped pretty-up Anton a bit.

Tom leaned as far away as he could. With his free hand, he reached into his jeans pocket, pulled out a pack of matches, and had started cleaning his fingernails with the cardboard corner when the backdoor of the courtroom opened.

Vincent Kelly, the local magistrate, stood in the doorway. He was a short fella, wore jeans and a plaid flannel shirt, and had red hair, pale face, and green eyes. Tom knew he was one of the many cousins of King Kelly, the state trooper, from the lengthy family history King had given him when they were drifting in a boat near Seward last summer.

The magistrate cast his eye around the room. It was empty except for Tom, Anton and Larson. "Are you Tom Sinclair?"

Tom tried to stand, pulling against Anton's dead weight. "Yes, sir."

"Got a call for you in my office." He turned to Larson, who was sitting in a chair looking bored. "Unhook Mr. Sinclair and send him in."

"What am I supposed to do with the other guy?" Larson asked.

"You stay there and watch him."

A baby district attorney entered the front door wearing a blazer that was too roomy for him although the sleeves were too short. A backpack was slung over one shoulder.

Magistrate Kelly waived him over. "In here, Counselor, we need a word."

Larson unlocked the handcuffs. Tom stashed the matches in his pocket, shoved his shirt tail in, and combed his hair with the palm of his hands. The magistrate was still holding the door open when Tom stepped through ahead of the baby lawyer.

Across the hall was an open door leading to a small office. Tom wandered into it and waited for the others. When he looked out the window, he felt disoriented. He wondered if he'd lost time. The sky was nearly black. Through the distortion of water washing down the glass, he saw spruce trees bending in the wind. The ocean he knew was there was invisible in the gloom.

Magistrate Kelly rounded the desk and took a seat. He picked up the phone handset, and said, "Putting you on speaker, King."

King Kelly had found Tom handcuffed in a courtroom on a weekend. He was a better cop than Tom had given him credit for.

"Tom, are you there?"

"I'm here. What's up, King?"

"It's your lawyer, Maeve Malloy."

Tom's heart banged against his chest twice. He took a deep breath to calm it down.

"Something happen?"

"Not to her. Here's the thing, she's staying at a lodge across the water on Fox Island. Looks like someone got murdered there last night."

"Murdered? You caught the guy?"

"We don't know who did it yet."

"So why are you calling me? Why aren't you over there arresting someone?"

"No boats in or out of the harbor 'cause of the pineapple express. I can't get over there today. Maybe tomorrow, I don't know."

"She's alone?"

"She's alone with a bunch of other people. How quick can you get here?"

The magistrate said to the baby prosecutor, "What's the state's position?"

The kid rummaged through his backpack and pulled out a file folder. "Mr. Sinclair is charged with assault four."

"Not a big deal, Counselor," Magistrate Kelly said.

"I need to talk to the victim before I can make any recommendations," the kid said.

"Sure." The magistrate rose from his desk, stepped into the hall, and called into the courtroom, "Trooper, bring in Mr. Zakharov."

"Crazy Tony?" the young attorney said.

"That's the one," the magistrate said on his way back to his desk.

Static crackled over the telephone line.

"You still there, King?" Tom asked.

"I'm here."

"Is she okay?"

"She's okay."

Anton Zakharov was pushed into the room by Larson. The sour smell of vomit still followed the trooper even though back in the motel, he had washed Crazy Tony's puke off his shoes in the bathroom sink. The smell must have reached the magistrate because he gave Larson a frown. "You can stay in the hallway, Trooper."

Larson propped Tony against the door frame and stood behind him, holding him up.

"Mr. Zakharov, are you filing charges against this man?" Magistrate Kelly gestured to Tom.

Anton forced his puffy, blackening eyes open. His head swiveled on his neck as he looked around the room. "What man?"

"This man here," the magistrate pointed at Tom.

"Who's he?" Anton's head dropped, his sagging his weight against Larson, who stumble backwards, swore under his breath, and then braced him against the wall.

The baby lawyer said, "It appears Mr. Zakharov isn't pressing charges."

"Case dismissed," Magistrate Kelly said. "You're free to go, Mr. Sinclair. You too, Counselor."

"On my way, King," Tom yelled as he pushed past the baby attorney the eased around Larson who was still trying to hold up Anton. As he rounded the corner toward the exit, he heard Larson say "screw it" under his breath, then the sound of a body thumping on the floor.

***

MAEVE WAS JUST ABOUT to knock on Roger Wadsworth's door when she heard a man's voice behind her. It made her jump.

"Miss Malloy, is it?" Francis Nolan said. For a large man, he was able to sneak up on her without making a sound. Maeve took a step back. The big man was crowding her space. "Is there something I can do for you?"

"I don't know what's going on."

She stared at him. Someone's been murdered, that's what's going on. The last time she had seen him was in the kitchen, when Sister Ignatius was performing the Last Rites. He'd been there only for a moment and most likely had missed the discovery of the knife wound.

"It looks like Sheila Wadsworth was murdered, Mr. Nolan. We reported it to the state troopers. They can't come over here right now because of the storm, so I've been asked to collect everyone's statements. I'm sorry, but I have to ask you to remain in your room until we have spoken privately."

"Why you?"

"I'm an attorney."

"I thought you were the dishwasher."

"I was taking some time off," Maeve said. She knew the answer wasn't satisfying to anyone who had the nerve to ask, yet it was all they were getting. This story wasn't about her, it was about the dead woman. And there was something suspicious about the way this guy demanded attention when everyone else was content to wait their turn. "I can't talk with you right now. I have to ask you to return to your room until I can get around to you."

"How long will that be?"

"I'm not entirely sure."

Nolan looked down the hall both ways then turned back to her.

"Is there a problem, Mr. Nolan?"

"I think I'm in danger."

"In danger from whom?"

"That's the thing, I don't know. Whomever killed the young lady."

Nolan must have read a skeptical expression on Maeve's face. He appeared to be thinking, adjusting his strategy.

As he did so, Maeve considered that he would not have been the first person who, because of his skewed perceptions, thought that he was the center of attention. On the other hand, as she had seen before, the killer sometimes tries to ingratiate himself into an investigation in order to keep tabs and manipulate its direction.

"I'm certain I'm in danger," Nolan said, sticking to his theme. "It's a long story. When can I talk to you?"

"Please, Mr. Nolan, just go back to your room and lock the door. I'll get to you as soon as I can."

"Soon?"

"As soon as I can, sir."

Maeve watched Nolan as he went back to his room. She waited until she heard the locks clack into place before she knocked on Roger Wadsworth's door.

***

GRACE'S FINGERS WERE ON the keyboard when she heard Roger's door open and close. She looked up and listened. Maeve must be talking to Roger now. Her drying clothes itched but she didn't have time to change. She swirled the mouse making it come alive and it opened onto the page she had just found, an Alaska Supreme Court Order.

"Well, I'll be damned."

The Court had suspended, not disbarred, Maeve Malloy. So, she wasn't just taking some time off. She'd gotten into trouble during a criminal trial. Even though Grace knew a lot about trials and jail and what lawyers said and did with their clients, but she didn't know what on between lawyers.

Maeve had overlooked a note in her file. Some investigator had left it there to warn her that her client's witness was lying. She didn't see it so she let the guy testify. After her client was acquitted, she found the note and didn't tell anyone. Not that it mattered, according to the Supreme Court, because double jeopardy prevented a retrial, but they were pretty pissed that she didn't tell the judge anyway. Something mumbo-jumbo about her conduct giving an appearance of impropriety and causing the public to doubt the veracity of the legal process.

Wasn't that what lawyers were supposed to do? Hide the bad evidence? Grace couldn't see what Maeve had done wrong.

Then Grace got to the interesting part. Maeve missed the note because she was drunk every night during the trial. Afterwards, she went to rehab. She'd gotten sober long before anyone found out about the note but the Supreme Court was still pissed off about her drinking. That's a laugh. They're all drunks: the lawyers, the judges, the cops. Being a drunk was okay. Getting caught being a drunk wasn't. What a big old pile of denial!

Maeve Malloy was a sober alcoholic. Funny, she hadn't mentioned that either. Grace tucked that little bit of information in her mind for later use.

Grace needed to get her plan back on track. Sheila's death had screwed everything up. Bernie was freaking out because she thought the cops were going to find the grow operation. She had good reason to worry, they probably were going to find it. And when they busted the grow, they could take the lodge away from her. And then her big fat windfall would go up on smoke.

Iggy was floating around being all holy. She could be counted on to corral everyone together. Then she'd take control, make it her own show. Let her. Afterwards Grace could do her own thing.

Before she put her plan into action, Grace would have to come up with another way to get Maeve Malloy, suspended lawyer and sober alcoholic, out of the way.

Chapter Thirteen

WHEN MAEVE KNOCKED ON Roger's door, Lester answered. Behind him, Roger Wadsworth was sprawled across a twin bed, a highball glass in hand. The other bed was still made. It would have been Sheila's.

The expression on his face was distracted. Lester slipped out as soon as Maeve came in, promising to go straight to his room and stay there until she could interview him, right after he checked on the generator. The lights flickered.

Maeve had a legal pad in one hand, a pen in another, her cell phone in her pocket, and was about to interview a grieving, and possibly drunk, widower. She might as well be practicing law again. Her stomach soured.

With Lester gone, Maeve waited for an invitation to sit. Roger didn't seem to notice her standing there.

"Mr. Wadsworth," Maeve said to get his attention.

Time stretched out before he reacted. He seemed to wake with a start, fumbling the glass in his hand. He put the glass down and pulled himself upright on the bed.

"We talked to the Troopers. They asked me to collect information from everyone so I need to ask you a few questions," Maeve said. She took the desk chair and dragged it to his bedside.

Maeve pushed the record button on her phone app, put the phone on the end table, and began to take notes. "You are aware that I'm recording this interview, Roger?"

He nodded.

"I'm sorry. I need you to give me an audible response." How easily that phrase rolled off Maeve's lips.

He frowned. "What was the question?"

"You are aware that I'm recording our interview?"

"Yeah, sure."

"So, to recap what I said before we began recording: the Alaska State Troopers have asked me to interview all the guests. Before we start talking about what happened last night, could I get some background information?"

"Sure."

"Where do you live?"

"Los Angeles."

"What do you do for a living?"

"I'm an oil engineer. I work on the North Slope, two weeks on, two weeks off."

"How long have you been married to Sheila?"

"Ten, twelve years. Something like that."

In all the years Maeve had interviewed men and women, men never remembered their anniversary and women had it on the tip of their tongues. The logical conclusion was that marriage was more important to women than men. Marriage changed their lives. They changed their names to reflect their new identity. Whereas the only change in a married man's life was he had gotten a live-in housekeeper. Maybe that was harsh. Maybe dreams do come true. If they did, Maeve hadn't seen it yet.

"Your birthdate?"

"April 8, 1977."

"Your wife's full name and birthdate?"

"Sheila Rose Wadsworth."

"Her maiden name?"

"McNair."

"Just like Bernie's maiden name. Are they related?"

"Their sisters. We're here for a family reunion."

No one had mention it to Maeve. On the other hand, why would they? She was just the hired help.

"What was her birthdate?"

"June 6 or June 8. I forget the year."

"Perhaps you could check her identification."

"Oh, right, sure." He swung his legs off the bed, pushed himself up, and looked around. A bright yellow purse was on the bathroom floor, open. He retrieved it. He put it on the bed and stood over it.

"Mr. Wadsworth?"

"Sheila doesn't like me going through her purse."

"May I?"

Roger handed the purse to Maeve.

It was the tidiest purse Maeve had ever seen. A set of BMW car keys. A tube of lip gloss. A bright yellow wallet that matched the purse. On the bottom, a few flakes of tobacco.

Maeve opened the wallet, found Sheila's drivers license in a plastic window, and took down the information.

"Did Sheila work?"

"She was an engineer too. Civil."

"I'd like to talk about what happened. Is that alright with you?"

Roger nodded.

"For the record, that's a yes?"

"Yes."

"When was the last time you saw your wife?"

***

LESTER CLOSED ROGER'S DOOR, looked down the hall, saw no one, then headed toward the kitchen. When he stepped into the lobby, he found the nuns sitting by the fireplace reading. It gave him a start. Sister Iggy looked up from her book, smiled at him, and looked back down again. The crazy little one didn't notice him.

Didn't the Malloy woman tell everyone to stay in their rooms? Why are they so special that they don't have to do what everyone else does?

He didn't trust nuns. What a strange Catholic thing, women cutting off their hair, giving up sex, wearing ugly clothes. He'd seen them in flocks back in Chicago and never thought he'd have one in his home, much less as an in-law. Back when he hooked up with Bernie, Iggy wasn't a nun, she was a cop. He wasn't sure which was worse.

He stopped in front of the reception counter and caught Grace's eye. Another someone who was so special she didn't have to go to her room. Seems like the only ones that did were Roger and Lester, the men. What was that about? Did the Malloy woman think Roger or Lester killed Sheila?

Grace was at her desk in that little office. He pointed toward the kitchen. Grace nodded.

He passed through the dining room, saw food laid out on the buffet, grabbed a muffin, and walked into the kitchen as he ate.

"You're dropping crumbs all over the floor," Bernie said without looking up. She was chopping celery with a vengeance, whacking the ends off, then hacking them to bits. She wiped her eyes with the back of her hand, she had been crying, and went back to work.

"The cops are coming," Lester said. "What are we going to do?"

"Has the lawyer interviewed you yet?" Bernie asked.

"Nope. I don't know nothing. What's she got to ask me?"

"She's talking to everyone. She has to. Go to our room and wait."

"Yeah, but..."

"Yeah, but nothing. Tonight, you and Roger get past that bear somehow and take down the grow. You can't burn it in this weather. Besides, she'd smell it. You can bury it in the woods. Even if the cops go back there, in all this mud, they won't see new digging. If you wrap it up good enough, we can dig it up later and sell it."

"Yeah, but what do I tell her?"

"That Grace was in our room playing cards until two in the morning. Then she left and we went to bed. We didn't hear anything. We didn't see anything. Got that?"

"Cards, got it." He opened the small fridge, took out a bottle of beer, and knocked the cap off on the countertop.

"I wish you wouldn't do that," Bernie said.

"Bummer." Lester saluted her with the bottle and walked back out the swinging door.

***

"When was the last time you saw your wife?" Maeve asked again.

"You mean alive?" Roger spat the words at her.

Maeve didn't know how cops managed with emotional witnesses. It's like Roger was waiting for the chance to make something Maeve's fault. To vent his anger and frustration on her. And it was her job to absorb it, if she wanted to get the facts. "Yes, sir."

"Last night. Here in our room." He dropped back onto the bed.

"What were you doing?"

"Reading."

"What was she doing?"

"She was in the bathroom when fell asleep. Next thing I knew it was morning."

Maeve had heard them arguing. "What time was that?" she asked.

"Couldn't tell you."

"What did the two of you talk about?"

Roger took off his hornrims and set them on the nightstand. He rubbed the reddened dents on the bridge of his nose, then ground his fists into eyes. He put the glasses back on and turned to face her. "When?"

"After dinner, before you fell asleep."

"Nothing special."

"The thing is, I'm trying to figure out why she went outside last night."

"She goes outside to smoke. She thinks, thought, I didn't know she still smoked cigarettes, like I couldn't smell it on her. So she'd sneak around."

"Did you argue?"

"Why do you ask? Are you accusing me? Do you honestly think I killed her?"

"I'm sorry, Mr. Wadsworth, I have to ask these questions. I wish I didn't have to. You understand the troopers need this information documented when it's still fresh in everyone's minds," Maeve said. "Was there an argument?"

Roger shrugged. "Not especially."

Maeve waited. Roger squirmed. Maeve checked to make sure the phone was still recording. It was.

Roger reached for the bottle of whiskey on the nightstand. He pulled another measure, took a sip, stood, and walked two paces to the window. He looked outside. The clouds were so dark and low that it looked like night. Waves of rainwater surged across the landscape. Runoff poured in sheets towards the bay. Moving the body wouldn't have compromised the investigation. Any evidence out there was gone by now.

Roger stuck one hand in his pocket and took another sip. "What were we talking about?"

"Did you argue?"

"I believe I said no."

"Back in the kitchen, you said it was all your fault."

"Look, shouldn't you be trying to find out who killed my wife? I've told you everything I remember. I don't know what else to tell you."

Maeve gave Roger a moment to collect himself. "I know this must be difficult, Mr. Wadsworth. These are important questions or I honestly would not be bothering you."

Roger scoffed and took a big swig of whiskey.

"When we were all in the kitchen, why did you say it was your fault?"

"Did I?"

"In the kitchen. We all heard you. What did you mean by that?"

"It was always my fault. Everything was my fault. I'm sure if Sheila explained it, she could tell you how it was my fault. It was easier to apologize when something happened."

When she was practicing criminal law, Maeve had seen many abusers and victims and she always marveled at how readily victims accepted responsibility for the violence. Roger Wadsworth could be such a person. Someone who had developed a Pavlovian response to any stressor: an apology. Or, he had murdered his wife and regretted it.

"Here's the thing, Mr. Wadsworth. I was down the hall in the gym last night and I could hear you arguing all the way down there."

"That wasn't arguing, Miss Malloy. That was how Sheila talked all the time. You have to, had to, know her. That's just how she is...was. No one paid attention. Look, shouldn't a cop be asking these questions?"

"They can't make it over here until the storm passes. I need to document the basic information as soon as possible. It's protocol. You understand."

"Why you?"

"Because I am familiar with the procedure. I only have a few more questions. Then I can leave you in peace."

Roger looked into his glass, then to the neatly made twin bed where Sheila would have slept.

"Sir?"

"Sorry, what's the question?"

"Did she say anything about meeting someone?" Maeve asked.

Roger's eyes widened, then he stared pointedly at Maeve. "I don't know what you're getting at."

"Did she say anything like she was going to leave your room and go outside to meet someone?"

"Oh, that's what you mean," Roger said. "No, nothing like that at all."

He put the drink down on the nightstand. His body curled inwards and he bent over.

Maeve wanted out of there. She didn't like her own emotions and she sure as hell couldn't handle anyone else's.

"I'll find someone to sit with you."

***

MAEVE CLOSED THE DOOR to Roger Wadsworth's room slowly, feeling the cushion of air resisting her, pulling through it gently so the sound would not disturb him. The door to Francis Nolan's room cracked open. He stuck out his head and beckoned towards her.

That's when she heard scratching at the exit door. A tree branch, maybe. But there were no trees nearby. The owners had cut down the recommended twenty feet around the lodge for a firebreak. She had seen the firebreak when they brought out the body. The sound came again, louder, grating.

Nolan heard it too. "What is it?" Maeve held up a hand to silence him. Something thudded against the door. Scratch. Another thud. The door shivered from the impact.

The bear.

Maeve stumbled backwards, crashing into the wall. Another thud, harder this time. The exit door creaked.

"Bear!"

"What bear?" Nolan asked.

"The bear is trying to break in!" Maeve shouted, hoping the others would hear.

"A bear is trying to get inside? Why? What are you going to do?"

"Go away, bear!"

"What am I supposed to do? You have to help me!" Nolan was hiding behind his door, only part of his face visible.

Maeve couldn't take her eyes of the door, willing it to hold. She heard Grace's lopsided jog coming round from the lobby. Lester appeared on the stairs, a beer in his hand. "What the hell?"

More scratching, like sawing now. Another thud. The doorframe cracked, a cloud of splinters bursting into the air. "Go away bear!"

Lester dropped his bottle. The shotgun was propped up in the corner next to the exit. He strode down the hall, grabbed the gun, and took position a few yards away, racked and aimed.

Roger came out of his room. "What?"

The nuns and Bernie arrived.

"Scat, bear!" Grace yelled. Bernie joined her. "Scat!"

"You have to do something!" Nolan said. "He's going to get me." Grace planted a hand on his chest, shoved him inside his room, and slammed the door shut.

"Keep yelling, everyone!" Bernie said. They were all shouting now. "Go away bear! Scat! Go home! There's nothing for you in here!"

The creaking stopped. The thudding and scratching stopped. They were still shouting. Lester dared a glance over his shoulder at Bernie. "Shells?"

Bernie grabbed Maeve's arm. "I'll get the shells. You go look outside, see if you can spot that bear." Maeve followed Bernie up the stairs. When they got to the top, Bernie pointed to the far end of the hall. "All the rooms are open. Go look."

There were four doors on the second floor. When Bernie opened the first door on the left, Maeve caught a glimpse of an unmade bed, a collection of empty beer bottles littering the room and the heavy scent of marijuana. The room on the right was standing open. It was filled with building supplies, two by fours, and cardboard boxes filled with tools.

She opened the door to the last room on the left. It was empty, covered in a heavy layer of dust. She brushed cobwebs off her face as she crossed to the only window. It looked out onto the path into the woods. Rain was coming down in sheets. Ancient spruce trees swayed in the wind. There was nothing on the ground. Had she imagined the noise, spooked from everything that had happened, and scared everyone needlessly? No she hadn't and she hadn't imagined the door frame splintering.

She crossed the hall to the last room. It had two windows, one on the opposite wall and one overlooking behind the lodge. She wiped the side window with her sleeve to clear condensation. The cold moisture soaked her hoody sleeve. Waves churned in the bay. Dark clouds roiled. When lightening flashed, the earth below illuminated. She couldn't see the bear.

Out the back window, she could see the place where they had found Sheila. The bear entered her view. It had come away from the lodge. It paced around where the body had been. It scratched at the mud, stood on its hind legs, sniffed the air, dropped to the ground, and swiveled its massive head in the direction of the lodge.

Maeve met Bernie in the hallway. "It's out there, hanging around just outside the exit."

"Must have watched us bring her inside," Bernie said.

When they got downstairs, the shouting had stopped. They all seemed to be straining to hear.

"He's out there," Bernie said into the quiet. She handed the box of shells to Lester. "Nail the sonofabitch if he comes in."

A deep gash ran up one length of the door frame. "Won't take much for him to get through," Lester said.

"You have a bunch of wood upstairs," Maeve said. "We'll nail up a barricade." She ran back up the stairs, followed by the nuns.

Maeve grabbed the top two by four and began dragging it down the stairs. The nuns together picked up one board and followed her. On the second trip, Maeve grabbed a cardboard box with tools and nails and handed that to Clare to carry. Maeve and Iggy drug two more boards downstairs. When they came down the third time with more wood, Bernie was holding a board while Lester drilled it into place. Grace was standing a few feet away, the shotgun in her arms pointed at the ground.

The drill whined to a stop, the battery dead. "Shit." Lester tossed the drill away and dug into the box. He pulled out a handful of nails, put them between his lips, and picked up a hammer. He lined up a nail, gave it one tap, and then slammed the hammer into it twice, driving it into the wood. He pulled another nail from his mouth, lined it up, pounded it in.

Lester and Bernie worked that way in silence; she held the boards in place while he hammered. They had built a second frame around the door with the boards secured to the log wall and he was nailing the boards across the exit into that frame. She and the nuns went upstairs for more wood. After they had brought down all the wood and Lester had covered the door with what he had, he stepped back to take a look.

With one hand, he grabbed one of the boards and pulled with all his weight. It didn't move.

Nolan was in the hallway again. "Is that good enough?"

"It's going to have to be," Lester said.

"What if he gets in?"

They turned to look at him.

"It's just some wood and nails. A brown bear weighs four hundred to five hundred pounds. He could beat that door down if he wanted to."

"Since when you know so much?" Grace asked.

"I took a class in wilderness safety. I had to, for when I was taking photos for my book."

"A class?" Grace blurted.

Bernie said, "He has a point."

"Fine," Grace said. "We'll take the furniture from my room and stack it up against the door. At least it'll slow him down."

"Where will you sleep?" Iggy asked.

"I can sack out in the office. No big deal. Slept in worse places." Grace opened the door to her room. The women drug the mattresses of the beds and stacked them against the door first, then pushed the dresser and nightstands against that, then tilted the bedframes on the ends and leaned them against the pile. Lester stood at a distance, the gun ready. Nolan watched, peeking from behind his room door. Roger stood in this doorway, looking lost.

Grace dragged out the last piece of furniture from her room, her desk chair. "Lester, you might as well take a load off."

"What now?" Nolan asked. "Do we just sit here and wait?"

Grace slowly turned to face Nolan. He pulled his head back and closed the door.

"Dammit, I wanted to hit him again. Don't look at me that way, Iggy, he's been getting on my nerves since he showed up."

"I'll go make coffee," Bernie said, stepping between Grace and Iggy.

"I'll pray for you," Iggy said.

"You just do that," Grace answered.

Iggy stepped to Roger's side and stroked his arm. "Try to get some rest."

"If you don't need me for anything."

"We'll let you know." She showed him to his room and closed the door behind him.

That left Maeve standing in the hall with Grace, Iggy, and Clare. Tears were streaming down Clare's face and stained her gray habit with dark splotches. Iggy put an arm around her shoulder. "You were very brave, Sister. It's over now. The police will come in the morning and take us away from here."

***

MAEVE FOUND HER NOTEPAD on the floor where she had dropped it when she first heard the bear. Her cell phone was in her pocket. She followed Grace into the manager's office behind her desk. Grace clicked the mouse a couple of times. The fan wound down as the computer shut off.

Maeve sat in the visitor's chair without being invited. Her knees were suddenly weak. A cold sweat had broken out all over her body. She wanted to vomit. It was just adrenalin, it would pass soon. She had felt it before the time she was attacked in her parking lot and again the time when someone shot at her. This too would pass.

"Is there something I can help you with?" Grace asked.

"I still need to take your statement."

"Seriously? There's a bear prowling around out there and you want to play Sherlock Holmes?"

Maeve turned on her cell phone recording app. "Can I get your full name for the record?"

"Miss Mary Sunshine."

Maeve leaned back in her chair. "You know, I don't want to be here either. But a woman was murdered. I would think you would want to get to the bottom of it. Most people would."

"What the hell is that supposed to mean?"

"Are you going to cooperate or not, just say so, and I'll let Trooper Kelly know." Maeve knees felt like jelly but she pushed herself to a stand. What she really wanted to do was go lay down, not in the room right next to the exit that the bear was prowling, her own bed – the one in her condo back in Anchorage. Screw it. King could get his own damned statements.

She was halfway out the door when she heard, "Grace Louise Miller."

Maeve stopped. She should at least give this woman a chance to cooperate. She sat down again and started her recording app.

"Is that a married name?"

"Yup. My maiden name was McNair."

"Just like Bernie and Sheila, right? So you were part of the family reunion?"

"Bingo."

Grace went silent. Information would have to be pried out of her.

"Your date of birth?"

"October 19, 1962."

"How long have you been on Fox Island?"

"Since late spring."

"Where did you come from?"

"Illinois."

"And what brought you to Alaska?"

"I was looking for a new place to go and Bern invited me up." Grace shrugged. "Alaska's always been on my bucket list so I thought, why not?"

"Where were you when Sheila was killed?"

"I was with Bernie and Lester in their room, playing cards."

"Who won?"

"We weren't keeping score."

"How late did you stay in their room?"

Grace scowled. "Maybe two a.m.?"

Out of the corner of her eye, Maeve noticed a school photo of a little boy hanging just inside the door, positioned so that only people in the office would notice it. He had dark unruly hair and bright blue eyes and was wearing a superhero T-shirt. He looked eager to please the photographer with his best smile.

"Who is that?"

"My son, Danny."

"And where is he?"

"Back in Illinois?" She said it like a question, like she was hinting it was irrelevant and none of her business and she didn't understand what Maeve wanted. Maeve didn't know why she asked about the boy either. Trying to warm up Grace with small talk, perhaps. It seemed to be backfiring.

Grace looked middle-aged to Maeve, far too old to be the mother of a little boy. "He must be grown-up by now."

Grace leaned back in her chair. "Why didn't you tell us you were a lawyer?"

There was no getting away from her past. No one asks for your resume before they order a German chocolate cupcake with toasted coconut icing.

"I already explained that. This isn't about me, it's about Sheila Wadsworth. Would you answer the question, please?"

"Do you have something to hide, Ms. Malloy?"

Maeve put down her pen and sat back. She wasn't going anywhere until she got her answers. And Grace couldn't leave this room without crawling over her. So they were stuck.

"Well, I mean, you are as likely a suspect as anyone here, aren't you? Yet your buddy at the trooper station asked you to do the investigation. What a great opportunity to hide evidence, isn't it? Shouldn't someone be asking you if you knew Sheila and had a reason to kill her?"

"I've known the trooper for a few years. So, he trusted me to collect everyone's statements."

"If you're a lawyer, why are you working as a dishwasher?"

"I'm thinking about a career change."

Grace laughed. "To dishwasher?"

Maeve sighed. "This job was a lark to get out of town. No, not dishwashing, something else. Something way far away from the law."

"And now you're playing lawyer," Grace said. "Or cop. How does it feel?"

"I'm doing a favor for a friend until the authorities can reach us. I've been honest with you. How about you return the favor?"

"Fine."

"Did you kill Sheila?"

"My sister! You got a lot of damned gall to ask me a question like that. Like I said, I was with Bernie and Lester. Ask them if you don't believe me." Grace looked sincere enough. Yet Maeve sensed that Grace, despite her antagonism, was all too comfortable with Maeve being an attorney and not remotely intimidated. This interview reminded Maeve of her early days as a public defender, interviewing clients in jail with far more legal experience than she had toying with her for sport.

"Did you know anyone who had a reason to kill her?"

Grace considered the question. "No one that I know had any reason to kill her. She was annoying, that's for sure. Isn't it usually the husband? What's his alibi?"

"I talked to him. I can't share his or anyone else's statements with the other folks here."

"You mean the other suspects."

"I don't want to start a fight. I'm just doing this favor for Trooper Kelly because he asked. If you insist, yes, the other suspects. Everyone's a suspect until the evidence points to someone in particular."

"Except you."

"Except me."

"Because you're local and we're all....what do you call us? Cheechakos? Is that the right word?"

"That is the right word. It means 'newcomers'." Maeve considered Grace's point. It was sarcasm yet had a ring of truth to it. This lodge was filled with tourists and newcomers. Grace, Bernie, and Lester had no ties to Alaska. No one knew anything about them.

"Then I should cooperate so you can find out who killed her and stop suspecting me."

"Exactly."

"What do you need from me?"

"Tell me everything you know about everyone and why they're here."

"Already did," Grace said, flicked a switch on the computer and it powered up. "So, if you don't mind, I got a lodge to run."

Chapter Fourteen

WHEN TOM WALKED INTO the police station conveniently located in the same building as the courthouse, the duty sergeant looked up from the game he was playing on his phone. "They let you out?"

"Looks like it," Tom answered. "I need my stuff."

The officer dug through a file drawer, pulled out a large manila enveloped marked "Sinclair, Thomas", and dumped the contents onto his desk: Tom's wallet, cell phone, and Rolex watch.

"Where's the truck keys?"

The cop pulled a sheet of paper out of the envelope and scanned it. "No keys listed."

"Shit."

Tom grabbed the cell phone, fired it up, and punched the contacts list. Damn, he couldn't remember that girl's name again. It was a month of the year. He started at the top and hit on it quickly: April. There was a photo next to her name he had never seen before: a selfie, a full frontal naked picture taken in the bathroom mirror while she sucked on a finger. She must have grabbed his phone when he wasn't paying attention. Maybe he had fallen asleep for a few minutes. The photo struck Tom as vulgar. It made him feel dirty.

He didn't have time to take a shower. He needed his truck and he needed out of Homer. Right now.

Tom punched the speed-dial. April answered, "Tom?"

"They let me go."

"Where's Anton?" she whispered.

"Sleeping it off, last I seen him," Tom said. "I need you to do me a favor. Are you still in my room?"

"When I went back to the motel to get my stuff, the manager came by and said he was throwing you out. He don't tolerate fighting. And you owe him for the busted-up furniture."

"Great, I'll get with him when I get back."

"Where are you going?"

"I have to run up to Seward."

"In this mess?"

"Friend of mine's in trouble. I need to get there ASAP. I need my truck."

"What friend?"

"Doesn't matter," Tom said. "Where's the truck?"

"What kind of friend?"

"She's my best friend, okay? I need that truck. Can you swing by and pick me up?"

"Sorry, I can't get off work. I'm the only one here."

"Like how busy can it be in this weather?"

"I'd lose my job if I locked up."

"Okay, fine, I'll come to you."

Just then the door opened and Officer Larson came in, half-pushing, half-dragging Anton. He tossed Anton into a folding chair, then stretched out his back.

"Listen, can you give me a lift?" Tom asked.

"He's not a taxi service," the duty sergeant said.

Tom ignored him. "Larson, would you look outside? I got to get to Seward right now and if it weren't for you, I'd been gone half an hour ago. Like you got something else better to do? Just take me back to the café."

Larson glanced at Anton draped across the chair, then at his shoes that still stank of vomit. "I got to go home and change uniforms. I'll be back in twenty," he told the duty sergeant.

"Pick me up some coffee, would you?"

"Didn't you hear? I'm not a taxi service."

As Larson drove to the café, Tom tried Maeve's number. It rolled over to her voicemail. "Dammit," he said under his breath.

"Problems?" Larson asked.

"Lady friend of mine's in trouble," Tom said. "Can't you make this thing go any faster?"

"I'm a cop."

"Put on the siren."

"We're almost there," Larson said as he pulled his SUV around the corner and the café came into view. The lights were off. The closed sign had been turned to face out the window. "What the...?"

"She must have gone home," Larson said. "Who's going out for coffee in weather like this?"

"So where's my truck?"

Larson cruised around behind the café and pulled in next to Tom's truck.

"Thanks," Tom said as he jumped out of the SUV.

"Want me to wait?" Larson nodded at the truck.

That's when Tom saw the damage. The windows were rolled down and rainwater was pouring in over the roof into the cab. The windshield had been busted in, a crowbar left on the pavement nearby. Tom looked inside. He found the keys dangling from the ignition, the truck engine idling, almost out of gas.

He ripped the keys out of the ignition and spun around, looking for April. She wasn't around that he could see. He leaned his head against the cab roof. He needed to think. Rain poured down the neck of his shirt, streamed between his shoulder blades, spilled out his shirt sleeves.

Larson rolled down the passenger window, leaned across, and yelled, "Need a lift?"

***

MARCH 18, 2003

The Clarion

Early this morning, police were called to the scene of a motor vehicle accident on Route 31. Witnesses state that the driver of a west-bound motorcycle was traveling at excessive speed and lost control. He struck a sedan traveling in the opposite direction head-on. The authorities say that intoxication appears to have been a factor. The sedan driver escaped with minor injuries. The deceased is Daniel Johnson of Chicago, Illinois.

***

MAEVE HAD THE FEELING that Grace got more information than she had, and now she had shut down now. "I'll get back to you later."

"Later," Grace answered.

She checked on Lester. He was sitting in the chair, the shotgun across his lap, reading a comic book. "How's it going?"

"Quiet," he said and pulled the hank of mustache into his mouth.

When she passed through the lobby, she saw the nuns. Clare had fallen asleep on the couch. Iggy was sitting in a chair next to the fireplace, working a crossword puzzle. She looked up and nodded.

A gnawing hunger she had been ignoring turned into a burning sensation. Maeve realized she hadn't eaten, or even had any coffee, this morning and it was almost noon.

The lobby led straight into the dining room, and Maeve could see that Bernie had laid out a brunch on the serving table. Maeve clipped her pen to her legal pad, tucked it under her arm, slipped her phone into her jeans pocket, and walked to the buffet.

She took a plate, loaded it with a muffin and a slice of melon, carried that to a far table where she left it and the legal pad, then went back to pour a mug of coffee from an urn. She was alone in the dining room although judging by crumbs and coffee rings on the other tables, other occupants in the lodge had eaten. So much for staying in their rooms as she had asked.

The storm seemed to be letting up now. It was still raining, not as hard, and the sky was a lighter gray. This was only the second day. A pineapple express could last three days or more. At best, she could hope that it would let up enough by tomorrow for King to arrive and take over the investigation.

And then, what would she do? She was out of a job, certainly. Even if Bernie had a change of heart about Maeve's former profession, the lodge would be shut down for a long time. Going back to Nelson & Associates as a paralegal was untenable. The other paralegals had ostracized her. The librarian, barista, and cupcake lady fantasies were fun, yet it struck her that after a while she'd find she wasn't satisfied. Deep down in her soul, she was a white knight. It was probably a character defect, possibly something diagnosable by a mental health professional, maybe treatable.

Since she had taken over this investigation, she felt useful again. In a real way. The collection of evidence in an impartial, organized manner would lead to the discovery of the murderer. Maeve wasn't working for the prosecution. She was working for Sheila

Wadsworth. She was giving Sheila the voice that had been stolen from her, the ability to identify who had destroyed her life. It was important work.

Maeve peeled the paper wrapper from the muffin, broke a chunk off, and took a bite. Crumbs choked her. She washed it down with coffee that had become tepid and bitter sitting in the urn. She held her breath and took another big swig. Back in the old days, she didn't drink alcohol for the flavor, she drank it for effect. Same thing with bad coffee.

She finished the muffin, refilled her mug, and settled back at the table. She wanted to review her notes. Before doing that, she needed to check the battery on her cell phone. She pulled it out of her pocket, saw that she was down to twenty-five percent, made sure all the apps were off, and slipped it back into her pocket.

On the legal pad, she had arranged the notes as if she were taking testimony at a trial. At the top of the first page, she had written pertinent information: Sheila Wadsworth's name, and suspected time of death, sometime between when she had argued with Roger and had been found the next morning. Sheila had gone outside while Maeve was working out between 8:00 and 10, walking right past the gym door. Maeve wouldn't have heard her, having the headphones on. There was no way to pinpoint the time.

It occurred to Maeve that she had written down her own statement which she'd better do while it was still fresh in her mind. A full, formal statement wasn't necessary right now but at least she should make some notes about what she knew from her own experience before her memory was tainted by what she had later learned. After dinner, everyone convened in the meeting room for Nolan's slide presentation. The power failed. Lester and Bernie left to fix the generator. The meeting broke up and Maeve went to the gym around 8 p.m. She heard voices in the hall. When she left around ten, the backdoor was standing open with a trail of water disappearing into the hallway. She closed the door, as Lester had told her to do because of bears, and locked it, and then went to bed. Then when everyone was in the kitchen early this morning, Roger came in looking for Sheila. And that's when she realized that Sheila must have gone outside. Maeve raced outside. The others followed. And they found her.

She didn't need to write down that Sheila had bled to death from a knife wound to her abdomen, that image was engraved in her mind.

Maeve had seen plenty of autopsy photos yet never before had she seen a corpse, smelled the tang of blood mixed with a fetid stink of a post-mortem bowel movement, while incomprehensively willing the dead woman to come alive and breathe and everything would be okay.

It would never be okay. Sheila Wadsworth had been murdered. And someone in the lodge had stolen the chef's knife, followed her outside, and taken her life. This was no accident. It was premeditated. Right in the middle of a family reunion. What was it that writer said? The past is never dead. It isn't even past.

Maeve had first interviewed Mary Bernadette Parker, also known as "Bernie." Bernie manifested an admiration for an idealized romantic image of the Native American culture as it used to exist. The shaggy hair, the beaded earrings, the Native-inspired T-shirts, the talk of living off the land. What was she rejecting from her past?

What was it about the Native American culture Bernie identified with? Being close to nature?

Bernie was married to Lester, who reeked of pot. Maeve had yet to talk to him, but by what she had seen, Bernie was overly optimistic about his ability to partner with her in building this lodge. He must have overstated his construction skills when they were dreaming their dream. He had shown an open animosity towards Sheila when telling her the stories about the bear, at the same time ridiculing her for her wildlife ignorance and trying to frighten her. He clearly enjoyed it.

Bernie's alibi had been that she and Lester and Grace were playing cards in the room she shared with Lester until two in the morning. She said they had played five card stud. She didn't say who had won and Maeve forgot to ask. She'd remember the next time they talked.

Maeve flipped the page to Roger, the second witness she had interviewed. He worked for an oil company on the North Slope as an engineer, two weeks on, two weeks off. The last time he saw Sheila alive was in their room. He figured she went outside for a cigarette. There were smashed butts in the mud near the door which supported his theory.

His alibi was that he was asleep in bed when Sheila was killed. Not verifiable. He could have easily followed Sheila out of the lodge, grabbed the knife on his way, sick of her shit, and stabbed her, then went back to bed. And given the amount of alcohol the two of them had drunk, he could have done it in a blackout.

He was certainly apologetic the next morning when her body was brought inside. Maybe there had been other things he did in a black-out. Beaten her, destroyed furniture, wrecked cars. Maybe he assumed he had killed her.

It was interesting that when everyone else heard Roger and Sheila fighting, Roger claimed that was just how they talked to each other. No big deal.

Maeve would like to know more about their history before they came to Alaska. Was there a history of domestic abuse? Had Sheila gone to the hospital for treatment? Did her coworkers notice bruises?

Grace, the manager, was the third witness. Maeve had come to think of her as a biker chick, not that Grace talked about riding motorcycles. It was her hard-ass demeanor, too tight black T-shirt, too tight jeans, visible tattoos.

Grace's alibi was that she was playing cards with Bernie and Lester until two a.m. She didn't say what game they played and said no one kept score. Which is just the vague kind of thing a sophisticated criminal would say because it was less likely someone else would contradict her.

Maeve brought the coffee mug to her lips and noticed that it was empty, not realizing when she had drunk it. While she was refilling it, Bernie stuck her head through the swinging door. Bernie took a look at Maeve, the expression on her face like she had smelled something bad, then scanned the table.

"How's the food holding out?"

There were still half a dozen muffins, a plate full of melon, a large bowl of strawberries untouched and little containers of yogurt sitting in a melting bowl of ice.

"Plenty left," Maeve said.

"I'll put sandwiches out in an hour or so. You think anyone is hungry?"

"They haven't eaten much yet. Sooner or later, they will be."

Bernie retreated into the kitchen. Maeve went back to the table and flipped back to her notes on Bernie. Most folks, with the exception of Sister Iggy, had been hostile to Maeve once they learned she was a lawyer, and Bernie was the worst. She was also the one who was concerned that a search would turn up some other criminal enterprise.

Were Lester and Bernie broke? Perhaps rebuilding the lodge cost more money than they expected so they supplemented their income illegally. Growing pot. Selling it somehow, even though they didn't know anyone in the state. She made a note to mention it to King. If they were moving pot, he probably knew about it. In a small town like Seward, everyone knows everyone else's business.

Maeve still needed to interview Francis Nolan, Lester, and the nuns.

During the entire time she was reviewing the evidence, she had not once thought about herself. Finally, relief.

She loathed the upcoming interview with Francis Nolan. He was demanding. People like him wanted control and there was nothing you could do. If you wanted information, you just had to go along for the ride.

She flipped the legal pad closed, clipped her pen to it, took one last slug of coffee, and pushed away the chair.

***

As Maeve tapped on Francis Nolan's door, she could hear a television droning from inside his room. It was turned off. She listened hard again for his footsteps, remembering how he'd snuck up on her in the hallway before. Had she been so wound up in her thoughts, she hadn't heard him? Or was so light of foot, he hadn't made a sound?

The door opened without warning. He stood a few feet away, wearing a white shirt open at the neck revealing a crew-neck t-shirt and a buttoned-up blue cardigan buttoned up over a pair of black slacks.

"Is this a good time?" Maeve asked.

"What about the bear?"

"It's gone for now."

"What if it comes back?"

Maeve gestured down the hall at Lester lolling on a chair with the shotgun broken across his lap. "Lester's sitting right there, see? He doesn't think it could break down the door, but if it does, he's ready."

Nolan stood back and pulled the door wide open. As she walked past him into the room, she saw a red spot dotted his throat. He had nicked himself shaving near the Adam's apple. There was the faint scent of whiskey, so light it was almost like aftershave that had worn off. Did everyone in this lodge drink except for her?

"Please, have a seat," he said.

The room was identical to the other rooms. Twin beds, a dresser, a desk and chair, end tables, a television on the dresser, a few framed photographs of Alaska landscapes on the walls. These photos were of Denali, the Great One, the tallest mountain in North America, hundreds of miles north of Seward. She took the chair, spun it around, and sat.

He remained standing, his back almost against the wall. He was as far away from her as he could get without leaving the room.

Maeve turned on the recording app, put the cell on the desk, and flipped the legal pad to a fresh page. She explained that Sheila Wadsworth had been murdered, that the police would arrive after the storm broke, and she was asked to conduct initial interviews. Would he mind answering a few questions?

"What kind of questions?"

"Your name."

"Francis Michael Nolan."

"Date of birth."

"September 15, 1959"

"Occupation."

"Retired."

"And you're an author?"

"After my retirement, I wrote a book about Pacific Northwest wildflowers. I took the pictures myself."

"What did you do before you retired?"

"Is that important?"

"I don't know what's important or what isn't. I'm just helping out the troopers until they get here."

"Why you?"

"Because I'm an attorney."

Nolan's weight shifted subtly. He seemed to be considering something.

"You mentioned before that you thought someone was trying to kill you."

Nolan perched on the edge of the farthest bed.

"That's true," he said. "At least I think it's true."

Maeve nodded to him to go on.

"This murder. Why that poor girl? She was nobody. I mean, she was somebody of course. Still there was no reason anyone would want to kill her."

"Did you know her?"

"No."

He had answered quickly, and now waited for her to ask the right question. Why would someone want him dead? She'd get to it.

"How do you come to the conclusion that no one wanted to kill her, Mr. Nolan?"

"You saw her. Who could she threaten?"

"Do you believe someone feels threatened by you?"

"Believe! You sound like I'm making this up, like I'm paranoid. I am not, I assure you. I know the truth. And they don't want the truth getting out."

"Who doesn't want the truth getting out?"

"Don't you want to know what the truth is?"

Maeve had a feeling once he steered the discussion around to his story, she would never get her questions answered. "In a minute. First I want to know from you, who do you believe they are?"

"There! You said it again. Believe. You think I'm crazy."

"I'll rephrase the question. Who do you think is targeting you?"

"I can't be sure just yet. One of them. Maybe all of them."

A vision of hitman nuns with plastic sniper rifles secreted in their clunky old-fashioned suitcases struck Maeve as humorous. This probably wasn't the first time someone thought Francis Nolan was odd.

"The nuns?"

"How can you be sure they're nuns?"

She had taken their word for it. She'd convey the information to King and he would confirm their stories. Meanwhile, she was going in circles with Nolan. She'd just have to let him have his say and then she could ask the questions King wanted answered.

"Mr. Nolan, tell me your story. That's what I'm here for. What is this truth that you know? Why would someone want to kill you because of it?"

"You said you're an attorney, right?"

"Right."

"So everything I say to you is confidential?"

"Not in this instance, Mr. Nolan. Our communications are only confidential if you are seeking advice from me."

"I have a case. A case with some very interesting facts." And then without giving Maeve enough time to protest, he scooted to the bed next to her, sat so close their knees nearly touched and told his story.

***

BACK IN JAIL, GRACE had learned the best way to control people was to keep them rocked back on their heels.

She strode into the kitchen. Even as the door swung back and forth on its hinges with a rhythmic whomp-whomp sound, she launched into Bernie. "What is wrong with you?"

Bernie put the hoagie she had just buttered face down on the grill and took a sip of red wine. "What do you mean?" She looked confused.

"You're joking, right?" Grace said. "You didn't tell the Malloy woman about us being sisters."

"None of her business."

"Lucky for you, I figured it out when she came to me and covered your ass. But let me tell you this much: you were the first person she talked to. If anyone's stories don't match yours, she's coming back to you."

"What about Iggy?"

"She knows when to keep her mouth shut."

"What do I do?"

"Too late now. Stick to your story."

"What if I tell her I forgot?"

Grace laughed. "Who your family was? Sure thing! No one drinks that much, Bern. Look it, if you change your story now, she's going to think you have something to hide and she's going to keep digging. And if she keeps digging, you know what she's going to find?"

"She isn't going to find anything. Lester's taking care of it tonight."

"How?"

"He's going to bury it."

"Long time between now and tonight."

Wearing Bernie down didn't take as long as it used to. Either Grace was getting better at it, or Bernie was tired. Grace reached into her jeans pocket and pulled out the wad of tissue.

"We need the Malloy woman out of the way. She'll finish her interviews and then let everyone out of their rooms before dinner. When everyone's done eating, we take our drinks into the lobby, sit in front of the fireplace, unwind. She doesn't drink alcohol, so you offer her a hot chocolate." Grace put the package on the counter and opened it, revealing four little blue pills she'd stolen from Francis Nolan. "You put these babies into her hot chocolate, stir it really good so they dissolve."

"What are they?"

"Sleeping pills."

Bernie stared at the pills. "Are four too many? She might overdose. What if she dies? I'll get blamed."

Grace had no idea how many pills were lethal. "Don't worry about it. I looked it up on the internet. They're harmless. Two is the recommended dose but it's okay to take four."

"You sure?"

"Absolutely!"

"And then what?"

"And then when she passes out, we got Francis Nolan to ourselves."

Chapter Fifteen

SISTER IGGY THOUGHT THEIR room had grown a little too chilly, so she had herded Sister Clare to the lobby where a fire burned in the stone hearth before the bear tried to get inside. After everything settled down, she brought back to the lobby. She was sure Maeve wouldn't mind. They were still isolated from the other witnesses.

Once settled in front of the crackling fire, Sister Clare soon drifted to sleep. The bear ordeal had been too much for her. Her hands were shaking violently as they helped bring down the building supplies. By the time the barricade was finished, she was sobbing. At least in sleep, she seemed to have some peace. Iggy watched her, wondering what she dreamed about. There was no telling what went on inside her mind, waking or sleeping. As Iggy watched, she heard a noise from the direction of the office and saw Grace standing behind the reception counter giving Iggy a pointed look. Iggy smiled back at her. She knew how much that irritated Grace.

It had started when they were kids. For a long time before Sheila came along, there had just been the three of them, Bernie, Iggy, and Grace. Grace was the youngest of the three and the one always trying to start a fight. Bernie was the one who tried to achieve, earning their mother's approval by working hard. And Iggy was the peacemaker. Sort of.

One time they were playing kickball in the street when their mother called them in for dinner. Bernie immediately went. Iggy knew she would set the table, pleasing their mom. The neighborhood kids started drifting home. Grace was mad because it was her turn. She was standing in the street, refusing to come inside, with the big, orange kickball lodged in the crook of her arm.

"You can be the first kicker when we play tomorrow," Iggy said. They were the last two kids in the street.

"Tomorrow's Sunday," Grace said. "No game."

"Then the next time we play. I promise."

Without warning, Grace hurled the ball, slamming it into Iggy's face. She fell on the hot asphalt. Bits of gravel dug into her bare elbows. As she pushed herself to stand, eyes watering, warm blood streaming down her face, a dark blur rushed past. Then she heard a smack and Grace's scream.

Their mother had slapped Grace. She grabbed Iggy's upper arm so tight, it hurt. Iggy was hauled to her feet, and she caught a glimpse of the red handprint on Grace's face, the tears welled in her eyes even as she refused to cry. Their mother pushed Iggy into the house, leaving Grace alone in the middle of the street.

It had always been like that. Grace got mad and attacked. Someone got hurt. Then Grace got hurt worse. That one thing that infuriated her was appeasement. She didn't want understanding. She wanted to get even.

Iggy felt her right cheek burning. She was suddenly aware the side of her body closest to the fire was hot and the side facing away was cold. The smile she'd given Grace had faltered, her muscles straining to hold it in place. She would not break their stare-down. She would sit like that until Grace made her next move.

Grace scowled at her, pulled the office door closed, and then walked through the dining room into the kitchen.

Iggy placed her book on the end table carefully so as not to disturb Clare and pulled herself to a stand. Her knees squeaked but Clare didn't wake. Iggy walked behind the reception counter, into the manager's office, around the desk, and pulled open the bottom drawer that Grace had stared into earlier that day.

A gun was in the drawer. She should have known. Grace never intended to turn Francis Nolan over to the authorities. She wanted to get even. An eye for an eye. A life for a life.

Iggy took the gun and slid the drawer closed. Her hand wrapped around the familiar heft as easily as hugging an old friend. She held the pistol close to her side, hidden in her skirt folds, then walked out of the office and into the corridor. She would stow it in her room until this whole thing was over.

No, that wouldn't work. If Grace discovered the gun was missing, she'd know that Iggy had taken it. She'd search Iggy's room, find it, and carry out her plan. What could Grace's exit strategy be once she'd murdered Nolan? Sit down and wait to be arrested, then go back to prison? Run away? Far more likely she planned the ultimate exit, suicide. Grace must not find that gun.

Lester seemed to be dozing in his chair. With the shotgun on his lap, she didn't want to startle him.

"Do you need to take a break?" Iggy asked.

Lester sniffed and snorted, shaking himself awake. "What's that?"

"I could watch the door for you if you need to stretch your legs."

"My legs are fine but I sure could take a piss. You don't mind?" He got up and handed her the shotgun. "Back in a few."

"Take your time. Got some coffee."

"Right," Lester said as he climbed up the stairs. When Iggy heard a door on the second floor open and close, she laid the shotgun on the ground.

Iggy couldn't hide Grace's pistol in Nolan's room. Maeve was in there with him. She could hear their voices. The gym? Then anyone could find it. Grace's own room? That would be ironic. Grace would never think to look there. She tried the knob. It was locked.

She went to the last room on the right, Maeve's. She reached for the metal knob. It was cool, damp. She turned it slowly, waiting for the halt of a lock. The clicking of the mechanism ran up her arm, too small a sound to be heard, as the knob spun. And then the door opened.

***

WHEN THE GLOVEBOX DROPPED open, Tom's gun almost fell out. It slid precariously close to the edge and scooted closer with every bump he took. He slowed the pick-up truck down, leaned over, shoved the gun back in, and slammed the door. The force felt like nails driving through his busted hand.

It was the only rig Tom could find. Larson had dropped him off at the house of a guy he'd met at an A.A. meeting. The guy was a shade-tree mechanic and had some beaten-up rigs in his yard. He didn't want to lend Tom a vehicle. After all, Tom had only been in town just this summer and folks came and went in Homer, Alaska. Those that went sometimes didn't come back. Tom didn't have time to use his charm on the guy, so he ended up leaving his Rolex as a guarantee. The watch would buy four of these trucks. Or better yet, the guy could afford one nice one if Tom didn't come back.

So, Tom had left his watch, took the truck, swung by the motel just long enough to get his pistol and a carton of cigarettes, jumped back into the truck, tried Maeve's number again, no luck, and headed north on the only road out of Homer.

It was the same pistol Tom had used when teaching Maeve how to shoot. They were on their way back from the Seward prison. The prison had a ridiculous name, Spring Creek, that made it sound like a spa, and it sat like a castle nestled against the mountain range. There was a guy in there who wanted Maeve to handle his appeal. They spent the entire morning driving down there and then three hours on the visit, mostly waiting.

Turned out the guy didn't have any grounds to appeal. He was just hoping if he conned some smart lawyer into looking at his case, they'd find something.

After the interview, they grabbed a steak at the only decent restaurant in Seward and then headed back to Anchorage. Along the way, Tom decided it was time Maeve learned how to shoot. When he turned down a side road, she'd asked, "Where are we going?"

"Little side trip. You in a hurry?"

"Depends on how long this side trip is. I drank a lot of coffee during lunch." She had. So had he.

"We'll find you a tree."

"We'll find me a restroom."

"Outhouse good enough? There's one a few miles down the highway."

She rolled her eyes. He took that as a yes.

When he found the spot he was looking for, he reached into the console and pulled out the pistol he'd stashed.

They climbed out of the truck and walked until they were so close to a fallen log, he could have hit it with a rock.

He told her what to do and she did it. Leveled the gun at the log and squeezed. The pistol kicked back, almost flying out of her hand. Dust flew up yards from her target. She was such a girl.

When he put his arms around her to show her how to hold the gun, he could feel her heart pounding. The vein in her neck throbbed. A sweat broke out on her forehead.

She didn't like shooting, he could see that, and that was exactly why she needed to learn. Doing what you're scared of made you tough. He couldn't watch over her twenty-four seven so she needed to take care of herself. Alaska ain't no theme park.

"Slow down your breathing," he had said quietly.

Maeve took a deep breath, her body filling the space within his arms. Her sweat soaked into his shirt. Her hair smelled like flowers.

The truck lurched to the side and the glovebox banged open again. He must have hit a pothole. He got the truck righted, focused on the feel of the steering wheel in his hands, figured no harm done, or not much at least, and vowed silently to pay attention to the road. He was never going to get to Maeve if he wrecked this truck. This time, he kicked the glovebox door shut.

The wipers scraped back and forth. If there was any rubber left, you wouldn't know it by the scratching noise they made. And they had no effect on the water pouring across the glass.

The wipers weren't the only things that didn't work. The heater fan was busted. On the passenger side, you could see pavement through the floor. The brakes were soft. The damned cigarette lighter was missing. And it reeked of grease and dirt.

Still it was making pretty good time as Tom drove north. Even with the storm trying to bat him across the road from time to time, he was doing at least sixty miles an hour and faster when he could.

Tom pulled a cigarette out of the pack lying on the bench beside him and jammed it in his mouth. Then he reached into a coat pocket, pulled out a book of matches, bent one match, and struck it on the graphite with his thumb. The flame bloomed, blinding him temporarily. He loved that acrid stink that seared his nostrils. It told him that in the next big inhale, he'd get a hit of smoky high. Tobacco gave him what he needed. Calm when he was nervous. A jolt when he was tired.

Right now, he needed to know that Maeve would be okay, safe and close by.

He held the fire to the cigarette, sucked until he could see the ember glow, then shook out the match. He tossed it to the floor, then with both hands on the wheel and the cigarette in his mouth, he squinted through smoke while he took another drag.

The wipers scraped again and for a few seconds the glass was clear enough to see. There was something strange on the road ahead. With sheets of rain coming down at an angle, it was hard to say what it was. Then Tom understood. Two half-ton pick-up trucks were parked cross-wise on the road blocking both lanes.

He slammed on his brakes. They went straight to the floor and his rig kept going. He pumped and pumped and finally got some resistance. The truck slowed. He pulled a hard right making it swing around and slide to a stop.

What idiots set up a roadblock?

The glovebox door had flown open again and his gun was on the floor. When he reached for it, wondering whether he should put it back or take it with him to meet these jokers, he noticed that an almost full bottle of Russian vodka had rolled out from under the seat. Figures. That shade tree mechanic had probably stashed it when he was drunk and had forgotten.

Four guys stepped out from behind the trucks, each carrying a rifle. They all wore slickers like commercial fishermen, hoods obscuring most of their faces. They had long scrawny beards, some blonder than the others.

"Fuck this shit." Tom said. He grabbed the pistol. He opened the truck door, stepped into the storm, and slammed the truck door behind him, keeping the pistol hidden at his side.

"What's this bullshit?" he yelled over the roar of the storm.

One of men stepped forward and yelled back. "You're Tom Sinclair?"

Tom looked around. If he dropped that guy right now, the other three would have him sighted before their buddy hit the pavement.

"What of it?"

"You're running from the law."

"What law?"

"In Homer town. You were arrested for assaulting my brother Anton and somehow you broke out of jail and now you're on the run. We're here to make sure you pay your debt."

The three other guys hiked their guns up, waist-high. These guys needed satisfaction and they needed it now or Tom wasn't going to get out of here alive, much less to Seward.

"Where did you hear that?"

"April."

Figures.

If he wasn't on his way to rescue Maeve, he would gladly have gotten into a shootout with these characters. He wondered if any of them had ever shot a human being, if they could really point their guns at a beating human heart and pull a trigger. On top of that thought came the realization that they probably shot plenty of moose. One less dead American wouldn't matter much to them.

"American" was what Old Believers called people who weren't of Russian descent, ignoring the obvious irony that if they were born in America, they were American too. He wasn't quite sure what they believed that made them different from anyone else. All of his contact with these men were in bars, after-hours joints, and whore houses, where men generally didn't talk about their beliefs.

They had a village close by. Tom had heard they moved to Alaska a long time ago trying to get away from Communists. They all looked alike: as pale-skinned as a halibut's belly.

Blonde or reddish hair. They weren't many of them and they had lived in America for a hundred years. There must have been a lot of cousins marrying.

They dressed in old-fashioned Russian clothes. Men wore long scraggly beards and tunics with high collars, sometimes embroidered. Their womenfolk wore long dresses with aprons and caps. As a group, they preferred to stick with their own, live in their villages, teach their children in village schools. Sometimes you'd see the whole family in Costco or at the Alaska State Fair.

The men made money by commercial fishing. They came into Home and hung out at Billiken's, a skanky bar near the docks, to get drunk and chase American girls while their women folk stayed home making all those pretty clothes. Tom had met plenty of these men, bought them drinks, and gladly relieved them of their hard-earned money in a card game, including one guy named Boris.

Today was not a good day to die. Not yet, at least.

Remembering that bottle of vodka, Tom yelled, "Hey, any of you guys know my friend Boris?"

Chapter Sixteen

"I NEED SOME ADVICE," Nolan said to Maeve. "I have a case. It's against the Church. Are you sure this is confidential?"

Maeve was suspended from practice. She couldn't represent anyone. She couldn't even consult. She certainly could not promise someone confidentiality, and even if she could, she was not sure she wanted to extend it to this man who she'd only met the day of a murder and who was pompous, evasive, and had an uncanny ability to sneak around.

"No, Mr. Nolan, this discussion is not confidential. I'm not your attorney. I am not giving you advice. I am interviewing you about a murder."

"Okay, don't give me advice. Just tell me what you think."

"That's the same thing."

He kept talking. "I have a case against the Church. I was a victim. Me. I'm not sure you understand how it works. When I was a teenager, you went to seminary when everyone else went to high school. I was thirteen. You live with priests and the other boys, away from home for the first time, just when a young man is waking up to his feelings." He blushed. "You know what I mean. And do you know what they did to you?"

She held up her hand. "Mr. Nolan, this conversation is not confidential."

"That's fine. Tell anyone you need to. They rape you, Miss Malloy. That's what they do. Everyone knew what went on. One time, I was asked to help carry a box of books to the storage room. As soon as I got in there, the young priest, Father Jimmy we called him, a teacher at the school, closed the door behind us. Then he knelt. When I started to kneel too, he stopped me. He grabbed me by the hips so hard he left bruises. I didn't know what I was supposed to do. I guess I was stunned. Then he unzipped my pants." Nolan's voice had become soft, boy-like. His face, a mask void of expression.

The storm's constant thrashing had been in the background for so long, Maeve hadn't noticed it in a while. In the silence of the room that followed Nolan's revelation, thunder rumbled in the distance. She looked out the window, searching for lightening and saw a soft glow behind the dark clouds. She remembered how, as a kid, she used to calculate the distance. One Mississippi, two Mississippi, three... Then the rumble again.

Nolan continued. "And while he was doing that to me, another priest, Father Leonard, opened the door. And do you know what he did?"

Clearly, she did not.

"Without a word, Father Leonard closed the door again, and left me alone with that man. Father Jimmy looked up into my eyes, smiled, and then kept going."

He waited for a response. He apparently needed a reaction.

"I am so sorry," Maeve said. What else do you say to a man when he tells you something like that? It sounded trite even if she meant it. She hoped he heard that in her voice.

Nolan's face tensed. "And that's when I knew I was doomed."

He was still sitting on the edge of the bed, his hands clasped between his legs, knuckles white from strain.

"So, I was a victim." He looked directly at Maeve. "Then someone said horrible things about me, things that weren't true. Lawyers got involved. And the Church made me into a scapegoat. After all the years I had given to it. Performing masses every week. Listening to confessions. Visiting the sick. Funerals. Herding wild children in after-school activities. Basketball. I can't play basketball. I don't know the first thing about the game. I'm not complaining, mind you. This is the life I chose. I wanted to shepherd the flock. Priests don't punch a clock you know. Being a priest is your entire life. And your family's. My grandmother wanted me to rise through the ranks. A simple parish priest wasn't good enough. She always wanted a bishop in the family."

"And they took that life away from me." He snapped his fingers. "Just like that. Thank God my grandmother didn't live to see this."

Maeve looked at the legal pad in her lap. She hadn't taken notes. She couldn't see how any of this was relevant to the death of Sheila Wadsworth. If it was, she wasn't likely to forget what Nolan had just told her. Besides, her cell phone was still recording. Everything he said would be stored in its memory.

"I'm sorry, Mr. Nolan, I can't help you."

"Maybe you have a friend in Illinois. The statute of limitations has been abolished. I can sue the Church now. For everything. For what those priests did to me."

Maeve didn't have any friends in Illinois. Arthur Nelson would know if anyone in Alaska was also licensed there. She'd ask him as soon as she got home. "I'll check around for you when I get back to Anchorage."

Maeve looked at her notes. She had his name, birth date, and his background information. And no alibi.

"One more question, Mr. Nolan. Do you know any of the other guests here?"

"Never met any of them. The manager, Grace, contacted me through e-mail."

"What were you doing at the time Sheila Wadsworth was murdered?"

"That's two questions."

"You're right. It was. Could you answer the question please?"

"I was in my room asleep, I suppose. I had taken a pill my doctor prescribed when I
heard her arguing with her husband down the hall. The next thing I knew, there was a
commotion in the kitchen and I found all of you standing around the body."

No alibi, then.

***

LESTER WAS RIGHT WHERE Maeve had last seen him sitting in the hallway. The gun was
across his lap, a comic book was in his hands, and a cup of coffee was on the floor beside
him.

"How's it going?"

"All quiet on the western front," Lester said.

"Is this a good time for us to talk?"

"Suit yourself."

Maeve went into her room and dragged her desk chair to the hallway. She started her
phone's recording app and gave him the preamble, that she was collecting information
on behalf of Trooper Kelly in the aftermath of Sheila Wadsworth's death. Lester said
he understood and agreed to have his statement recorded. She had already gotten the
background information from Bernie so she skipped to the heart of the question. Alibis.

"Could you tell me what you did last night, Mr. Parker?"

"Mr. Parker was my dad. Call me Lester."

"Lester. Could you tell me what you did last night?"

"You were there. We ate dinner."

"Go on."

"Then I came back to our room. I was just sitting around, doing nothing, I guess, can't
remember."

Smoking a joint was Maeve's first guess. "Relaxing?"

"Yeah, right, relaxing. And then the lights went out."

"You were with us in the conference room when that happened."

"Oh, yeah. Now I remember." That hank of mustache hair found its way into his mouth. He chewed on it for a few minutes. "I tinkered with that for a while. You want me to tell you what I did to it?"

"I wouldn't understand if you did."

"Ain't rocket science. Anyway, I got the thing going again and came back inside. By then, your little meeting broke up. When I came back inside, Bernie and Grace were in here playing cards. So I started playing with them."

"How long did you play?"

"Must have been two a.m. when we finally called it a night."

That was exactly what Grace had said. And exactly what Bernie had said.

"What were you playing?"

"Texas Hold 'Em."

But, that was not what Grace or Bernie had said.

"Is Texas Hold 'Em anything like Five Card Stud?"

"If you don't know any better, I guess."

"You three play Texas Hold 'Em a lot?"

"What's a lot? Sometimes when things get slow, we play."

As far as Maeve could tell, things were always slow at Fox Island Lodge.

"Who won?"

"Grace. She always wins. I ain't got no poker face."

Someone was lying. Maybe everyone.

***

"My name is Boris," said the Russian who did all the talking.

"Hey, Boris, you remember me. Tom. We wasted a few nights in Billiken's."

"Ah," Boris said, nodding, "Billiken's." He took a minute to digest the information, "Tom, the fisherman?" It looked like Boris was remembering Tom. Not that he remembered the money he had lost to Tom, he would have been too drunk, but instead that he had a good time when they played cards. That was because Tom made sure that the guys he played with always had their drinks topped off and pretty girls hanging around them. So even though Tom fleeced a lot of men, they always came back for more.

Tom hadn't mentioned during those nights that he used to work for a lawyer. With folks who made it a point of pride to live outside the law, his past association would make them cautious. He didn't want cautious. He wanted to be their best friend. And it was true. He was a fisherman.

"That's right," Tom said, "out of Homer."

There was a subtle shift in the men. Something only an old street fighter would see. The two with Boris dropped their shoulders and their weight sagged into their heels. Boris pushed off his hood letting the rain batter his head but also letting Tom see his face. "Tom, my friend, what are you doing out on a night like this?"

"It's not what you heard. Say, Boris, it's kind of wet out here. I got a bottle of vodka with me in the truck. Want to get out of the rain?"

Boris jerked his head in the direction of his truck. The Russian hung their rifles on the back window gun rack and clambered in, Boris in the driver's seat, the other three in the back.

As soon as Tom climbed in with the bottle he'd retrieved from his truck, he stuck out his hand to the men in the back. "Tom," he said.

Boris said, "These are my cousins, Alexi, Sergei and Yuri." They each shook Tom's hand in turn. He couldn't tell them apart except for the balding one with the big scar in his scalp. That was Yuri.

"Nostrovia!" Tom shouted the Russian's traditional drinking toast, having no idea what it meant. He'd heard drunk Russians shouting it in bars. Then he uncapped the bottle and handed it to Boris.

"Nostrovia!" Boris said before he took a big gulp and passed it to the guys in the backseat.

"Nostrovia!" each one shouted, holding the bottle aloft before drinking and then passing it on. When the bottle got back to Tom, he passed it to Boris again. He didn't drink. They didn't care. More for them.

Boris took a hit off the bottle and passed it to the backseat. "So, Tom, what is the problem in Homer?"

"You know women. She got the story confused. Sure, there was a small disagreement with Tony but we worked it all out. The cops let me go. Soon as he wakes up, they'll let him go too." At least Tom figured they would. It'd save the Homer police from having to feed him. Nothing would piss a cop off faster than having to leave the comfort of a warm jail to find take-out for a prisoner.

By that time, the bottle had been passed back to Boris. "Women!" he said, shaking his head the way men do when they're sharing their bafflement. "What can you say?" Boris asked philosophically.

"Can't live with them," Tom said.

"Can't live without them," Boris finished. He lifted the bottle in salute to Tom and took another swig.

"Say, Tom," Yuri shouted. "Didn't I see you in Talkeetna one time?"

"Maybe," Tom said. "I been there."

"You know that pretty girl Sandy? The bartender in Talkeetna?"

Tom lit a cigarette, offered one to each of the men. They all took a cigarette and lit up. Tom cracked a window. He really needed to get out of here and soon. Right after these guys got to feeling like he was their best friend, so they wouldn't shoot him in the back on his way to his truck.

Sure, he knew Sandy. Sandy Douglas, a bartender, could bounce a drunk from a bar as good as any biker could. Tom and Maeve had met her when they were investigating her husband's death, their client accused of the murder. For a while, Tom had thought about getting to know her better. When she got busted dealing pot, he decided to let that one go. There was always another one sooner or later.

"Yeah, I know her."

"Feisty!" Yuri said. The bottle had come back to him. He took a swig and passed it on.

"Feisty, that's for sure."

The Russians on either side of Yuri punched him and laughed.

"Is there a joke?" Tom asked. "I don't get it."

One of them sang out, "She broke a bottle over his head and he still loves her!" Yuri, a little embarrassed, fingered the scar with a hand that bore a wedding ring. He laughed along, not as loud.

All at once the jolliness faded. The men were getting tired. Party over.

"You fellas coming into Homer soon?"

"Depends," Boris said. "On the fishing."

"When you do, look me up. I'll buy you a drink."

Tom reached for the door handle. Boris offered the bottle to him. "Keep it," Tom said. "And drive safe. Don't want to get picked up for DUI."

Boris scoffed. "No cops out tonight."

Tom looked up and down the road. No cops, no cars, no one at all. In the twin beams of Boris' headlights, raindrops ricocheted from the blacktop, glittering before they disappeared into the gloom.

"Nostrovia," Tom said as he climbed out of the rig. He promised himself he'd make up the lost time.

Back in the truck and heading north again, it had only been about ten minutes since he left the Russians when Tom noticed the temperature gauge starting to rise. He didn't know if it was a radiator leak or low oil, not that he could do anything about it now. He had no way of fixing either. So he kept driving, letting the rig coast downhill and trying to be as gentle as he could as he pushed it uphill.

He was about two-thirds up a grade, praying the truck would make it, when he heard a bang. He ducked out of reflex. Then he realized it wasn't someone shooting at him. The piece of shit truck had thrown a rod.

It never made it to the top of the hill. The engine stopped turning and the rig coasted to a stop. Tom jammed on the emergency brake before it started rolling downhill.

He pulled his cell phone out of his jeans pocket, speed-dialed Maeve's number and got nothing. Her phone must have been turned off. He speed-dialed King's number and got nothing again. That's when he suspected he was stuck in some black hole, where cell phone coverage didn't reach.

He slipped the pistol into the back of his jeans, pulled on his denim jacket, still soaked from his meeting with the Russians on the road, flipped the collar up, and started walking.

Chapter Seventeen

MAEVE FOUND THE NUNS sitting in big leather chairs, each with a book in her lap and a cup of tea on nearby end tables. A fire crackled in the over-sized hearth. She knew they had been stationed there since she first called King Kelly. She should have herded them back to their rooms, like everyone else, yet deference had stopped her. When would she grow out of the lonely kid sitting at her desk, hands and knees clasped, while Sister Mary Patience patrolled the classroom with a ruler hidden in her sleeve?

No harm. As long as the others stayed in their rooms, there would be no opportunity for collusion. Yet a suspicion nibbled at her. Sister Iggy knew she could manipulate Maeve and took advantage of it. She was getting played, by a nun no less. If she wasn't careful, someone was going to get hurt.

Not the nuns, though. Who would hurt a nun?

As Maeve walked across the lobby, her phone made a thunking sound, notifying her that a text had arrived. She pulled it out of her pocket and read. *What's going on?* She felt her heart patter and heat rise to her cheeks. She looked at the number. It was King and her heart settled back into its usual rhythm. Tom hadn't called her since long before she left Anchorage. Weeks it seemed. Or maybe she had called him to tell him about her plans. When they had spoken, their conversation was awkward, interrupting each other, halting tentatively. They didn't know how to talk to each other anymore. He said he had to let her go and he'd call her back. He never did.

She tapped in a reply. *Almost done. Will call soon.* When she looked up from the phone, the nuns were sharing a smile.

"Do you need to take a call?" Sister Iggy asked. Clare giggled.

"It wasn't Tom," Maeve said.

"This Tom of yours must be special."

He was to Maeve. Or he had been. She wanted to talk about him to anyone who would listen, even if they didn't know him. It might be better that way. That would give him anonymity. No awkwardness as they were unlikely to run into each other. Maybe later she would indulge herself. Right now, she needed to finish her inquiry and report back to King.

Maeve dragged an ottoman toward the fireplace closing a triangle of herself and the two nuns. She set her phone on record and flipped to a new page on her legal pad.

Sister Iggy kept a finger in her book for a placeholder. "Is there any news about the bear?"

"Lester says he hasn't heard anything."

"Is it typical for bears to abandon their quarry?"

"I'm not a bear expert but from what I understand, the bear probably thinks the remains belonged to him. Sometimes they will cache their food and come back for it later. He isn't happy she was stolen from him."

Sister Clare picked at her face, watching the exchange.

"So we can expect him to return."

"It's good that we're prepared."

"But we aren't, really. Prepared, that is. Lester nailed up some wood but is that enough to keep a bear out? What if he gets past Lester and comes inside?"

Maeve had a vision of giant angry carnivore loping into the lobby, Lester shooting at it from behind, the shotgun spray hitting everyone and everything but the bear.

"It'd be better if you took cover. You could hide in the manager's office."

Clare spoke. "But won't he find us there?" Her voice sounded old and young at the same time, creaky from disuse but tentative. It was the first time Maeve had heard her speak.

"Chances are he'd head for the kitchen, where the food smells come from. Bears are about eating. That's pretty much all they think about."

"Is Bernie in danger then?"

"Honestly, Sister, we all are if the bear gets in."

"Let's pray that he doesn't."

"Good idea."

With that, the nuns slipped onto their knees. She thought Iggy's prayer suggestion was a figure of speech, that she hadn't really meant it. They were looking at her, waiting for her to join them.

Maeve put her phone and legal pad on the coffee table and knelt. When she planted her knees on the bare wood floor, sharp pains, like broken glass, ground inside them. She shifted her body trying to find relief and felt the thin cover of skin between her bone and the floor slither. Chilled air drifted past her hips and thighs on its way up the chimney. She was cold, her knees hurt, and she wondered how long this was going to take. Iggy crossed herself. Clare and Maeve did as well. Iggy began praying aloud.

"The light of God surrounds us,
The love of God enfolds us,
The power of God protects us..."

That's when Maeve tuned out. Her mind floated over the lodge with a bird's eye view of the interior. There was Lester guarding the exit, turning a page in his comic book. Roger in his room, flat on his back, stared up at the ceiling. Nolan sat on the edge of a bed, transfixed in the horror of his childhood. Grace in the manager's office, tapped away at her keyboard, stopped and craned to read something on the monitor. Bernie with a glass of wine in hand, stood in the kitchen, her eyes trained on the walk-in fridge door. Inside that fridge, Sheila Wadsworth was wrapped in a tarp, her face pale gray, drained of life. And out there in the woods, prowled the bear.

"Amen," the nuns said.

"Amen." Maeve said. She crossed herself and opened her eyes. The nuns rose effortlessly, swept their skirts smooth and sat back down in the chairs. Maeve pushed herself back onto the ottoman with somewhat less grace. Her body felt like a collection of levers that she wasn't quite sure how to manipulate.

"We'd be happy to answer your questions, Ms. Malloy," Sister Iggy said. "I'm not sure how helpful we can be."

Maeve turned on the cell's recording app. "First, I'd like to know how you knew that I was a lawyer."

"Trooper Kelly addressed you as 'counselor'."

Right. He had. At the time, it didn't occur to Maeve that Iggy would have heard. Or that she would have understood the reference.

Iggy touched Maeve's hand lightly. "May I make a confession?"

The nun is a murderer? Maeve found herself holding her breath. That was ridiculous. "Certainly."

"I was a police officer before I joined the convent. I joined the force because I wanted to help people. Then one day, it struck me out of the blue: I wasn't helping anyone. The system is designed to isolate the offender from society. It never fixes the problem. I wanted to catch young people before they offended, save them before they were lost, try to guide them towards productive lives."

"Noble intention," Maeve said, wondering what Iggy was getting at.

"I suspect you are at such a crossroad in your own legal career."

"Everyone seems curious about that."

"Naturally. We have this image of lawyers, smarter than everyone else, educated, powerful, earning lots of money. Most people are intimidated by lawyers, and at the same time, fascinated by them because we can't really see what you do. A mechanic takes a car apart, replaces a broken component, and reassembles it. A doctor takes your temperature and gives you some pills. But a lawyer just talks."

"We do a little more than that."

"That's not what it looks like to people who don't understand your profession. What they see is that you have interposed yourself into the system, you have made yourself necessary, but they don't know why because they have no idea what you are doing or why they should pay you. You might as well be charlatans."

Maeve tried not to take offense. The profession was misunderstood and that many unscrupulous lawyers had earned the derision they deserved. She had believed she was different from the bad ones but there was no denying she had made a mistake. A really big one. She drank through a criminal case. Not during the day, but only at night to fall asleep. On the eve of the last day of trial, Tom had found evidence that her client's alibi was perjured. He tried to warn her before their boss sent him out of town so he clipped a note to the file. She didn't see his note because she ran into court hungover and didn't look at the file. So her client was acquitted and went on to kill someone. The blood of that murdered man was on her hands.

So when the bar association found out and ordered her suspension, she didn't fight. Time off from practice had given her time to think. About the law. About herself. About where she fit in. She knew the cupcake lady fantasy was nothing more than that, an amusement, a distraction. But she hadn't felt ready to face who she was and what her purpose in life should be. Was she really cut out for the law? Was she smart enough, tough enough, good enough?

Sister Iggy put her book on the floor, clasped her hands, and leaned forward. "While I was working as a police officer, I spent quite of bit of time with lawyers. It's unusual to see one working as a dishwasher."

Maeve heard herself speak before she had time to screen her thoughts. "I was suspended."

There was no shock on Sister Iggy's face, just concern, so Maeve went on. "Because of something that happened. I got an acquittal for a client and then he went on to murder someone."

"How have you atoned?" Sister Iggy asked. She had dropped the last few words of the question off, yet Maeve, the lapsed Catholic she was, knew what there were. The whole question was, "How have you atoned for your sins?"

"I visited the family and made amends, said how sorry I was." A mere apology was so inadequate.

Sister Iggy waited for more.

"And when the bar found out about it, I accepted its judgment."

Iggy's hands were still clasped in her lap. Maeve wondered what she had to say to get her to open them. She shrugged.

"It's clear to see you are in pain," Iggy said. "You still carry the weight of this tragedy."

"I'm not sure anyone could get past it."

"This man who died, what was his name?"

"Manny Reyes."

"How was he killed?"

"My client, former client, was shooting at another drug dealer and Manny just got in the way."

"An innocent bystander?"

Maeve nodded.

"This murder is not your cross to bear, yet you still seek redemption."

"I don't know that it's redemption I want." Maeve had no idea why she had made the choices she had, working as a paralegal, quitting, taking this kitchen job. There was a big difference between wandering and hiding.

"Why else would you humiliate yourself with manual labor?" Iggy asked.

"It's honest work, Sister. There's nothing humiliating about it."

"Penance?"

A few Hail Marys wouldn't fix what had happened to Manny Reyes. "The bar suspended me."

"A suspension isn't a disbarment, am I correct? You could go back to practice after the suspension is over. What would you need to do?"

"If I wanted to practice law again? I'd have to fill out a form, someone would approve or disapprove it."

"When can you do that?"

"Anytime. The suspension was over a few months ago."

"Why haven't you?"

"It's not penance, Sister. It's purgatory. I'm stuck. I don't want to go back to the same life. If I do return to law, I want it to be different this time. I thought if I just waited long enough, I'd feel some kind of change inside me and then I would know."

"Know what?"

"How not to make mistakes."

"You take yourself with you wherever you go."

No shit.

"I let a dangerous man out on the street. I fought for his freedom. I allowed myself to be used. I should have seen it coming."

"And if you had, would you have done anything different?"

All these months of obsessing over the story and she had skipped over that question. She didn't want to think there had been a choice. She wanted to be the victim, powerless, trapped by her circumstances, and suffering the consequences.

But she had had a choice and she had made the wrong choice. She had not opened the file because she thought the case was sewn up. There was no more work to do than show up and go through the motions. She needed to own that decision. It wasn't her drinking that kept her from looking at the file, it was her grandiosity.

Bless me, Father, for I have sinned. I have been a self-centered asshole.

Maeve realized that she had lost track of the conversation. Sister Iggy was no longer leaning towards Maeve confidentially. She was sitting upright, the teacup in her hands. She wore a sage expression, seeming to have intuited Maeve's stumble upon the truth.

"How can I be of help to you, Ms. Malloy?"

"Please, call me Maeve."

"Certainly," Sister Iggy said.

"Can I get your legal names – that is, before you joined the convent?"

"My name was Teresa McNair," Sister Iggy continued to look at Maeve placidly, like a cow in deep grass.

"Like Bernie, Grace, and Sheila. Why didn't anyone tell me about this family reunion before?"

Iggy shrugged. "The topic never arose. At dinner you asked us why we had come to Alaska and we answered your question. We came here to see Lord's bounty."

Would a nun lie? Maeve didn't want to think about it.

"Okay. Why did you call yourself Sister Ignatius instead of Sister Teresa?"

"Traditionally, when a young woman joined the sisters, she chose the name of a saint she emulated. Saint Ignatius of Loyola had been a military man, enamored with heroism. He was wounded in battle and during his recovery, realized how dissatisfying his aspirations had been. Then he was blessed with a new ambition, to devote his life to God. He was one of the founders of the Jesuit order. He seemed a fitting choice."

"And Sister Clare?"

"Margaret Monaghan," Sister Iggy said. Sister Clare confirmed her name with the faintest of nods.

"What do you do?" Maeve asked.

"I am a social worker in a homeless youth shelter. Sister Clare is one of our administrators."

"Like a secretary?"

"More like a chief financial officer."

Sister Clare wasn't dimwitted after all. Just odd. Very, very odd.

"When was the last time you saw Sheila alive?" Maeve asked.

"Last night. To be precise, the last I saw her was when she went to her room."

"Did you speak with her?"

Sister Iggy paused to reflect. "Not directly, no."

"Did you hear her going outside last night?"

"No, sorry. As nuns, we have a fairly strict schedule and generally, we both go to sleep immediately after night prayers."

"What time is that?"

"Prayers are concluded by 9 p.m."

"So from then until this morning, you didn't hear anyone going out the back door?"

"Is that when you think she left?"

"When I went to the gym at 8 p.m., the back door was closed. If it'd been opened, I would have noticed. When I went back to my room, it was open and there was a trail of water going down the hall."

"How far did the trail go?"

"It disappeared before it reached any of the guest rooms." Maeve considered her next question. "So, Sister, what did you do when you were a police officer?"

"I was a detective."

"Homicide?"

"Major crimes," Sister Iggy said. "Do you have any suspects?"

"It has to be someone in the lodge. That was as far as I got. Do you have any ideas?"

Sister Iggy didn't hesitate. "Only a troubled soul would commit such a heinous act."

The wind was still howling overhead and rain battered the lodge. Underneath the noise was a high-pitched noise. Clare shrunk into her chair. "What's that?" Her voice was barely above a whisper.

Another noise, a shriek. It sounded like a woman screaming. Maeve found herself crossing the lobby. She leaned across the reception counter. Inside the manager's office, Grace was frozen over the keyboard. Their eyes met. As Grace rose, Maeve jogged across the dining room into the kitchen. There was another scream as she pushed the swinging door open. She found Bernie standing in the middle of the kitchen, a long knife raised. If it hadn't been one of the women, then it had to be one of the men.

Maeve crashed into Grace as she left the kitchen. She rounded through the lodge and into the hallway. Lester was on his feet, the shotgun ready to fire pointed at the ground. Roger was in the hallway. Nolan was standing in his door. "What is it?"

The shriek sounded again then ended abruptly.

"Well it's none of us," Lester said.

"Then who was it?" Nolan said. "I thought there wasn't anyone else on the island."

"There isn't," Lester said. "That cow the bear took down, she had a calf."

"Shouldn't you do something?" Nolan asked.

"That's the great circle of life," Lester said. "Best not to interfere. Besides, it's too late. Nothing you could do now but put it out of its misery."

They all went quiet.

"Better it than us," Lester said. "Old Smokey's going to be too busy for a while. I'm taking a break." He ambled down the hall and climbed the stairs to the second floor.

***

JULY 31, 2007

The Clarion

BREAKING NEWS: The Roman Catholic Church settled several lawsuits against it this morning. The settlement was announced on the courthouse steps during a recess after a jury had been selected. The Church will pay 50.3 million dollars to twelve victims or their estates. The exact amount of each settlement will be determined later.

The Church has been scandalized for years with allegations of child sexual abuse committed by priests. This is just one of a number of lawsuits that have been filed across the country. It is estimated that the Church will eventually pay in excess of one billion dollars in settlements and judgments.

Chapter Eighteen

TOM HAD BEEN WALKING for forty-five minutes. His right hand was busted for sure. The aching spiked every few seconds. The hand was swollen and wouldn't make a fist.

His denim jacket and jeans were soaked. His flannel shirt, underwear, and socks were soaked. The gun stuck into the back of his jeans was cold and dug into his flesh. With every step, his feet squished inside his cowboy boots and water streamed out from the stitching along the sole. The boots were ruined. That was okay if they got him to where he needed to be.

A pair of headlights, like pinpricks, flickered through the downpour. As they grew larger, Tom could make out a truck cruising toward him at about thirty miles an hour. Its lights scattered long reflections in pooled rain and rippled where water washed across the tarmac.

The red Ford F-150 slowed as it approached Tom, then pulled to a stop beside him. Tom waited as the driver's window rolled down.

A man wearing a baseball cap, horn rim glasses, and two days growth stuck his head out. "Where you headed?"

Tom walked up to the side of the truck and noticed two rifles hanging in the rack mounted on the rear window. "Seward."

"Hop in. I'll give you a lift."

Tom walked around the front of the truck, pulled open the passenger door and hauled himself in. "Thanks for the lift."

"No problemo. Name's Rider."

"Thanks for the lift, Rider. Tom." Rider squinted as he gave the truck gas. Even with the wipers flapping back and forth as fast as they could, only a few feet of road were visible. Now inside the truck, Tom could see Rider was older than he'd appeared at first. He had fleshy jowls draped along his jawline and a rotund beer gut between him and the steering wheel.

"Crack your window," Rider said. "You're steaming up the truck."

Tom moved his knee so he could reach the crank. That's when he saw the stickers on the glovebox. Swastika. Confederate flag. Some other evil looking symbol he didn't recognize. Goddamned survivalist. One of those tax-protesting nutjobs with guns and canned goods stashed in a bomb shelter somewhere behind a rickety cabin, hoping and praying for anarchy. The woods were full of them.

A year or so ago, Maeve had been appointed to defend one of them for threatening a judge, a federal offense. His name was Wilfred J. Thurston. He had just been arrested and was cooling his heels in Cook Inlet Pretrial when the call came. Tom had been lolling on the couch reading the paper. Maeve was playing solitaire on the computer. They packed up, drove down to the jail, submitted to the long procession of signing in, waiting, being herded down locked corridors and into a visiting room. When they got there, a fat white guy with two days stubble in an orange suit was waiting for them. Maeve introduced herself and Tom.

"You're the lawyer?" Thurston asked.

"Yes, sir," Maeve said while she was propping a legal pad on her knee to take notes.

"What about him?"

"He's my investigator."

Thurston gave Tom a snide look, one that said no self-respecting man would work for a skirt. Tom tolerated it because he didn't want to make trouble for Maeve.

"I'm representing myself. I don't need a lawyer," Thurston said.

"That's fine, Mr. Thurston. The court has appointed me to assist you in the event..."

"Ain't no bitch helping me."

Maeve took a beat. Tom could practically hear her saying the serenity prayer in her head. "Mr. Thurston, the federal judicial system is fast-moving and very...."

"I said, ain't no bitch helping me!"

Maeve looked up at Tom. He knew what she was thinking. They didn't need a new case that badly. Tom nodded.

Without a word, Maeve slipped the legal pad back into her briefcase and stood. Tom pounded the door for the guard to let them out.

Thurston represented himself at trial. The jury came back in two and one-half hours, just long enough to order lunch and eat. He was doing three years in a federal pen, working on his own appeal, no doubt.

Tom laughed.

"What's so funny?" Rider asked.

"Nothing."

"What the hell are you doing out on a day like this?"

"On my way to Seward. Like I said."

"Walking?"

"Truck broke down."

Rider nodded.

"You're going in the wrong direction," Tom said.

"No, I ain't. I'm on my way home, outside of Nikiski."

Tom knew it was his imagination. Still, sitting in a truck with a Nazi taking him out into the deep woods, he thought he heard the sound of banjo music.

He pulled out his cell phone, wiped it off on the seat, and hit the power button. He'd call King, let him know what's going on. Just so this guy knew Tom had friends who would look for him. Maybe King had some other cousin tucked away in the woods who could come get Tom.

"Who you calling?"

"Friend of mine's waiting for me," Tom said, then added, "A state trooper."

The phone was dead in his hand. Tom hit the power button again. Nothing. Damned thing was soaked through.

Tom had a choice. He could sit in this truck cab and wait for Rider to take him wherever he was going, overpower him, and take the rig. Or, he could demand Rider pull over right now and let him out so he could start hitchhiking, which would be the politically correct thing to do. He needed to get to Seward now.

Assault and grand larceny versus walking in the rain for the next day and a half, when all the while Maeve was trapped with a killer.

Screw it. Option number three. Tom reached back into his waistband, pulled out his pistol. "Pull over. Now."

***

BACK IN HER ROOM, Maeve dropped the legal pad on the desk, herself in the chair, and called King Kelly. He answered on the third ring.

"What d'ya got?"

"The lodge is owned by Mary Bernadette Parker, maiden name McNair, DOB December 7, 1960, and Lester Alvin Parker, DOB January 23, 1972. They cashed in their retirement and bought the lodge. The plan was to live off the land and supplement their income with guests. Unfortunately, business seems to be slow. And Lester smells like pot all the time."

"We've been keeping an eye on them," King said. "Figured they had a grow op. Some guy comes in pretty regular, stays one day, and leaves again. They think no one sees them but there's only one way across the bay and that's by boat. Just like clockwork, the day after the guy comes in, good old Lester drops his friend off at the harbor at 7:30 a.m. The guy gets into the rental car he left in the harbor parking lot and then drives out of town."

"Were you going to do anything about it?"

"Decisions like that are above my pay grade," King said. "What else do you have?"

"The manager's name is Grace Louise McNair Miller. She's Bernie's sister."

"Old biker chick?"

"Or looks like one. Wears lots of black. Tattoos. Walks with a limp."

"We seen her too. She comes into town once in a while. You got a DOB for her?"

"October 19, 1962."

Maeve heard the sound of keyboard tapping as King repeated the date to himself. "Got it. Any other employees?"

"That's the lot. And we have five tourists counting the dead woman."

"Give me the victim first."

"Sheila Rose McNair Wadsworth, DOB June 6, 1977."

"Wait a minute! They all have the same last name?"

"Right. It was supposed to be a family reunion."

"And one of them bumped off a sister?"

"The youngest sister."

"You suppose one of them did it?"

"Sorry, King. I don't have enough to go on yet. I'm just giving you what I've learned so far."

She heard King tapping away on his keyboard, then a pause. "Okay. What else you got?"

"Sheila worked as an engineer in or around L.A. Like I said last time I called you, we found her outside in the rain, a bear playing around with her. At first we thought she had been mauled. When we got her inside, we saw she'd been stabbed and I found a chef's knife in the mud. So she must have been dead for a while before the bear came across her."

"Anyone else?"

"Sheila's husband, as far as I can tell, Roger Wadsworth, DOB April 8, 1977. He's an engineer too, works on the slope. Two on, two off. They had taken a cruise up and booked into the lodge as one of those add-on excursions the cruise ships offer."

"Does he have an alibi?"

"Asleep in bed. Everyone heard them arguing the night before. He said they were just talking. Then he said he went to sleep and had no idea she'd left the room. Or why she would have gone outside when we had all been warned that a bear was hanging around."

Sheila hadn't believed Lester's story about the bear.

"Sleeping alone is not the best alibi," King said. "But lots of innocent people are sleeping alone at night when folks get murdered."

"Why would he follow her outside, grab a knife along the way, and kill her? Come to think of it, it's not on the way. They'd have to go through the lobby and dining room and go into the kitchen to get the knife. They could go back out through the kitchen door or retrace their steps and follow her out the guest hall exit. That's not heat of the moment stuff, that's premeditated. Most of the time, spouses murder each other in the middle of an argument, right? Going out of his way to get the kitchen knife doesn't fit in with heat of passion."

"Gotchya," King said. "Go on."

"I told you about the two nuns. Sister Mary Ignatius formerly known as Teresa Mc-Nair, DOB September 23, 1961 and Sister Clare is Margaret Monaghan, DOB February 23, 1977," she said slowly so King could take down the information. "They work in a homeless shelter in the Midwest. Sister Ignatius is a social worker and Sister Clare is an administrative assistant. By the way, Teresa McNair of them used to be a cop."

"There's lot of things I think I might like to do when I'm not a cop anymore and being a priest wouldn't be one of them."

"To each his own, King."

"Did the nuns confess?"

"Nope. They were both in their room with the lights out when Sheila was murdered. Saw nothing. Know nothing. And that leaves Francis Nolan."

"What can you tell me about him?"

Maeve reviewed her notes. She hadn't written down what Nolan had told her about the priest abuse. She knew he hadn't wanted her to share that. He tried to get her to assure him it was confidential, and she warned him that it wasn't. She couldn't see how it had anything to do with Sheila's death. What possible connection could there be between a young seminarian abused thirty years ago and a woman stabbed to death in the Alaska wilderness yesterday? None she could think of. The only reason he told the story was to interest her in a case against the church.

"He used to be a priest," Maeve said. "Now he's a self-published author. Some book about wildflowers of the Pacific Northwest."

"Wait. You got a priest and two nuns stuck in a remote lodge in Alaska, all from somewhere else. That's a mighty big coincidence. Is he there for the family reunion too?"

"No, he was invited to do a seminar. Says he's never met these people before. I think they were hoping to attract more tourists."

"What's his alibi?"

"In his room, in bed asleep, like all the rest. Except for Bernie, Lester and Grace. They said they were up playing cards. Thing is, their stories don't match."

"Oh, how's that?"

"Grace said they were playing, but she didn't say what game. She was certain they hadn't kept score. Bernie said they were playing Five Card Stud but didn't say who won. Lester said they were playing Texas Hold 'Em and Grace cleaned the other two out."

"Sounds like someone cooked up a story, and all three of them couldn't keep it straight," King said.

"That doesn't mean one of them, or two of them, or even all of them killed Sheila. Could be they just were somewhere they shouldn't have been and didn't want me catching on."

"Such as?"

"Such as that pot grow operation you talked about. Like I said, Lester smells like pot all the time. He's high, for sure, but more than that. It's like he's covered in residue."

"How's a nice girl like you know what pot smells like?"

"It smells like burning tea or rope. I read about it in *Ladies' Home Journal*."

King let that hang. He knew that she was a recovering alcoholic. Everyone knew it. She hadn't made a big deal about her occasional recreational use of illicit drugs. Like most other law students, she had been exposed. Unlike other law students, she had indeed inhaled. When she quit drinking, she quit everything else too.

"I got what I need for now," King said. "Will you be okay until we get there?"

"How long? The bear is prowling around outside the back door. He already tried to bust into the lodge."

"What stopped him?"

"Lots of yelling. Lester boarded up the back exit as best he could. He's sitting there now with the shotgun, just in case."

"That's about all you can do. Late morning is the earliest we can get there, I'm guessing. The storm's supposed to pass over some time tomorrow. The tail end of it won't be so bad and we can take the boats out."

"Sure, I can make it until tomorrow. I'll lock myself in my room. Is it alright if I tell them they are free to wander around the lodge?"

"Seems to me they wouldn't want to with a murderer on the loose."

"I don't have the authority to lock them up," Maeve said. "You know that." Besides the only people following Maeve's instructions were Roger and Nolan. It seemed convenient for Roger, an introvert who'd rather drink alone in his room anyway. Nolan, on the other hand, was scared of everyone, convinced that he would be next. He'd stay put.

"I don't like it," King said. "Give me a call if..."

The call was cut off.

Maeve checked the battery. Zero. "Dammit."

She plugged the phone into the charger. The little light that should come on was black. She pushed the plug into the outlet. Checked the charger. Nothing happened.

She turned the wheel on the desk lamp back and forth. No response.

The generator was down again.

Maeve would just have to wait until Lester got it fixed, got her phone charged, and then she could call King. Meanwhile, she could always use the landline in Grace's office if she had to.

Chapter Nineteen

MAEVE SHOULD TELL EVERYONE they were free to go about their day, not that there was much to do. When she stepped into the hall, she saw Lester's chair was empty. She waited for a few minutes by the door, hoping he'd come back. He didn't.

She knocked on the Nolan's door. He opened it a few inches. His eyes were wide. "Is there any news?"

"I finished taking statements so everyone's free to move about."

"What! What about me? They're coming for me."

Maeve did not think anyone was out to get Francis Nolan, and certainly not a pair of hitmen disguised as nuns. He was a narcissist. He saw himself as the center of every story. Self-absorbed. Self-centered. Kind of like she was with the death of Manny Reyes, except she was different, she had perspective and she was capable of change. Apparently, he was not. Having him in his room was one less person she'd have to keep an eye on. Although King hadn't asked her to watch the others, she was certain he would have if the call had not been disconnected.

"You can stay in your room. Keep the door locked. I'll bring your dinner. Be sure you know who it is before you open the door. The state troopers will be here late morning. They'll take over the investigation and boat you back to Seward. So you might want to get packed early. We're all leaving."

"What's for dinner?"

"No idea."

"Can I order something?"

Lots of luck with that. "Bernie is overwhelmed as it is, Mr. Nolan. This has been upsetting for everyone. I suggest you make do."

He stuck his head out to check on Lester. "Hey, where'd he go? Isn't he supposed to be watching for the bear?"

"I'm sure he'll be back soon."

"Yeah, but what if the bear comes in before he does?"

"He'd make a lot of noise. Lester would hear it and come. He's probably just using the restroom. Maybe you'd like to stand watch while he's gone."

"And do what? Where's the gun?"

"He must have taken it with him. You could yell out if you hear anything. I'm sure Lester will come running."

Nolan pulled back into his room. "I think not. One more thing, how are they going to get us out of here with the bear trying to get us?"

"They'll have guns. I told Trooper Kelly what was going on. They're used to dealing with wildlife. It'll be fine. I'm sure."

"I'll just wait inside my room."

"Good idea."

The next room was Roger Wadsworth's. He didn't answer the door. He was probably sleeping off his morning drunk.

Maeve found the nuns in the lobby exactly where she had left them, both reading. When she approached, Sister Iggy looked up from her book. "Any news?"

"I've spoken with Trooper Kelly. He says we're all free to move about the lodge. The troopers are coming over tomorrow morning."

"The storm?"

"The worst should have passed over by then."

"That is good news."

Sister Clare looked up from her book and tapped Iggy on the knee.

Iggy said, "Sister Clare wants to know about the bear."

"All quiet."

Maeve stuck her head into the manager's office and gave her the news.

Then she found Bernie with Lester in the kitchen. She hadn't told Lester he was free to move around. The shotgun was leaning up in the corner by the back door.

As soon as she walked into the kitchen, Bernie spoke. "I know you told everyone to stay in their rooms, but Lester's got to work on the generator."

"Did you fix it?" Maeve asked Lester.

"Almost," Lester said.

"Any sign of the bear?"

"Nah, chances are he's working on that calf he took down. It should keep him busy for a while."

"Shouldn't we have someone by the exit?"

"I see no reason. Take turns, if you like. I need stuff that needs doing." With that, Lester retrieved the gun and ambled out of the kitchen towards the lobby.

"Do you need any help with dinner?" Maeve asked Bernie.

Bernie spiked a sidewise glance at Maeve. "Got it all under control, thanks. Just doing cold foods since we have no power and we need to clear out the fridge. The buffet will be set up around six. Thanks for dropping by."

And there you have it. Some people were never going to like Maeve. Maybe it had nothing to do with her. Maybe it was them.

***

Dear Mom,

Sorry I haven't written in a long time. I've been really busy with school and serving mass after school and playing basketball in the city league. Father Frank is the coach. He's really cool. He's taking the whole team camping after the season is over. We're going up to the lake and we'll get to go swimming and sleep in tents. Sheila's mad because she wasn't invited. It's for boys only, so there.

Got to go.

Love, Danny

***

GRACE HELD THE LAST letter Danny had ever written. Lines creased the paper up and down and side to side from having been folded into a tiny square. It was like that when she first received it in prison.

She remembered the day when that letter came. Danny hadn't written in a couple of months. She had called Bernie the week before and asked why.

"He's busy," Bernie had said, dishes clanging in the background.

"Too busy to write his mother?"

There was a long pause. Grace wasn't his mother anymore, legally. She knew that. She was just the woman who had carried him for nine months, who had vomited every morning of every day of the pregnancy. It was her belly he had rolled around in, poking her in the ribs with an elbow or knee. It was her body that was torn apart when the doctor ripped him out. She thought she was going to die. And then they placed the baby in her arms and all the pain was gone. She was exhausted, and exhilarated, full of hope, and scared to death.

She wasn't his mother anymore because the adoption had gone through. Bernie had promised nothing would change, that it was only a convenience so that Bernie could sign paperwork, permission slips and things. And since Grace wasn't getting out of prison before Danny turned eighteen, it only made sense.

There had been a subtle shift even before the judge signed the papers. His letters were shorter and came less often. When she called, he was never around, always off on some afterschool activity or over at a friend's house.

The last time they talked was awkward. She had called on a Sunday evening right after dinner, the time when he was most likely to be home. He had answered on the second ring.

"Hello?" he'd said. He sounded a little out of breath. He was at that age when teenagers ran to catch the phone.

"Hi. It's your mom."

"Oh." That was all he said. Oh. There was disappointment in his voice.

"Who'd you think it was?"

"No one," he said. He was lying, and not very good at it. At the time, she figured he had been expecting a call from some girl.

A thousand what-ifs ran through her mind. Girls chasing him. He was a beautiful boy, after all. He'd take what was offered. Would he get busted for statutory rape? What if he picked up a disease? What if he got some girl pregnant? Would Bernie make him get married and get a job? Or would he take off, just like his dad had done.

Girls. She wished now it had been so simple.

She had tried to ignite a conversation. "How have you been doing?"

"Fine."

Silence.

"What have you been up to?"

"Usual stuff. Nothing special."

In the background, she heard Bernie ask, "Who is it?"

"It's your sister," he said, then added, "Grace."

"Your mom," Grace said.

"Right."

"Are you mad at me?" She wondered what Bernie had said to him about her, about the adoption. Did he think she had abandoned him?

The line crackled. Danny must have twisted the phone's chord. Then she heard a hollow sound when he covered the mouthpiece. A muffled conversation took place between Bernie and him.

"Look," Danny said. "I have to let you go. I got homework to do."

"Sure, Danny. Love you."

The line went dead.

Before that day, in each and every phone call, he had asked, "When are you getting out?" Even though he knew the answer, he asked anyway. It was like a ritual with him. And she would give him her expected release date. He would be thirty-six years old when she was paroled.Then they would talk about the things they would do together: go to Disneyland, buy matching motorcycles, get an apartment of their own.

She was waiting for him to ask the question, but he didn't. Maybe he had forgotten. Maybe he was distracted. If she knew he wasn't going to ask, she would have led the conversation around to it, just to let him know that he was still her son and they would be together again someday.

She called every Sunday night after that. The line was always busy.

How she missed the days when he was a little boy and she was the only person in his world. How, after dinner, he crawled into her lap and laid his head on her shoulder, drifting to sleep while they watched TV, and then she'd carry him to bed.

When this last letter came in, she had taken it back to her cell. She sat on the cot, slipped the letter out of the envelope that had already been slashed open by the guards, the letter presumably read and put back inside. She had held the paper close to her face so she could smell that musky scent that boys gave off. Her boy, Danny.

She sniffed the paper now. She thought she picked up a trace of that smell. Or maybe it was wishful thinking.

When she had first read the letter, she felt better. He'd just had an off day when she had talked to him. Who wouldn't, with Bernie chirping in their ear? After she got out, they could be a family again. At least they could see each other, do things. At the time, she hoped she could go see him playing basketball. Funny. Not funny.

Bernie should have known. There was nothing she could have done about it, being in jail, and not being Danny's legal mother anymore. She should have known and she should have told someone.

Bernie should have known, too. She was right there, every day. How could she not have seen the signs? Or did she see them and ignored them on purpose because she was afraid of rocking the boat, losing her cushy diocese job. Grace think Bernie had traded Danny's safety for a paycheck. And when it all came out in the open, it was Bernie who got the money. Not that Grace would have traded Danny for a million dollars.

Bernie got rich and Grace lost her son. No, not lost. He was stolen from her. It wasn't fair.

Grace wanted justice. She was entitled to it. An eye for an eye.

***

KING KELLY HAD JUST finished talking to Maeve when he heard a crashing sound outside. He got up from his desk and went to the window. A tree had fallen across the road. He'd call the road crews and add it to the list.

He stretched. He'd been sitting in that chair so long, it felt like his body had been molded into its shape. He scrubbed his face with both hands, trying to startle his brain into alertness.

The mug on his desk had a brown rim near the top, marking the fill line. Black liquid pooled in the bottom. He picked it up and slugged down the dregs. The coffee was cold and flavorless.

He toured the office lazily on the way to the kitchen for a refill. He had been at his desk since the pineapple express began moving in. It wasn't a huge surprise. The meteorologists had been warning them for a few days that it was headed in their direction. Then at the last minute, it veered northward. They had expected to get wet, but not like this. Seward was bearing the full brunt of the storm now.

It wasn't the first time, so they were ready. The local grocery store and restaurants had stocked up on supplies. The one road in and out of town would flood so no one was going to rescue them. Not by road. Not by boat. Not by plane. They were on their own.

All emergency personnel were on duty to handle whatever crisis might come up until travel was restored. Trees falling down. Babies getting born. Old folks getting sick. Stray tourists falling off mountains. No one had expected a murder.

King stretched his aching back muscles and sat back down in the desk chair where he had been answering the phone non-stop. It had been pretty busy right up until Maeve called and then suddenly it was quiet. He opened up the computer's search engine and got to work.

He researched the folks at the lodge with Maeve. There was little to be said about Sheila Wadsworth. She had a driver's license issued in California where she also had a BMW sports car registered and owned a house with her husband, Roger Wadsworth. Roger had the driver's license and an old SUV in his name.

Bernie and Lester Parker had previously lived in Chicago where they had incurred nothing more serious than a few speeding tickets. And then he hit on Grace Miller.

She was a gold mine.

Grace Louise Miller, formerly McNair, had been in trouble since she was a teenager. Over the years, she racked up a progressively more serious list of convictions. She'd started off with minor consumption of alcohol. Disorderly conduct. Shoplifting. Concealing stolen goods. Possession of controlled substance. Distribution of controlled substance. Assault. Aggravated Assault.

And bingo! Murder.

King punched Tom's number into his desk phone. Tom picked up on the first ring.

"Where are you?" King asked, still surfing through the world wide web.

"Just a few miles out, should be there in an hour. What's going on?"

"Found a convicted murderer at the lodge. Grace Miller. She just got out of prison. Did ten years."

"Is she the one that killed the broad?"

"Give me a break, Tom. We got no one over there yet. All I got is the statements Maeve took and their alibis."

"Did this Grace have an alibi?"

"Playing cards with two other folks."

"You believe it?"

"Totally bogus. Between her and the others, they couldn't agree on what game they were playing or who won."

"Did you tell Maeve what you told me?"

"Hadn't called her yet, wait hold on, let me see if I can get through." King pulled out his cell phone and dialed Maeve's number. Nothing happened. "She was running out of battery when I talked to her. Maybe she turned it off."

"Maybe," Tom said. A heavy silence hung between them as if someone had just walked into the room with a gun.

The station door opened, a gust forcing it out of the hands of the trooper entering. The door slammed into the wall, embedding the knob into the sheetrock. The trooper pushed the door shut again, pulled off his poncho, and hung it on a hook. The bottoms of his pants were soaked as was the top half of his shirt and his cuffs. His light brown hair was plastered to his head. Rivulets poured down across his face.

He wiped his face with a hand. "Bad news," he said.

"What bad news?" Tom said over the phone.

"What bad news?" King asked.

"Cell tower's down."

"Cell tower's down," King told Tom. "Pretty soon you'll clear the next tower, and then you'll be out of range. Get here as quick as you can."

There was no response.

"Tom?"

No response again. Not dead air like when someone disconnected a landline. Just silence.

"Shit."

Chapter Twenty

GRACE STARED AT THE computer screen. She only had a few minutes of charge left on the laptop and then she was off-line until Lester got the generator fixed. She wondered if she should print what she had found so she could read it later. What if someone else found the news articles? They'd know what she was doing even if they had no business snooping in her office.

She hit the print button. As the ancient machine ground out paper, she reread one of the articles. It was about Maeve Malloy and a murder case she had defended the year before. Her client was some homeless guy. The cops said he had killed his drinking buddy: an open and shut case. Nevertheless, she persisted. As it turns out, she was right. She found the real killer and the judge dismissed the case against her client.

Before the truth came out, some nut case had attacked her in her office building parking lot. The guy objected to her defending a criminal. Not a big believer in justice for all, apparently. She had fought him off. He'd gotten caught and was doing time.

Grace knew a little bit about criminal law. Hardly ever did a judge dismiss a case against someone in the middle of a trial. And, she'd never heard of a defense attorney who bothered to find the true killer. This Maeve Malloy must have been brighter than any lawyer she'd ever met. And tougher too to fight off some whacko like that.

Both articles had finished printing and were strewn all over her floor. Grace got up, collected the paper, put it in order, and shut down her computer just before it died, then sat back to read the second article. Maeve had rescued a boy, fighting off the kidnappers, and found out who had murdered his mother. Smart. Relentless. Like a pitbull.

She was no one to be taken lightly. Grace was glad she had found those sleeping pills. Bernie would put them in Maeve's hot chocolate tonight and Grace would have a few blissful hours to carry out her plan without interference.

She didn't give a damn how tough Maeve Malloy was. Once Grace had finished what she'd come for, she wouldn't live long enough to get arrested.

She folded the articles in half, pulled open the bottom drawer of her desk to drop them inside for safekeeping, and saw the drawer was empty. Her pistol was gone.

***

Iggy entered the kitchen carrying two used dinner plates. The kitchen counters were covered in foods that should have been refrigerated: milk, cream, cheese, meat, chicken, fish.

"Over there," Bernie jerked her head toward the sink. She was beating the hell out of a blueberry mixture, whipping it up to look like whipped cream. Blue and fluffy.

"What are you making?"

"Eskimo ice cream. I need to use up the blueberries and anything else in the fridge. With the power out, that stuff isn't going to last."

With the power out, the body was going to get ripe, too.

"Neither will Sheila," Bernie said, as if she read Iggy's mind. "We can't haul her outside, even cache her up in a tree. The bear will get her. The only thing I could figure on was taking out all the food in as few trips as possible to keep from letting too much cold air out. Then I moved all the ice and frozen goods in there. Hopefully they'll help keep the room cold. Sorry, there won't be any crushed ice for margaritas tonight."

"What are you talking about?"

"It was a joke."

Iggy was worried about Clare following her into the kitchen. She had seemed absorbed in her book, a biography of St. Francis, yet she had the most disconcerting way of walking in on Iggy without making a sound. She hadn't talked to Clare about the plan and hadn't decided on the best way to approach her yet. Clare had been especially stressed since they arrived. Withdrawn for longer periods of time. Picking at her robes, her face. Chewing her nails. She had recognized Nolan, even if he didn't seem to know her. When Iggy tried to talk to her about it, Clare had shut down.

"Did Maeve tell you the police would be here tomorrow morning?"

"Yup."

"Then tonight is our last chance."

"I already went over it with Grace," she said as she covered the bowl with cling wrap. "After dinner, you invite everyone into the lobby so we can talk about what happened, *process it*, or whatever you want to say. Or maybe a celebration of life. We'll all have drinks and then when Maeve nods off, we'll get her to her room, and have Nolan to ourselves."

"She doesn't drink alcohol."

"What girl doesn't like hot chocolate? It'll make her sleepy."

Bernie was up to something, no doubt egged on by Grace. Iggy didn't like it. "Why would a cup of hot chocolate make Maeve sleepy?

The door swung open banging into the cabinet beside it. Grace entered with paper in hand and a fierce look on her face. It was a good bet that Iggy had discovered her pistol was missing.

"Never you mind," Grace said. "Just do your part."

"These things are carefully orchestrated," Iggy said. "We can't just launch a frontal assault on him."

Grace leaned against a counter and crossed her arms. "Fine. You run it, we always said that. You talk first and decide who talks next. I go last, got that?"

"What about Lester and Roger?" Iggy asked. "Are they going to sit in? Do they want to share their experiences?"

"They're busy," Bernie said.

Iggy understood. She had known all along that Bernie and Lester were growing marijuana in their cabin. They needed to supplement their income. Remodeling the lodge had taken all of the settlement funds and they were broke. Iggy wasn't a cop anymore. She no longer felt bound by the pledge to uphold law and order. There were so many more evils that law and order could not address, and those were her battlegrounds.

She understood, too, that Bernie and Lester had to hide the evidence of their grow operation before the police arrived. And Roger, who was flying back and forth from California to his job on the North Slope every two weeks, stopping in to visit with Bernie and Lester, was probably smuggling the marijuana for them and had as much incentive as anyone to avoid detection.

"Sister Ignatius," Grace said. "We need to talk."

***

MAEVE FLOPPED DOWN ON her bed. Then she remembered to lock her door. She got up and turned the lock. As she pulled on the door with all her weight, she wondered if Lester had ever fixed it.

On her way back to her bed, she opened the bottom drawer of her dresser to get out her big book of Alcoholics Anonymous. There was a pistol in the drawer. Not hers, she didn't have a gun. They scared her.

She'd only fired a pistol once in her life, the time Tom took her out for target practice. He said she needed to learn how to shoot given her tendency to attract danger. She didn't like shooting. She didn't like how you could go from pointing a loaded lump of metal at someone, feel one quick urge, and the trigger was pulled.

Murder did not just snuff out a life. It did not just rob someone of their future. It ripped a hole in a family and the community that could not be healed. Shattered. Scarred. Never healed.

Point. Bang. Dead. An entire new universe would then organize itself around the loss.

Maeve found herself staring at the pistol. Sheila hadn't been killed with a gun. So why was someone hiding one? And why her room?

And what did that person plan to do with it when she or he came back for it? If they were saving it for a bear, you'd think someone would have pulled it out when they retrieved Sheila's body.

Or maybe Francis Nolan was right. Maybe someone was out to get him.

If she went to the manager's office and use the lodge's phone to call King and let him know, then someone might overhear her. She sensed it was better to keep it a secret for the time being.

Only one thing was certain: the gun was hidden sometime after she put the big book in her drawer. Someone could have sneaked into her room even before Sheila was killed, while Maeve was in the gym or working in the kitchen and not keeping track of everyone's whereabouts. Or after Sheila's body was found while Maeve was taking statements. The only person who had stayed put was Roger. Every other occupant of the lodge had been roaming around.

That gun could have been hidden by anyone at any time. In fact, Sheila could have while Maeve was working in the kitchen.

All she could do was make sure they had to look if they wanted to find it again. Maeve carefully slid open the closet door, slipped the pistol under a folded blanket on the shelf above the hangers and pulled the door closed again.

Meanwhile, she knew where it was and how to get to it. Fast.

***

"Sister Ignatius," Grace said. "We need to talk."

Iggy had not been looking forward to a confrontation with Grace although she knew it was coming. Grace would find the pistol was missing and there was only one person who had the nerve to take it from her. It wasn't like Grace to walk away from a slight.

Iggy led the walk from the kitchen to Grace's office at her own pace. She could feel Grace behind her, a churning mass of heat and conviction. If there was one good thing Iggy could say about her outlaw sister is that when she made a plan, she stuck to it. The problem was, Grace's plans generally ended with someone getting hurt.

It was Iggy's actions that had brought them to this point. Grace had found out about the repeal of the statute of limitations and approached Iggy about confronting Nolan. Iggy suspected from the beginning that she wasn't going to let Nolan live after he confessed. It wasn't her nature. She had an exacting sense of justice. It could have been the result of social influences once she had fallen into a life of crime. At the same time, wasn't it also possible that Grace was attracted to that milieu as it synced with the paradigms she had already constructed? Chicken. Egg. Did it matter?

When Grace had proposed the plan, Iggy saw the opportunity. If managed properly, it could be therapeutic and didn't have to end in more death. Grace's ostensible goal, to have Nolan prosecuted, wouldn't heal anyone. The criminal justice system didn't address the victim's needs beyond awarding a meager financial restitution which was rarely paid. So even if Nolan confessed and was turned over to the authorities, what good would that really do for the people he'd harmed? Not just the children who suffered his abuse. What about the families torn apart by guilt and recriminations? That is exactly what Grace suffered from. What she needed was a redemption from her self-imposed hell.

Iggy entered the small office dominated by Grace's desk and assessed the power position in the room. The desk was it and Grace would angle to occupy it.

She turned and stood blocking Grace's entry into the room.

Grace gestured, shooing Iggy to one side so she could get by.

She didn't move. "I will assure Nolan's attendance tonight if and only if you do one thing."

"What's that?"

"Don't say another word."

With that, Iggy pushed past Grace and strolled back to her room. It was time for prayer.

***

Iggy blew past Grace in a swirl of gray robes and veil. Iggy had the gun. That was all she needed to know. She kissed her fingers and touched them lightly to Danny's photo before entering the room, then moved around the desk and settled into her chair.

Her leg was aching. The prosthesis didn't fit right anymore. She pulled it off and massaged the stump, wondering what it would feel like to be whole again. It would feel like nothing because you don't think about how your body parts feel until you lose one.

Her last clear memory of being whole was before the motorcycle accident. She had picked up some guy in a bar. It was past midnight. She threw her leg over her Harley and he climbed on back. The road glistened from rain that had fallen earlier that night. The city air smelled clean for once, washed of car exhaust and the stink of people. She'd had a just few beers. She was feeling good.

The guy wrapped his arms around her tightly as she pulled out. He kissed her neck. She told him to knock it off, she needed to pay attention to the road. She was gliding through a right turn when the idiot groped her breast. She could see it all in slow motion now. She clamped down on his arm with her own to stop him, pulling the bike's front wheel slightly to the left. And that was when the machine slid out from under her and she was falling through air.

When she woke up a few days later, the first thing she saw were white tiles on a very high ceiling. She didn't know where she was. Then she saw the drip bottle on a stand next to her bed and felt the intravenous needle in her arm. Her skin around the tape holding the IV in place burned. Her head felt like it weighed a hundred pounds. It fell back into the pillow when she tried to lift it. She waited a few minutes, mustered her strength, and pushed herself up a few inches. That's when she noticed her legs didn't feel the same.

At first she didn't know they had taken off everything below the knee because of all the drugs she was on.

A nurse came into the room and flicked the I.V. line with her fingernail. "So we're awake now, are we?"

The woman was a bitch. Grace had been in the hospital before when she had Danny. Everyone was nice to her then. Not this one. She stood as far away as she could while she did her checks, her face taut. She wouldn't meet Grace's eye.

"Water?" Grace asked.

"I'll talk to the doctor, see if you can have some ice chips," the nurse said and went away.

Grace must have fallen asleep because the next thing she remembered was a cop standing over her bed.

"I'm placing you under arrest on the charge of homicide," he said, then he read the Miranda warning from a card. "When you're released from the hospital, you'll be transported to jail."

The last thing Grace remembered was pulling her bike onto the wet road. "What are you talking about?"

The cop flipped open a stenopad. "Everett Manley, a passenger on your motorcycle, died at the scene of a one vehicle accident. You were driving impaired. You are being charged with his homicide. When you're released from the hospital, you will be transported to jail pending prosecution."

The guy on the back of the bike, the horny bastard who had caused the accident, was dead.

The bedside tray was empty. The bitch hadn't even brought back ice chips.

Danny had been living with Bernie already when that happened. Grace had just gotten out of jail from a drug bust and couldn't support him yet. She was trying to get her life back together. She had gotten a job tending bar a few nights a week and from there she was hoping to work her way into a day job and then maybe management. When she was making enough money, she would make a nice home for the two of them. It never happened. When her attorney started talking about a deal, Bernie insisted Danny would be better off if she was his legal mom. So Grace gave him up. That was a mistake.

Iggy would deliver Nolan tonight and she had stolen Grace's gun. No problem. When everyone was at dinner, Grace could go into Iggy's room and take it back. And if she couldn't sneak away, she could get a knife from the kitchen. It's not like anyone was going to stop her.

She wouldn't have to do it while they were all together. She could wait until he had gone back to his room and locked himself in, thinking he was safe.

What Nolan didn't know was that Grace had the master key.

Chapter Twenty-One

LESTER SQUATTED NEXT TO the generator, rain dripping off his anorak hood, pelting his back and shoulders. He looked over his shoulder one way and then another. He had scanned the woods for sign of the bear as he left the lodge and saw none, but he couldn't be too careful. Even with the shotgun leaning up against the housing just an arms reach away, the bear could be on him before he had a chance to react.

He tore the last shred of duct tape off its cardboard roll and pressed it like a bandage onto the generator. The housing had been scraped by Bernie's shotgun blast when they brought Sheila's body in from woods. At first, Lester thought it was going to be okay, but now there was a tiny stream of gas jetting from it.

The edges of the tape curled up as he watched. He lifted the patch, dried the side of the machine as best he could with his shirt tail, then pressed the tape down again with all his might.

His knees were muddy and cold from kneeling in the dirt. Rain poured down his neck under the anorak. His soaked t-shirt clung to him. He eyed his handiwork one last time. It'd have to do. He was out of duct tape.

Lester stood, wiped his hands off on his jeans, picked up his toolbox and the shotgun, and spat. He let himself in the kitchen door just knowing what that old cow would say and she didn't disappoint.

"You're tracking mud through my kitchen!"

"The generator's fixed. You want me to start it up?"

"Later tonight on your way up to the cabin."

"When's dinner?"

"In half an hour. Now you go back outside, come back in the other way. Take off your filthy boots and go upstairs and get cleaned up."

"Yes, ma'am!"

"Don't you give me back talk."

"No ma'am!"

Lester reached into his jeans pocket for another plug of chew, stashed it into his cheek, and then did as he was told.

After he took a tepid shower and changed into dry clothes, he stopped in at Roger's room.

"You and me got work tonight."

Roger struggled to pull himself out of bed. He massaged his head. "Where?"

"Up at the house."

"How are we getting past the bear?"

"Taking the shotgun. We'll be fine."

***

BERNIE WHACKED A KNIFE into an onion, slicing it in half. It'll be over tonight. The fumes didn't bother her eyes; they were perfume to her. Light, clean, acidy. Chopping until she had a pile of miniscule identically sized pieces was satisfying. It was something she could do. No one appreciated how good she chopped. Or cooked. Or planned ahead. Or kept a roof over their heads and food in their stomachs. Not Lester. Not the kids when they were little. Not even when they were grown and should have known better. And, not Grace, that's for sure.

She and Lester had fought about taking Grace in. They had just moved to Alaska and were living in the cabin. The summer days were unbelievably long. Bernie had spent the day putting fence up around her little vegetable patch while Lester and a crew worked all day on the lodge.

She had just pulled a red salmon out of the oven when Lester came in for dinner. He was alone. Usually the crew ate with them before taking a boat to their homes across the bay.

"Where are the guys?" Bernie asked.

"Went home already. We ran out of sheetrock. They're going to the builder's supply store and bringing some back with them tomorrow," Lester said. He slapped a stack of mail on the kitchen table. The letter on top was from the correctional institution where Grace was doing her time.

"Didn't take long for your sister to find us," he said.

"I wrote her. She was going to find out anyway. When she got out, she'd go to the house and one of the neighbors would have told."

"So what's she want?"

"How the hell should I know?"

Bernie pulled off her oven mitts with her teeth and opened the letter. Out of the corner of her eye, she tracked Lester as he slid the pot tray off the fridge top and rolled a joint. Some men kiss their wives when they come home. She'd seen it on TV. Not Lester. Right after he walked in the door, he rolled a joint.

She read the letter.

Dear B, I'm getting out in a few months. My parole officer says he needs the address where I'm staying....

Her gut churned. She put the letter down. She had worked so hard, trying to do the right thing. Like filing the lawsuit against the church. She couldn't let them get away with hurting kids. People had to know. It wasn't her fault she ended up with a pile of money. She never expected that to happen. She thought about giving it away, but what would that prove?

Even before then, she felt bad for taking Danny in. If she hadn't, he would have ended up in foster homes. He was just a little boy. It wasn't fair to him. Grace had practically abandoned Danny. She was too busy drinking and drugging to raise him and then she was in and out of jail. You'd think she'd be grateful someone took her boy in. Not Grace. She acted as if Bernie had stolen him.

It was horrible what that bastard had done to Danny. But how was she to know? No one told her the warning signs.

Even before then it was like everything was her fault. Her mother's anger. Iggy and Grace fighting. Grace getting into trouble. She thought if she worked hard enough and did all the right things in the correct order, everyone should be happy.

Lester took a long drag from the joint, held his breath, and then pursed his lips, allowing a tiny smoke stream drift from his mouth. "So what's she want?"

"To come here."

"You're not going to let her. She's a whole lot of trouble."

Like he'd know.

Bernie had met Lester just before Danny died and long after Grace went to prison. She hadn't dated until the kids were older. Who had the time? Her friends kept encouraging her to meet men, as if she knew how.

Then suddenly Lester was there all the time, sitting at her kitchen table drinking coffee. He was one of the maintenance guys at the church. She had barely known him before she had hired him to do some repairs around the house. She knew he was a pothead from the things he said even though he didn't smoke around her. He helped her through Danny's death. When she figured out what that bastard had done, Lester listened. The next thing she knew they were married. She remembered waking up one morning, wondering when he was going home.

Funny, he lost his job just about the same time the settlement money came in. Somehow that was her fault too.

"It's family business," she said.

"Oh, like I'm not part of the family? We're married. Until death us do part. Remember that?"

Suddenly he looked like a stranger sitting at her table. Where did he come from?

Her life had been spent taking care of her sisters and Danny and she was happy to do it. This guy wasn't one of her kids. And here she was feeding him, washing his clothes, and listening to his whining.

"She's coming to live with us and that's final."

She didn't have to take Grace in. How could she let her own sister go to some halfway house? She didn't turn her back on Danny. She wasn't going to turn her back on Grace. It was only right she had invited her.

Grace sure as hell didn't act like she appreciated it. From the minute she got here, she was the same old Grace. Maybe sober. Maybe older and slower. Clumping around on that fake leg of hers. Meaner than ever. She had that same old attitude she had when they were kids, acting as if she got cheated. She blamed Bernie. For what? All Bernie did was take up the slack when Grace was partying her brains out.

She had tried to make it up to Danny. If he'd been younger when he came to her, maybe he wouldn't have bonded with Grace. It would have been easier if he hadn't. She could have raised him as her own child.

He was so angry when he first moved into Bernie's house. He said he needed to go home and take care of his mom when she got out of jail. That time she was only doing a year for a drug deal. When she got out, she took a job tending bar at night. There was no way she could get him to school. Who would watch him when she was at work? Bernie would, that's who. So he stayed at Bernie's house. It only made sense. Besides, how long would it be before Grace screwed up again when she was hanging out in a bar every night?

Bernie had been right. Grace got into trouble again just a few months later. The way the cops told it, she was drunk, hotdogging on her bike on a wet street, when she lost control and the guy on the back, no one knew where he'd come from, was killed. Grace went to prison.

She pushed the pile of minced onion aside with the blade. Warm tears were washing down her face. She wiped them away with the back of her hand. If anyone came in, she'd tell them it was from chopping onion.

So what was she supposed to say to Francis Nolan tonight? I trusted you. I was on my own raising two kids, working full-time, broke. Danny needed a father figure. And you came along. I thought you were the answer to my prayers. You were going to show him how to be a responsible adult. You were going to steer him away from his mother's lifestyle. And what did you do?

***

TOM SHOULD BE HERE any time now, King thought. He stood up, stretched his back, got another cup of flavorless coffee, and strolled around the muddy floor. Outside the constant rush of water was a white noise, drowning out the buzzing of overhead lights, the computer's humming, the clicks of the coffee pot's heating coil, even the creaking of King's shoes on the linoleum floor. It was spooky. The phones were still down. The only traffic through the station was an occasional trooper coming in to dry off before he went back out on patrol.

He put his mug down on the coffee-stained blotter, held the pistol on his hip in place as he sat down, and strained to hear the chair casters squeaking as he rolled across the floor. He felt a vibration in his shoe soles even though the sound didn't reach his ears. Was that how beluga whales heard? Did they felt the vibration of orcas soaring through water just before the kill?

A few days ago, a beluga had washed up on the beach. King was dispatched to stand guard and keep humans away until marine scientists arrived. It was too late to save the animal, it was dead already. King was trying to save curious humans. If a bear picked up the scent, it'd come to claim its dinner and kill whoever was standing in its way.

It took two full days for the scientists to figure out how to remove the body and get it done. Meanwhile King gave more marine biology talks to ogling tourists than he ever had in his life. Sometimes he felt less like a cop and more like a tour guide.

Another rush of rain drowned out his thoughts.

He woke the computer and got to work. He had already dug up everything he could online about most of the folks at the lodge and found nothing noteworthy besides Grace Miller's murder conviction. One thing he couldn't find was an explanation for how Bernie and Lester Parker, who had formally owned a beat-up house in a run-down neighborhood and shared one old pick-up truck, suddenly came into enough money to buy and fix up the Fox Island lodge.

King typed in Francis Nolan. He lived with a woman also named Nolan. She was a couple of years younger than him and they lived in a small house she owned in a middle class neighborhood. Could be his wife. He owned a Ford Fiesta he'd bought used. And he had self-published a guide to Pacific Northwest wildflowers. The events listed on his author website included weekend flea markets, crafts fairs, and holiday bizarres. The book's Amazon rating ranked it at number 555,376. Not quite the New York Times best seller list.

King surfed back to the search results and found several newspaper articles. Nolan had been named as a defendant along with the Catholic church in a lawsuit filed by various John Does who claimed they had been sexually abused by priests. A television news report was posted on the station's website.

The desk anchor, a pretty young woman with shoulder-length hair, said, "And now, breaking news about the priest sex abuse case. Over to you, Bonnie."

The scene cut to another pretty, young woman with thick shoulder-length hair standing in front of an ornate old building, holding a microphone.

She looked at someone beyond the camera, nodded, and then started talking directly into the lens. "The Roman Catholic Church today announced a settlement of the priest sex abuse case that was scheduled for trial later this year. The Church will deposit 5.6 million dollars into a trust account which will then be divided amongst the victims and the victims' estates through arbitration. One of the mothers has agreed to speak with us."

The view widened to show a shaggy-looking middle-aged woman standing next to the reporter. King recognized her. She came to town monthly, just like clockwork, the day before the mystery visitor would arrive, buying groceries, a case or two of wine, four cases of beer, and a box of cigarette rolling papers but no tobacco. Dead giveaway they were smoking marijuana.

And that's how the troopers knew the guy was coming. They figured he was the drug mule, carrying their harvest that had been grown on the island. Because who the hell imports cannabis to Alaska where the world's best was grown? Or so King had heard.

The woman on the screen was Bernadette Parker from Fox Island. Although she looked a little younger on television, King was certain it was her.

"How do you feel about the settlement?" the reporter asked, then flipped the microphone in Mrs. Parker's direction.

Mrs. Parker jerked her head back from the mic and looked at the cameraman.

"Mrs. Parker, when did you first learn about the settlement?" The reporter asked.

Bernie turned to the reporter. "It's been in the works for a while, but we just heard from the lawyer's office yesterday that it had gone through."

"Are you happy with how it turned out?"

"It'll never bring back my son..."

"And we won't mention his name because of confidentiality laws."

"Right. My adopted son, really. It won't bring him back. He died of in an accident just before the case was filed."

"When did you first suspect?"

"When it was happening, I had no idea. If I had known, don't you think I'd have done something about it? I was a faithful member of the church. And being a single parent, I was relieved when Father Frank... Oh, is it okay if I say his name?"

The reporter nodded.

Bernie went on. "I was thrilled when Father Frank took interest in my son. A fatherless boy needed a strong male role model. That's what everyone told me. Who could possibly be a better role model than a priest?"

Bernie looked at the reporter. The young woman waited for more to be said and then understood that she was supposed to respond. "You had no idea?"

"Why do you keep asking me that? What do you think I am? I had no idea. None. At his funeral, a witness came forward who said she saw Father Frank with my son and it looked suspicious. She didn't actually see something going on, only that she had caught the two of them alone and they acted guilty. I realized that all his problems started after Father Frank started hanging around. At first I chalked it up to a boy being a boy or maybe because he'd had a rough start in life. And then I found his poems. It was all there. He'd hidden them under his bed and he never let me in his room."

"When did you learn your son wasn't the only victim?"

"Months later. Our lawyers told me. The priest had abused a bunch of girls and boys in our parish, and in other parishes before. Whenever the church caught him, they'd just move him, hoping to bury the problem. They dumped him on us because we're poor. We need the services the church provides us so they figured we couldn't afford to rock the boat."

"But you did rock the boat."

"My boy was dead. I didn't want this happening to any more children."

Bile erupted in King's gut. His throat burned and he could taste the sick, sweet flavor of vomit. He paused the video, pulled a trash can out from under his desk and bent over it, waiting. After a few minutes, his stomach settled.

He sat back in his chair, sweating, letting the information filter down so he could go on. He grabbed his coffee to wash down his throat. Inside the mug was a bluish film of creamer slithered inside a bulging, glistening rim. Flecks of something floated on the surface. His stomach lurched a second time and he pushed the cup away.

He reached for the computer mouse and hit play.

The reporter spoke directly to the camera. "We called the church's attorneys before going on air tonight and were told there would be no comment."

Chapter Twenty-Two

NOLAN SAT AT THE undersized desk, his laptop's cursor blinking on a blank screen. What he needed was a title. Something catchy and memorable. And sinister. "My Life in the Seminary" was too dull. "Seminary, Sex and the Altar Boy" sounded like porn. "The Seminarian." Maybe.

When the church axed Nolan, the bishop's office had called him into a meeting at its law firm. A secretary showed Nolan to an empty conference room and placed him at one end of the table. She didn't offer him anything to drink.

A few minutes later, three lawyers filed in. An old man, a young man, and a young woman. He figured they were all attorneys because they were wearing suits, even the girl. He'd seen them before when he came in for interviews about the case. Someone must have introduced them but he'd forgotten their names.

The old one sat at the other end of the table. The other two took chairs to one side of him. The female lawyer set a legal pad in front of her and poised a pen over it. They were so far away, Nolan thought he'd have to yell to be heard.

The old lawyer did the talking. "On behalf of the church and diocese, I'm prepared to make you a very generous offer." No greeting. That was the first thing out of his mouth.

Then they all looked at Nolan. The young ones seemed to be holding their breath.

"Where's the bishop?" Nolan asked.

The two younger ones flinched. He must have shouted. When he looked at them, they both dropped their gazes. The female wrote something down. He couldn't see what she had written.

Nolan could tell something important was about to happen. If they were moving him to a new assignment, he would have been called to the diocese, not their attorneys' office. That's how it always worked before.

"The bishop will not be joining us. I have full authority to act on his behalf. As you know, there have been serious allegations against yourself and the church arising from your interactions with certain children."

"Not just me. There were others." The lawsuit had named three additional priests that had served in the diocese before Nolan arrived. Some of the claims were for abuse that had, allegedly, occurred decades before.

"I understand that." The old lawyer folded his hands. "We are at a point in the litigation where settlement is being explored. The trial date is coming up."

"Can't you get the trial date delayed again?"

"We've gotten all the continuance the court will give. It's put-up or shut-up time. If you choose to testify, and it is our very strong recommendation that you don't, you will be on the stand for days. The plaintiffs' attorneys would take your testimony under oath and it would be videotaped. They would ask you everything and anything, starting from where you were born and how you grew up, your time in seminary, your assignments, your duties. And, of course, your interaction with the children."

"They weren't really children." He had blurted that out. Nolan couldn't stand little kids. He had only worked with teenagers. Young adults, really, even if they were underage. Some of those kids knew more than he did.

All three lawyers exchanged glances.

The old one spoke again. "It would be a very unpleasant experience for you and given the number of attorneys involved and the multitude of claims, I anticipate your testimony could last at least three days. Maybe a week."

"Isn't there something you can do?"

"Time's up, I'm afraid. That is why we are meeting today. The church wants to put this behind it and move on. I'm sure you do too. And that brings us back to the offer."

The case had been going on for years. Nolan had been dragged to the law firm for questioning over and over again as new complaints were made, like he was some sort of criminal. There were children named he'd never heard of. The lawyers said they had proof he knew them. They had been on some team he coached or gone on some trip he chaperoned. How was he to remember every kid he met?

From the minute the lawsuit was filed, there were no more calls from the diocese office. No more requests to attend fundraisers. No more meeting with visiting dignitaries. The parishioners quit inviting him to dinner. In the hallways, people whispered and looked away when they saw him. He was a pariah.

Absolutely, Nolan would love to have the case over too. "What kind of offer?"

"The church is prepared to pay you one hundred thousand dollars."

He was confused. The church just didn't hand out money like that. He was expecting to be sent to one of those priest getaways for a few months where they'd make him talk to some therapists. And then maybe they'd send him out of the country. "Money? What for?"

"To settle any claim you might bring for wrongful termination."

"I don't understand."

The old lawyer pulled a document out of a file at his elbow and handed it to the young man who passed it to the woman. She flung the paper down the table. It whirled across the slick surface, then stopped just beyond Nolan's arm length. No one was going to hand it to him. He stood, reached, and picked it up.

The diocese letter was on thick paper. Ornate raised letterhead was flanked by a couple of gold and red symbols. He glanced across the one short paragraph and saw the words "notify" and "laicize."

He was too nervous to read. "What does it say?"

"Given the allegations, the church has no choice. You understand that were you to pursue a wrongful termination action, evidence would be made public that would be damaging to you and your future. So I've been authorized to give you this check for one hundred thousand dollars," he said tapping the file folder.

Nolan realized he was sitting in the same room with a check that would make him rich. He could deposit it in his bank account this afternoon.

"Before I can give you the money, you need to sign this agreement," the old lawyer said. He pulled a stapled sheaf from the folder and reached across the young man to hand it to the young woman himself. When she took it, he flicked a finger in Nolan's direction. She stood this time, walked over to his side, and placed the document in front of him, before retaking her seat.

Nolan scanned the pages. He caught certain phrases. "Laicize", again. They were throwing him out of the priesthood. "Agreement not to dispute disciplinary action." "Non-disclosure clause." And at the bottom, in bold letters, capitalized, "The undersigned acknowledges that he has read and understands the foregoing."

"What does it mean?" Nolan asked.

"Basically, it means you go away quietly and promise never to talk about the allegations against you."

Nolan would be delighted to never talk about the allegations again. To anyone. Ever. It had all been so humiliating.

"You said how much?"

"One hundred thousand dollars." The old lawyer pulled a check out and carefully place it on top of the file folder.

"Where do I sign?"

They gave him one hundred thousand dollars to settle a wrongful termination claim he hadn't made. They made him sign the non-disclosure agreement to get the money. They told him he couldn't talk about his time as a priest or about any of the kids who had accused him. That was fine with him.

There was a loophole, something those fancy, smart lawyers didn't think of. The agreement didn't cover the time before he was a priest and what had happened to him. The church's lawyers didn't know about that. They didn't want to know. They shut him down every time he brought it up as if they already knew what he would say and they didn't want to hear it.

He found himself standing in his sister's cramped living room wearing an outdated suit. Beside him was a suitcase from the church's thrift shop. A few days later, he found out that the alleged victims of his, who had attorneys, got more than two million each.

He was a victim too. But he didn't get multi-millions because he didn't have an attorney working for him. He had trusted the church to protect him.

The kids and their families all had lawyers. The church had the best lawyers money could buy. Because no one was looking out for Nolan, all he got was a lousy hundred thousand.

The money was gone. Nolan had no idea how much it cost to live in the real world, not that the amount they gave him was negotiable. The church's attorney acted like he was doing him a favor giving him that much. He had never supported himself, having gone straight from junior high into seminary. With his settlement, he bought a car, gave his sister some money to help out with the house, and invested the rest of it getting his book published.

He had no idea how to find someone to edit it, someone else to format it, an artist for the cover, and then how to market. So he'd hired a vanity publisher. They did all that but when it came to marketing, all they did was set up an author website for him that looked exactly like the websites of all the writers they published. Then he hired a publicist who, as far as he could tell, hadn't done anything. No speaking engagements. No blog tours. No conference panels. No reviews. The sales he made wouldn't fill his gas tank.

When he got the invitation to speak at this lodge, he thought he had finally broken through, been noticed. It turned out to be a ruse. They had lured him here because of what he knew. And they tried to kill him but they got that obnoxious woman instead. She was part of it. She tried to get him to go outside where someone was waiting to kill him. That explained everything. She was in on it. And when he didn't meet her and they must have mistaken her for him because it was dark and raining.

He was going to get off this island alive even if he had to use that lawyer-dishwasher as a human shield. And then he was going to tell his story.

He'd write a book, file his own lawsuit, and get millions of dollars. He pictured himself on Oprah, her sympathetic cooing as he told the story of his boyhood. And the closet where the seminary priests had taken him. Taken. Yes, that was the right word for it. They had led him to that room and then they had taken him.

He had gotten screwed. First by the priests and then by the church.

***

ROGER NEEDED TO SOBER up if he was going to work with Lester tonight. He had to help – he had no choice. If the cops found the pot, they would only have to dig a little bit to see that Roger visited the lodge once a month. They'd find out he had much more money than he earned on the slope and put two and two together. He should have never bought that yellow sports car for Sheila. It cost way more than he could afford on his salary. She'd wanted it so much and it had made her happy for a couple of days.

If he got charged with smuggling marijuana, he'd lose his job and everything he had.

His head was aching and his mouth felt like fur was growing inside it. He sat on the edge of the bed, rubbing the bridge of his nose where his glasses rested, braced for Sheila to fly out of the bathroom barking at him. It was quiet except for the rain. Every rush of downpour was like an electric jolt through his body.

Then he remembered. Sheila was gone. Dead. Never coming back again. Someone killed her. That's why the cops were coming and they had to hide the pot grow. He picked his glasses up from the side table and slipped them on.

The room felt empty without her. When he first saw her lying on the kitchen floor, he felt terrible. It had to be his fault. Everything was. She had told him so. Now, as he sat here, hungover, he didn't feel grief. He felt free. And guilty for feeling free. She was his wife. He would be the principal mourner at her funeral. Still, the quiet was nice.

Roger stood slowly, knowing that as he rose, the altitude would make his head pound. What he needed was a morning after cure: a drink and a few aspirin. Right after he took a leak. He looked at the bathroom, calculated how much energy it would take him to get there, and decided that he didn't need to go that badly.

Sheila's bed was still made. During their marriage, he had never crossed that invisible line between his side and her side, not since their wedding night. He had never learned to read her. He couldn't tell when she wanted him to initiate sex. All his fumbling seemed to be at the wrong times so he'd given up. When she wanted him, she had let him know.

Roger fell onto the mattress, sprawling across the entire surface. The bed was his now. All of it. He could sleep upside down if he wanted. He flapped his arms and legs as if he was making a snow angel.

Should he take her suitcase home when he left the island or just leave it? He didn't need her stuff. Why bother hauling it all the way back to California just to donate it to charity? Maybe the police would take her things as evidence, for D.N.A. or some other test, and then he wouldn't have to decide.

What about the poem?

It wasn't Sheila's poem. It was a poem Danny had given her not long before he died. She acted like she hated him. She said that when they were younger, before Danny changed, they were close. One time, she said, she found Father Frank and Danny in the pantry. It was obvious they didn't want her there. She said she never saw Father Frank do anything to Danny. And Danny never said he had.

So when Bernie made all those accusations, and then took all that money, it didn't seem right to Sheila.

Sometimes, even after Danny started getting into trouble, he had reached out to her. Treated her like he always did, like his little sister, even though she was really his aunt. The last time she saw him, at some family gathering, he'd given her this poem written on lined notebook paper and folded into a tiny square. Sheila thought Grace might like to have it, so she'd brought it. She didn't get a chance to give it to her. It was just like Sheila to pick a fight with everyone instead.

He rolled onto his side and crab-walked off the bed, careful not to rise too quickly so as not to aggravate the headache. On the closet shelf, he found Sheila's bright yellow overnight bag. He pulled it down onto the floor, sat beside it, and rummaged through the pockets. She'd be furious if she could see him. He felt another whiff of guilt, then freedom.

He found the paper folded into a tiny square and opened it.

The Pantry

In the pantry, nice and dark,
The perfect hiding place for little kids,
Jars and boxes of food on shelves,
No windows, just one lightbulb,
In the pantry where it was nice and dark.

In the pantry, nice and dark,
Where a boy could find peace,
Where he could read books about knights and dragons, wizards and warlocks,
Where he could imagine what life might be like if it was fair,
Beyond the nice, dark pantry.

Father found him in the pantry,
The man who loved him like a son,
He was growing now and needed to learn
Things beyond his understanding,
Who better to show him than the man
Who stood between him and the door
Of the nice, dark pantry.

Trapped.
Confused.
A tidal wave carried him away.
Drowning.
Scared.
I want to go home.

Before the door opened of the nice, dark pantry,
The monster said, "hush, don't tell a soul,
It's private, our little secret,

Special. Just for you and me."
Then the monster creeped out,
And closed the door
upon the mangled soul
In the nice, dark pantry.

Crap poetry, Roger thought. Didn't even rhyme. Then it hit him. Sheila was such an idiot sometimes.

Chapter Twenty-Three

THE TRUCK TOM WAS driving slid to a halt on the mud-slimed road. Rain had stripped the mountainside, washing dirt across the asphalt on its way to Resurrection Bay. That wasn't his worst problem. His worst problem was the swollen creek roaring across the highway in front of him. No way would this beater forge that water. If he tried, the current would lift the truck and flip it. He would drown before he could escape.

He checked his pockets to make sure he had his cigarettes and lighter, pulled his gun out of the glovebox, and got out of the truck. Might as well leave the keys in case someone comes along and needs to move it off the road when things dried out.

Sooner or later someone would return it to that separatist wannabe he'd dropped off by the roadside. Dude needed some exercise anyway. A walk would do him good. Tom had taken his cell phone so he couldn't find help too soon. He didn't need that guy and his buddies tracking him down. Lifting the phone wouldn't be a big deal to the cops when they charged him for stealing the truck at gunpoint. Grand theft auto, assault, who knows what. He'd deal with it later, after he found Maeve.

He dug out his own cell and tried Maeve's number. Good thing her number was on speed-dial because his right hand was practically useless, swollen, and ached from punching Crazy Tony's nose. He thumbed the number with his left hand.

No answer. It had been hours since he got King's call telling him that someone had been murdered at the lodge. Was she safe? Did she remember all the martial arts he'd showed her? Generally, her instincts were good. But for all Tom knew, and for all Maeve knew, everyone at the lodge was in on the murder. So all of them would have reason to silence her. A simple wrist release wouldn't help her against an organized attack.

He tried King's number. King could drive out and meet him on the other side of the creek once Tom got through. King didn't pick up.

He shoved the gun in his waistband and assessed the situation. As water poured down the mountainside, the creek got bigger, wider, and faster. His only chance of crossing would be to hike toward the peaks until he found a spot narrow enough to walk through or jump over.

He headed up. He was still in sight of the road when his foot slipped and he went down on all-fours in the mud. Pain shot through his right hand. The arm gave way and he face-planted in slimy mud. At least, he hoped it was mud. He was too close to the stream. The rushing water was taking bigger bites out of the bank with every minute.

He scraped the gunk of his face, grabbed a boulder with his good hand, and pulled himself a few feet to the side where less water made it through the tree canopy and thirsty cottonwood and alder soaked up most of the downpour. Tom got his footing again, checked to make sure he still had his gun, grabbed another tree trunk, and hauled himself up the mountain one-handed, one tree trunk at a time, keeping the creek within sight.

He had no idea what time it was. His Rolex was back in Homer and the heavy clouds made the sky unnaturally dark. This time of year, it should be light until ten p.m. He wasn't used to hiking. His heart wasn't used to climbing uphill constantly. Sometimes it thumped too fast and felt like it was going to crash out his chest, so he'd have to slow down and catch his breath. He wasn't getting any younger.

He passed a pile of bear scat, darkened from the blueberries it'd eaten. Tufts of hair were stuck in it from some unlucky moose that had traveled through the bear's gut. The hair would have upset Maeve. She was such a city-girl, he was amazed she hadn't brought home a bunch of dogs from the pound. At least she had the good sense to know she didn't have the time for a pet, being a trial lawyer.

He had helped pack up her office. The furniture was gone, some charity thrift shop had picked it up. The phones had been disconnected. Her two rooms felt eerie. Every footstep echoed. Their voices disappeared in front of them like the air had swallowed up their words. So when he wanted her attention, he walked over to where she was taping lids to bankers boxes filled with closed files.

"Have you thought about it anymore?" he asked.

"About what?"

"What you're going to do when you come back?"

"Who says I'm coming back?"

And that was it. She went to work for Arthur Nelson as a paralegal months ago.

One night a few days after the three month suspension was up, he had called her. "When are you getting your license back?"

"Who says I'm getting it back?"

"Did you talk to Nelson?"

"He's busy."

"You're his client. It's his job to work your case. When are you going to talk to him?"

"Haven't thought about it." She sounded remote.

So he gave up hanging around and got the job in Homer. She'd tell him what she was going to do when she was ready. And then he would decide what he wanted.

What if she decided to leave the state and start over somewhere else? That's what people usually do when they can't handle the hard life here. Would he follow her? He had lived in Alaska a long time. This is the place where he crossed from the criminal side of the street to the law side. This is where he got clean and sober. He didn't like to think about leaving, so he wouldn't until he had to.

Maybe he'd buy her a kitten. They weren't as needy as dogs.

Tom watched his footing as he trudged up hill. He came up on a line of brush that went on as far as he could see. Ten feet high with upcurved limbs. There was no time to go around, his only choice was through. He turned up his collar, pulled his head down, raised his arms to protect his face, and headed in.

When he broke through the brush, he found himself on top of a rise, facing a meadow. A cold breeze stopped him like a slap in the face. It streamed down his shirt and he could feel the hair on his arms stand up. In the distance, mighty as you please, a strip of prehistoric blue ice was nestled between two gray mountains. Exit Glacier. No way he was getting across that.

Tom headed west looking for the creek. Sweat stung his face were shrubs had scratched him. His right hand was practically useless now and hurt like a mother bear. His jeans and jacket were muddy and torn up from the bushwhacking. The denim collar chafed at his neck. His shirt was soaked from sweat and rain and clung to his chest and back.

He found the creek, now a knee-deep stream, and waded in. It wasn't like his boots could get any wetter. He stopped mid-way and splashed his face. He filled his cupped hands and drank from them. Water never tasted so good. He hoped it didn't make him sick. Did giardia live in streams this high up the mountain?

After he hauled himself to the far bank, he sat down on the rocks and pried off his boots. He drained the water out of them and pulled them back on. Then he pushed to a stand and let gravity carry him downhill.

***

A KNOCK ON THE door startled Maeve. She had drifted to sleep while reading in bed, closing her eyes just for one moment to rest them. The Big Book was splayed across her, still open to page 449, the passage about acceptance. As she drifted off, it struck her that for the first time since Manny Reyes died, she felt peaceful. Her perception had shifted while talking to Sister Iggy. It seemed like such a tiny change yet just enough that serenity had seeped into her.

Her sin had been grandiosity. She thought she knew it all. She would not be so careless in the future.

The knock came again, louder this time. Maeve threw off the covers, crossed the room to the door, paused to look into the closet, saw the gun was still there, and opened the door.

Francis Nolan stood before her. "When are you going to dinner?"

Maeve could smell baked meat and potatoes. Her stomach growled. "Are they serving yet?"

"Just started, I could hear them from my room. Are you coming? I don't want to go alone."

"I thought you weren't going at all."

"Why should I hide? I didn't do anything wrong. I didn't murder that girl. One of them did. Besides, I'm safer in the open, where everyone can see what's going on."

Maeve dearly wanted to visit the bathroom before dinner. "Then I'll see you there."

Nolan slipped in past her. He judder-stepped when he saw the unmade bed, veered toward the desk, and settled himself into the chair. "I'll wait."

***

NOLAN WAS STILL SITTING at her desk, drumming his fingers, when Maeve emerged from the bathroom, ablutions completed.

"Did I tell you about my new book?" he asked.

She was interested in his new book. She was picturing the stashed pistol. Someone would come looking for it later. So she closed the closet on her way out of the room to slow down their search. He followed and pulled the room door shut behind them.

"It's about my time in seminary," he said as they walked down the hallway. "A tell-all, that's what they'll call it. But it's the truth. I know it. They know it. And it's about time the world learns what's going on."

Maeve was about to ask who "they" were when she and Nolan rounded into the dining room. He was no longer walking beside her. Instead he was following in her wake. Every other person in the lodge was already seated. When Maeve and Nolan entered, they stopped talking and appraised the pair in stony silence.

Yet again, Maeve felt like everyone knew the joke except her. The fact that she could see them all at once was one consolation. No one could sneak away to ransack her room for the gun without her seeing them.

Going down the buffet, Maeve took a slice of roast beef, a modest amount of red potatoes, and salad, and made her way to a vacant table, her back to the wall. No one could leave, or murder Nolan for that matter, without Maeve noticing. By the time he joined her, the others had gone back to their meals with little discussion beyond "would you pass the pepper, please."

The collection of people stranded together in the lodge seemed smaller now that Maeve had gotten to know them. They were clumped into two small groups. Which of them murdered Sheila Wadsworth? It had to be one of them.

Bernie, Lester, Roger, and Grace were seated at one table. Bernie's examined Maeve, her look lingering even after she noticed Maeve staring back. What possible reason would Bernie have to slaughter her guest? It didn't make sense given her heroics when they recovered Sheila's body, guarding the rescuers, shooting at the bear. On the other hand, her alibi didn't make sense. Lester and Grace had vouched for her, yet their stories didn't match. The three of them didn't agree on what card game was played or who won.

No doubt, they were lying. Perhaps to cover up the marijuana operation, an innocuous sin given there had been a murder. Or they could be hiding their roles in Sheila's death.

Lester was slathering butter on fresh-baked dinner rolls with grimy hands. The shotgun was leaning in a corner. He shot Maeve a single look and then hunched over his dinner, forearms braced against the table. What reason would he have to kill Sheila? Besides, Lester was a pothead. For him, murder would be too much hassle.

And then there was Roger, Sheila's husband. He picked at his dinner, head down, pushing the food around with a fork. After Maeve's arrival, he didn't look her way again. He took another sip of a highball, then resumed rearranging his food.

At another table were seated the nuns, Iggy and Clare. The former cop turned soul-saver caught Maeve's eye and smiled at her. She seemed to know more about everything. Or was that just her spiritual demeanor showing?

Sister Clare was cutting her food into tiny pieces and balancing each morsel on a fork, then carrying it to her mouth one bit at a time. She lifted the cloth napkin from her lap, dabbed her mouth, folded it, and placed it next to her plate. Iggy noticed something about Clare and made the slightest movement in her direction. Maeve looked closer. On Clare's napkin was a smudge of red, corresponding to a red stain on her robes. Clare folded her hands, covering the stain.

Maeve couldn't imagine why Clare would do harm to Sheila. They had no apparent connection. And she had the best alibi of all, Iggy, the most forthright person of the lot.

That left Nolan, who was slicing into his slab of roast beef. Priests don't murder people. Do they? And if they did, why would Nolan murder Sheila? He caught Maeve watching him and raised his eyebrows in inquiry. Nolan claimed he had been lured here and acted as if he didn't know Sheila. If true, it was unlikely he had come to this place with the intent to murder her. If he was guilty, what sudden turn of events made him do it? Or was it a simple argument that had spun out of control?

Maeve sensed a disconnect in Nolan, as if his reality was conjured. Perhaps he was not outright lying, perhaps he lacked the ability to comprehend the truth, just as Maeve had with her role in Manny Reyes' death. He claimed he was the intended target of a diabolical plot. Was it true? A figment of his imagination? Or a clever way of deflecting attention from himself?

Was Maeve sitting next to a murderer? It wouldn't be the first time.

"Pass the pepper, please," Maeve said.

Chapter Twenty-Four

MAEVE'S ANALYSIS OF WHO, where, and when, rolled through her mind over and over as she finished her meal. She didn't want to miss something important. If Nolan was right, someone might try to kill him before morning. If he was lying, he could well be plotting to murder during that same time period. When she got back to her room, she'd review her notes and put the story into chronological order. Timelines helped her to understand the flow of the story – the sequence of events revealed causes and effects. Sheila's death was the culmination of a series of occurrences that were so intolerable to someone that the only solution was murder.

Good Catholic she was, Maeve always cleaned her plate. She was lifting the last forkful of food to her mouth when a wall of dove grey filled her peripheral vision.

"Excuse my intrusion," Sister Iggy said. "Since this is our last night together, I was hoping you would join myself and Sister Clare in the lobby for cocoa."

What Maeve really wanted to do was go back to her room, ponder the facts in solitude, and make sure no one stole that gun.

Yet, the lure of chocolate was strong. No less strong than Maeve's convent school discipline, where she had learned a suggestion wasn't really a request. Not that Iggy was herding Maeve like a schoolchild; still, one does not say no to a nun bearing cocoa.

"Delighted," Maeve said.

"And you're invited as well, Mr. Nolan."

Nolan surveyed the room. Something outside the window caught his eye. Maeve turned to look. She sensed everyone else turning too, the room suddenly hushed. The bear was no more than six feet away from the window, ambling toward the back of the house. His shaggy brown coat streamed with water. He stopped and shook it out like a dog. He could have easily come through the window, yet he acted as if he didn't know they were there. Clare huddled behind Iggy's back.

Maeve remembered the tracks she'd seen in front of the lodge. It had seemed so long ago.

Then the bear started moving again, slowly. He headed towards the tree line, entering the woods at the trail that led to the cabin. And then he disappeared into the forest.

Maeve heard whispers of fabric as people began moving again. A fork clanged against a plate. Someone let out a deep sigh. She was still watching the trailhead, wishing the bear to keep walking on and on away from the lodge.

"We'll meet you in front of the fireplace," Iggy said. She walked over to Bernie, who was piling used dishes on a cart, spoke into her ear and the two of them went into the kitchen.

Maeve picked up her plate and stood. Nolan stood as well, apparently intent on leaving his plate on the table. She picked it up too, piled the cutlery on top, and carried them to the bus cart while Nolan lingered. Then they walked into the lobby where they found Sister Clare sitting in the middle of a couch, leaving the two armchairs flanking the fireplace unoccupied. In one of the chairs was Iggy's book.

Maeve assessed the seating arrangement and Nolan appeared to as well. He took the armchair on the far side of the fireplace with his back to the prow windows, the gambler's seat. It had full view of the room. No one could shoot him in the back. It was the same position Maeve had chosen in the dining room so she could survey the diners.

He's a quick learner, Maeve thought. Or, more likely, it was the only seat he would take. Iggy had claimed the other chair by leaving her book in it. And, given his obvious aversion to women, he would not have sat next to Clare.

"May I join you, Sister?" Maeve asked.

Clare shifted to one side and patted the couch next to her.

The moment drew out awkwardly. It was getting dark again, unnaturally so due to the cloud cover. The storm's roar had subsided to the drizzle's crescendo and decrescendo. An evening just sitting there by the fireside, listening to rain, would have been a pleasant pass time under different circumstances.

Sister Clare sat head bent, hands in lap, still as ever except for with the faintest of smiles playing on her face. Or it could be gas like that old wives' tale about babies. The red stain on her robes had seeped and grown larger than a quarter with a ragged watery edge. She moved one hand to cover the mark as if she knew Maeve was looking at it.

The red blotch could have been juice from the roast beef. Or ketchup. Or tabasco sauce. Or something else. When Maeve was in convent school, tampons weren't permitted because they had been deemed sinful. Maybe Clare had a mishap. Why, then, hadn't she changed clothes?

Nolan cleared his throat, crossed his legs, and pushed himself more deeply into the depth of the wing-back chair. He began drumming his fingers again. From the corner of Maeve's eye, she could see him sending her imploring looks. For someone who had no reason to hide, he certainly was anxious out in the open.

Only a few moments ago, he had responded to Iggy's invitation as if it was a challenge. Now it seemed he was chickening out.

Perhaps he wanted Maeve to announce she was retiring and he would follow her. She could respond to his unease and suggest an end to the evening or she could wait for her hot chocolate.

Maeve got up, poked the dying embers in the fireplace, put another log on from the nearby pile and prodded again, ostensibly waiting to see if the new log would flame without help. Truth was, she was just keeping busy. As she was about to go see where Iggy was, she could hear the kitchen door swinging and a cart rattling across the hardwood floor.

"Have a seat, and I'll serve all around," Bernie said. Iggy took the chair she'd reserved for herself, placing the book on an end table. Maeve sat back on the sofa next to Clare. Bernie handed Iggy a plate with a thick slice of dark chocolate cake with chocolate frosting. "Suicide cake," Bernie said.

Maeve wondered if that recipe would work for cupcakes. Dense chocolate cake, heavy rich frosting, chocolate shavings. She'd tinker with the recipe when she returned home.

Home. That was the first time Maeve had thought about her little condo since she had arrived in Seward. She missed the split level with glass doors opening to a deck overlooking the lake, the loons who sang her to wakefulness every morning, and the rim of blue-gray mountains in the distance.

She wanted to go home.

Bernie handed her a plate of cake, which Maeve balanced on her lap. "Eat, eat," she said. "Don't wait for me."

She didn't need to be told twice. After Maeve got sober, she needed a way to knock herself out when she couldn't unwind. Drugs were out of the question. So, she'd developed the unhealthy habit of spiking her blood sugar with something chocolatey. The chocolate high on top of a sugar rush was guaranteed to make her happy right before she crashed and slept the night through. She wondered how long she could stay awake with this lethal combination of cake and cocoa.

As Maeve sliced into the cake, Bernie served everyone hot chocolate.

"It's a pity we weren't able to go on the nature trek," Iggy said to Nolan. "What kind of wildflowers would we have found?"

Maeve jerked herself awake. Her dessert was only half-finished when she was overwhelmed with sleepiness. Her head bobbed as Nolan's voice faded.

"*Andromedia polifolia*, commonly known as bog rosemary, a dwarf evergeen with pink urn-shaped flowers."

"Oh, dear," Iggy said. A hand reaching for the plate in Maeve's lap was the last thing she remembered.

Chapter Twenty-Five

WALKING INTO THE WOOD behind a bear was insane. "Are you sure about this?" Roger asked.

Lester was in the lead, the shotgun nestled in the crook of his arm. "We got no choice." He slowed a moment, leaned to the side, and spat. "Besides that bear can be miles away by now."

"Or not."

Lester didn't answer. Roger felt numb. He was just going through the motions, doing as people told him, because he had no will to resist. He wasn't still drunk from this morning – he had sobered up since then. The highball with dinner wasn't enough to get him drunk. It was because Sheila was gone. Roger didn't know how to act without her.

The woods grew murkier as they made their way up hill. The rain was fogging up his glasses so he had taken them off and stashed them in a pocket. He tripped on a tree root. He stumbled and crashed into Lester, who him back. "Watch where you're going."

"It's dark."

"No shit. You have the flashlight."

Roger had forgotten about that. Suddenly the weight in his hand was noticeable. He flicked the switch on and aimed the beam at the ground.

When they came around a bend, a rotting stench hit him. Lester stopped walking. Roger bumped into him again.

"What did I just tell you?" Lester said under his breath. He grabbed the flashlight from Roger's hand and played the light along the shadows.

A large dark lump blocked the path. Roger knew what it should be, yet he strained to make out the gloom-shrouded sight. A wind moved through the tree canopy, pushing drizzle onto them, and rainwater ran down the back of Roger's shirt. It felt like bugs crawling on his skin.

The moose had been gutted, her abdomen an empty cavern, and there were gnaw marks on the hindquarters. Her head was still intact as she stared vacantly into space. An image of Sheila lying in the mud with that exact expression flashed through Roger's mind. It couldn't be a real memory, because he hadn't seen her outside where she'd died. It was what Roger had seen in the kitchen and his imagination was playing tricks on him. Had to be.

All he remembered of that last night was her nagging. He'd quit listening years ago because there was nothing he could do to fix it. When they were first married, he'd try to talk to her, to understand what was going on, to make her happy. Then as soon as one problem was solved, she'd shift to something else. Later on in their marriage, she would dance from one complaint to another before he could solve the first one. At that point, he figured there was nothing he could do to satisfy her, so he gave up trying.

Last night was like every other night. She came into the room, harping about something. That went on for a while, then she went into the bathroom. That was the last thing he remembered.

When the lawyer-woman asked him what he was doing that night, he told her he had fallen asleep. He knew it was true because he woke up this morning. Sometimes, though, Sheila would tell him that he was talking and doing things he didn't remembered. He figured she made it up to have something else to bitch about.

"Another one of your blackouts," she said. "You drink too much. Why don't you know when to stop?" Talk about the pot calling the kettle black.

Roger pulled his raincoat up over his nose to block the stink. Lester began moving off the trail slowly, tense, as he worked the shaft of light in between trees.

"Is the bear out there?" Roger whispered.

"I don't see him," Lester said. "Keep your eyes peeled. It's your ass, too, if he catches us near his moose."

Slogging through knee-deep rain-soaked plants, they circled around the moose and then came back to the path uphill from her. The air there already smelled better. Roger's jeans, soaked from the knee down, stuck to his legs and itched. Maybe he'd leave them behind at the lodge, just take his toothbrush. He could leave Sheila's things there too. The women might want her clothes and stuff.

A new wave of exhaustion washed over him. All he wanted to do was lay down and take a nap when they got to the cabin. Lester wouldn't like that.

A few minutes later, the cabin came into view. Roger had been there before, many times. When he walked in the front door, it looked the same. The living room had been converted into a greenhouse. There were rows of pot plants, each in a white five-gallon bucket, under grow lights. They were so tall and leafy, it looked like a jungle.

In the kitchen was a table where the sorting, weighing, joint-rolling, and pot smoking took place. There Lester had spent many hours with Roger and Bernie getting high as they prepared the harvest for transport.

He didn't particularly like either Bernie, or Lester for that matter. He tolerated them because she was Sheila's sister and there was nothing he could do about that. She had been like a mother to Sheila. And although Sheila had complained bitterly about childhood injustices, mostly centered around not being loved as much as Danny had been, she was fiercely loyal to Bernie in a way Roger didn't understand. She always said she could talk shit about Bernie, but no one else could. As for the other two sisters, Grace and Iggy, she rarely mentioned them, and when she did, she said they weren't around.

Bernie was a pretender. All the fake Native American stuff. The T-shirts with eagles, mountains, and feathers. Posters of long-dead Indian chiefs hanging on her walls. The beaded earrings. The only genuinely Native thing she had was the silver bracelet she had bought at an arts fair in Anchorage.

One time when she was in the bathroom, Roger got up to get himself a drink of water. As he stood at the kitchen sink, something on the dreamcatcher in the window caught his eye. It was a tag reading "Made in China."

He thought it was funny. Sheila didn't. When he told Sheila about it, she unloaded on him. "So what?" she asked. "Everybody has their thing. Iggy's a nun. Grace is a loser. Lester likes pot. And you're a geek. So what if Bernie likes Native stuff. She isn't hurting anyone."

Still, Roger thought, there wasn't a Native American within shouting distance of the lodge. She might like their stuff, but them, not so much.

And Lester was no better. Nothing he fixed worked right afterwards. He didn't talk much. At first Roger wondered if that was because he was stoned all the time; lately he'd suspected it was because Lester knew he was an idiot and didn't want anyone noticing.

Bernie wasn't all bad. She had worked hard and she had raised Sheila and Danny single-handed. It was after Sheila had gone to college when Bernie hooked up with Lester. She had never had time for a relationship of her own with raising other people's kids, so if Lester is what she wanted to comfort her in her old age, who was Roger to object?

He couldn't imagine why any of them would want to kill Sheila. She was a pain in the ass, sure. Nothing new. Besides, if any of them had wanted to hurt Sheila, it would have happened before now. And despite everything, Sheila had never said anyone had hurt her. Or Danny for that matter. She had thought he was lying to get attention.

If one of her sisters and Lester didn't kill her, who'd that leave? The lawyer-woman? Nah. Had to be the priest. Roger really didn't like that guy's looks. Shifty, arrogant.

Roger followed Lester into the kitchen. On the table was a tray with a small pile of bud and a pack of rolling papers. Without saying a word, Lester slipped into his chair, flicked a paper out of the packet, held it in one hand while he arranged marijuana on top, then rolled it deftly into a nice big fat joint, while holding the whole operation over the tray to catch whatever fell out. Waste not, want not.

If there was one thing Lester could do well, it was rolling joints. The first thing he did in any social setting, not that anyone came around too much, was to roll a joint, impressing people with his skill. It worked. Anyone who saw him would be in awe, and pretty soon, extremely loaded, so if he said something stupid, no one would notice.

Lester lit the joint, took a deep draw, and held his breath while his eyes rolled slowly back in his head. He always did that. It was annoying.

"Dude," he said, bouncing his head like one of those old-fashioned dashboard toys.

Then he passed the joint to Roger, who took a hit. The smoke was hot and dried out his throat. A cold beer would be perfect. He got up, handed the joint back to Lester and checked the fridge. No food. No beer. Damn. It was going to be a long night.

Lester took two more hits before he handed the joint back to Roger and pulled two pairs of snippers out of a drawer. It would be Roger's last toke for a while. This was potent stuff and they had work to do, so he pulled in a bigger hit than usual. The smoke blew up in his lungs, made him cough and burned his throat. Lester snorted. Roger smiled back, embarrassed, and really wished he had that beer.

Still not having said a word, Lester handed Roger a pair of snippers and led him back into the living room. The night was long. They picked the buds, weighed them into precise quarter ounce piles and vacuum sealed them into little plastic baggies. When that was done, they pulled up the plants, root and all, and shoved them into black garbage bags. Used to be Bernie saved the leaf for "medicinal" purposes. Pot tea, pot brownies, cannabutter, cannabis caramels, cannabis cookies.

Once they had bagged the bud, Lester scrounged through some drawers and pulled out two rolls of duct tape. "We're going to bundle them all together and then wrap them up real good with this tape. Those drug-sniffing dogs will never find them."

"You sure about that?"

"Just shut up and get to work."

Whatever, dude.

When they were done, they had sitting on the table in front of them a big silver brick. Lester put it into a black garbage bag and then covered that with more tape. "It'll keep the pot dry." Then, Lester grabbed the half-smoked joint from the ashtray, leaned back, and lit up. It was about time. Roger had started to feel normal again and he didn't like it. Lester passed the joint and picked up the shotgun and flashlight.

"Come on, we need to get a move on."

Although the greedy bastard had plenty of time to take his hits, when it was someone else's turn, he couldn't wait around. Roger took a couple quick drags, and stood, with his lungs still full of smoke.

"Grab the shovel," Lester said, nodding towards a corner of the kitchen where several tools were propped up. "We'll come back for the rest."

When they stepped outside, it was even darker than before. Roger had no idea what time it was.

Lester walked up the hill a little bit. "Okay, start digging here."

"Why me?"

"Because someone's got to watch out for the bear. You ever shot a bear?"

"No, and as a matter of fact, neither have you. But your wife has. Maybe she should be out here."

"Yeah, well, it's my gun. I'm here and she isn't. So get to work. Besides, I can't have you tripping on some tree root and shooting me. Accidentally."

"Dude," Roger said, realizing how handy the word was. It could mean anything. In this case, it meant "what a rude bastard you are" but Lester probably thought it meant "you're right."

Once the mushy leaf litter was scraped away, the surface was damp and further down, the soil was dry. Roger dug a hole that was knee deep and six feet across.

"Good enough," Lester said. "Let's bring up the rest." They made several trips for the wrapped-up bud brick, the bagged-up plants, and the five-gallon pot buckets, Roger guiding with the flashlight and Lester in back with the shotgun. When they had it all lined up, Roger dumped the potting soil from the buckets into the hole, tossed in the garbage bags, carefully placed the bud brick on top and then backfilled with the dirt he had dug up.

He was covered in dirt and wet leaves. His palms burned. He looked at them. Even in the shadows, he could see he'd developed blisters that had burst and his hands were raw meat. His arms and back ached. Lester should have been doing the manual labor, not Roger. Lester was the handyman. He did stuff like this all the time.

"How are we going to find it again?" Roger asked. He knew the answer. He was pissed that he had done all the work so he wanted to jack with Lester, show him who was smartest.

"We could plant something on top."

"Like?"

"Bernie's got some basil in her little garden."

"That'd look pretty unusual one basil plant growing in the woods."

"Then all of them."

"Even more unusual," Roger said. "Everyone knows basil needs light. It wouldn't grow here. Even I know that. If I know, then the cops would know. They'd think it was strange and start snooping around. We need to triangulate a position."

"Triangle-what?"

Lester really was stupid.

"Look," Roger said. "I'll stand here and find three landmarks." He searched the forest and the back of the cabin for something that would stand out. He could see well enough; the sky in the east was starting to lighten already. It had to be almost four o'clock. What he needed were landmarks that would stand out in the dark or light, easy to find when they came back for the stuff whether at night or during the day. It felt good to be thinking again. It made him feel smart. Like he could do something without being told to.

"There," Roger pointed. "Bernie's dreamcatcher hanging in the kitchen window. See it?"

"Yup."

Roger spun around and looked deep into the woods. He checked his position. He was exactly in between the dreamcatcher and a fallen tree. "See the roots of that big old tree that fell over?"

"Okay, so?"

Roger spun around again, looking up the mountain. "And there's a boulder up there on the hill about a hundred feet up."

"Uh-huh."

"Go back to the house, stand next to the dream catcher, and walk towards that dead tree. When you can see the boulder up there on the hill, stop. I'm going to put a quarter here so we'll know if we got it right." Roger dropped a coin on the ground, covered it with some dirt to keep Lester from cheating, then stood out of the way.

Lester walked down to the cabin, stood directly outside the kitchen window where the made-in-China dreamcatcher hung, and walked slowly towards the fallen tree, glancing uphill every few steps. He slowed, then stopped, pointing at the boulder. "There."

"Great. Check your position. Are you between the dreamcatcher and the fallen tree?"

Lester looked from here to there and back at Roger. "Yup."

"Then you should be standing right on top of the quarter."

Lester squatted, scattered the dirt with his hands, and picked the coin up. "That's like magic!"

"That's engineering," Roger said. Maybe his hands were bloodied and blistered from digging, but who was the smart one now?

"Seems like a lot of trouble," Lester said. "Why don't we just leave the quarter here and come look for it?"

Yet again, Lester missed the point.

"Whatever, dude."

"We got some time," Lester said. "Let's go back inside and finish that doobie."

Chapter Twenty-Six

GRACE WAS HANGING OUT in the hallway where she couldn't be seen by the folks in the lobby, waiting for the signal. It'd been a half hour since she had doctored Maeve's hot chocolate in the kitchen. Behind her back, she held the framed photo of her son, Danny.

With the few minutes she had to spare, she let herself into Iggy's room with the master key and searched for the gun, looking under the beds, between the mattresses, in the drawers and cabinets, in their luggage. The gun wasn't there. She had found a small utility knife slipped between the mattresses of a bed. It couldn't have been the same knife that killed Sheila. That one was wrapped up with her body in the fridge. Maybe Iggy had taken it for protection, just in case blessing someone to death didn't work. She always was the sneaky one. Taking vows didn't change that.

Where the hell would a nun hide a gun? Grace didn't have time to think about it. So she went to her post and waited in the shadows for the signal.

A few minutes later, she heard it: Bernie saying, "Ah, look, she's fallen asleep."

Then Bernie said, "Up you go," like she was talking to a child who had drifted off in front of the T.V. A bit of moaning and stumbling followed, and then Bernie appeared, walking a drugged Maeve to her room. Grace pushed the door open for her, no need to unlock it since the lock never worked and waited for Bernie to drop Maeve on the bed. Then she followed Bernie back into the lobby.

You could just see it in Nolan's face when he saw Grace walk in. He got it. He finally got it. He understood now that they were all here for him. He wasn't escaping this time. His bodyguard was sleeping off a healthy dose of barbiturates. It was a delicious moment, something Grace would savor for the rest of her life.

"Good evening, Father," Grace said, drawing out the last word.

Bernie took the seat on the couch where Maeve had been sitting. All the while Nolan's eyes were on Grace. Recognition lit his face. He must have figured out who she was.

Although Nolan and Grace had never met, everyone always said Danny looked just like her.

Grace remained standing, behind the couch, blocking the only exit from the room just in case the sorry bastard tried to make a run for it. He wasn't going anywhere. Not until they were done with him.

"We are so glad you could join us," Iggy said to Nolan, always the gracious hostess.

His eyes darted from woman to woman, Bernie with her dangly beaded earrings, Grace in her jeans and t-shirt, then settled on Iggy in her nun's habit. She smiled at him warmly.

"I know you've met everyone here," she said. "Still I'd like to introduce them again to you. This is my oldest sister Bernadette Parker, maiden name McNair." She nodded at Bernie. "And standing behind her is our sister, Grace. And seated beside Bernadette is Sister Clare. Her lay name was Margaret Monaghan. Do you remember her? She was the nutritionist's daughter, worked with her mother in the kitchen every day after school."

Clare's posture which had been stiff as usual, seemed to come to life. She practically glowed at the sound of her name. Her head lifted a bit and she smiled, still not making eye contact.

Nolan was shaking his head. Did that mean no, he didn't remember her or no, he didn't like what was happening?

Clare's eyes blinked several times as if she was fighting back tears. Iggy noticed, too.

"She's changed quite a bit since you last saw her. Perhaps it's the habit that is confusing you. Clare, would you please remove your veil?"

Clare pulled the veil and headband off her head. Her fine mousy-colored hair was pushed away from her face, stuck in place by years of wearing the headdress. A few strands from the top clumped together and fell over to the side. She looked bird-like, fragile, vulnerable, just like that pig liked them. She turned her head slowly to face him.

"Never saw her before," he said. Grace could see the lie in his eyes. He knew exactly who Clare was.

Even as he said that, he seemed to force himself to look away from her. He took in Bernie, then Grace. Grace held his look. She wanted him to remember her for as long as he lived, however long that would be. He turned to Iggy. "What..." his voice croaked. He cleared his throat and started again. "What is this all about?"

"It's about atonement and redemption, Francis," Iggy said. Nolan stared at her for a long moment, then moved to get out of his chair. Grace stepped out from behind the couch, blocking his exit. She didn't have a gun, but she had her fists and knew how to use them. She squared her shoulders and dipped her head, beckoning him to come forward. Do it, bastard! Come and get it.

Nolan dropped back into his chair.

"We'll be happy to hear whatever you have to say, Francis, after we each tell our stories. Grace first."

"Danny Johnson was my son. You remember Danny. Don't deny it." She pulled the photo out from behind her back and held it up. "Look at him. This was when he was a little boy, his whole life ahead of him." She handed the photo to Bernie, who propped it up on the coffee table facing Nolan.

"Here's a poem he had written after he met you. My sister found this hidden under his bed after he died.

Like a swan beats his wings,
My mind escaped,
Like a smoky tendril dissipates,
My soul scattered,
Like last year's rose blackens and falls,
My heart withered.
Yet I go on.
Why?

"That is what you did to him. It wasn't just touching him. It wasn't just pleasing yourself with a boy. You reached into his heart and his mind with your sick shit and you twisted him, made him dark, made him hate himself, made him hate the world. Fucker. Babyfucker."

Iggy gave Grace a look but didn't interrupt.

"And he started drinking and drugging with a death wish. He didn't want to live anymore because of what you did to him, you twisted useless piece of shit."

Nolan was stuck to the chair like a bug with a pin through it. He didn't even squirm while Grace talked. He didn't blink, his eyes were wide like a deer in the headlights. Grace felt a surge of power. She was in that guy's head. Whatever she said now, he would live with for the rest of his life – however long that was.

She shifted to her good leg. "Iggy thinks you should have a chance to own up. I said, nah, Nolan will never apologize. Because he doesn't think anything he did was wrong."

His mouth flopped open. It felt like only the two of them were in the room. Her and Nolan. She was faintly aware of some sniffling nearby and torrential rainfall bashing against the ground.

There wasn't anything more for Grace to say. Iggy was wrong. This wasn't making her feel any better. She was unsatisfied, like back when she was drinking and using. She needed something, beer or pot or a line, to make her feel right again.

"Thank you, Grace," Iggy said. "I know how difficult this is for you."

Yeah, well, Grace thought. *I said my piece and that codfish pedophile is just sitting there.*

"Bernie?" Iggy prompted.

"Danny was my nephew," Bernie started. Grace felt a sudden softness for her. She hadn't said Danny was her son.

"He was living with me when he met you. I was working at the diocese office, book-keeping. You probably don't remember me 'cause I was mostly in a back office when you fannied about. I worked hard, long hours, taking care of Danny and my little sister after our parents died. So when you took an interest in him, encouraging him to become an altar boy, coaching the basketball team, taking him to swim meets and camping, I thought 'wow, here's a great male role model for the boy'. Sure, I was grateful to have someone take him off my hands for a few hours, but if I'd known."

Bernie stopped talking. She swallowed hard and scraped at her eyes. Grace wanted to reach out to her, touch her somehow, console her. She let one hand drop, her fingertips barely grazing Bernie's shoulder. Bernie took her hand, and held it tightly, her own fingers still wet with tears.

"No one told us. It wasn't the first time you did something like this. We found out later. And the Church knew. Oh, you betchya, they knew. You got caught before, and they just sent you somewhere else, finally dumping you on us because we were poor. No one important or influential in our parish, so they figured what the hell, no one would complain. And if they did, no one would listen to them. And the kids wouldn't ever tell. Not with all the shame. Not even Danny. It wasn't until after he died that we found out what you did to him. It was right there in his poems. I read your deposition. I know what you said. I have it right here."

Bernie pulled a piece of paper out of her pocket and read aloud. "I have absolutely no recollection of this reported abuse and I believe in my innocence." She looked at him. "Still saving your ass but everyone knows. Everyone."

Nolan had pushed himself as far back into the chair as he could get. "You don't understand."

"Like hell, I don't, you useless piece of shit!"

"I was a victim. I was a victim too."

***

IGGY HAD BEEN WATCHING Clare. When Nolan said he'd never seen her before, she winced. The veil was wadded up in her lap, her limp hands resting on top of it. Iggy tried to catch her eye to give her a smile, a show that someone here understood her pain, but Clare's look was fixed in the middle distance.

She had picked up Clare's story in bits and pieces over the years. Margaret Monaghan had taken the name of Saint Clare, who bore a life-long devotion to Francis and his teachings. Saint Francis and Saint Clare had a partnership, of sorts. One could understand how people might view their bond as marriage-like although the Church was quick to deny any kind of romantic love, much less intimacy.

In Clare's mind, there was a spiritual union between herself and Francis Nolan. Lord knows what he told her. It was apparent he had exploited her vulnerability. For her to hear that Nolan was a serial pedophile, and not the man of her dreams, would destroy her construct of reality.

Iggy had made a terrible mistake bringing Clare to this lodge.

Nolan's voice interrupted Iggy's thoughts. "You don't understand."

Grace was twitching like she was being electrocuted. "Like hell, I don't, you useless piece of shit!"

Nolan's voice cracked. "I was a victim."

Grace launched herself. She had to move around the couch before she could get to him. Iggy stood, blocking her way.

Nolan moved quicker than Iggy thought possible. Knocking his chair over, he shoved the couch Clare and Bernie were on between himself and Grace, pinning Iggy against the fireplace. Iggy felt the fire's warmth on the back of her legs. Pinpricks stabbed at her calves. Grace tried to climb over the jumble to get at Nolan.

"You're on fire!" Bernie yelled, pushing Grace out of the way. She fell to her knees and began batting at Iggy's skirt and stockings. The acrid smell of burnt synthetics filled Iggy's nostrils. With Bernie on her knees, the couch in her way and Grace blocking escape, there was nothing she could do but pray.

Clare twisted in her seat, her eyes following Nolan out of the room. "Brother Sun?"

Iggy now saw it all. Clare's repeated recitation of the prayer written by St. Francis, the Canticle of the Sun. In her mind, Nolan was Brother Sun, "beautiful and radiant in all his splendor", and Clare Sister Moon, "clear and precious and beautiful" and they had both been made by the Lord Most High forever traveling through the sky, not together, but sometimes within sight of one another.

"Brother Sun!" Clare squirmed and climbed over the couch. She ran after him and was out of the room, as her veil slid to the floor.

This was all Iggy's fault. Clare was on the precipice of a break-down. Nolan had burrowed more deeply into denial. And Grace was angrier, if that could be possible. No one had been redeemed.

***

GOING DOWN WAS A lot faster than climbing up, Tom thought. He might as well just sit on a mudslide and ride it all the way down. He couldn't get any more wet or filthy. Just as he began to seriously consider it, he tripped on something with his left foot, reached out with his right hand to catch himself against a tree, having forgotten that it was broken. Pain shot through his arm like icepicks. He jerked his hand back, tumbled, rolled through the mud, twigs cracking beneath him, until he felt his head crash into something hard, saw a flash of white light and then everything went black.

***

ROGER FELT SOMEONE NUDGING him. He was in that twilight between sleep and wakefulness, fighting hard to stay asleep. Sheila was trying to get him up, go do something on her honey-do list. It was his day off. He wanted to sleep.

"We need to head back down." It was a man's voice. Where was Sheila?

He realized his head was laying on a table, his neck aching. He opened his eyes and saw Lester.

Roger pulled his head up. A river of drool had run across his cheek. Bits of pot twigs and leaf were stuck to his face. He brushed them off. He straightened his glasses. "How long have I been out?"

"Long enough," Lester said. "We got to get back down before the others get up. There'll be hell to pay if someone sees us, Bernie'll see to it."

Sheila would too. No, Roger remembered. Sheila won't. He felt like he was floating. His wife was gone and there was no one to tell him what to do. He envied Lester. Bastard. He had everything. He had a wife.

Chapter Twenty-Seven

FRANCIS NOLAN WAS LAYING on his bed, fully clothed, bags packed. He was ready to go at first light.

The scratching on his door stopped. The whimpering too.

It had to be that crazy little nun, Clare. She had looked familiar but he couldn't place her at first. He'd worked with so many children. Hundreds over the years. How was he expected to remember each one?

He was safe in his room for the moment. It was just as he suspected. They had lured him here. Turns out they wanted him to confess. He thought he was done with all that after the settlement. No more court. No more depositions. It was a blur. Two, almost three years, of strange faces and strange places and everyone staring at him like he was last week's fish dinner.

One thing he remembered clearly was the instructions the Church's attorneys had pounded into him: fake confusion. "I'm sorry, I don't understand the question," he would say to the plaintiffs' lawyer, "Could you rephrase that?" Or sometimes, for variety's sake, he would say "I'm sorry, I have no recollection of this reported abuse. I believe in my innocence." Over and over he said that. Hours and hours. Days and days.

When he first testified, he was terrified. He had spent a lot of time with the Church's attorney, rehearsing what could be expected, one attorney pretending he was the plaintiffs' attorney, another attorney acting as his counsel, a paralegal pretending she was a court reporter. So when that first deposition got under way, he knew what to expect. He still remembered the first question.

"What is your understanding of the Church's sexual harassment policy?"

He countered with his "I'm sorry, I don't understand the question." When he recited the memorized response, he was terrified that something bad would happen. But nothing did.

The attorney smoothed his tie, then asked, "Before you met my client, had you abused any other children?"

"Objection!" the Church attorney said.

"I don't understand the question," Nolan said. They weren't children and it wasn't abuse.

"What don't you understand? The word 'children'?"

The lawyer was trying to make him look stupid. He wasn't stupid. He wanted to know what did he mean by "children"? Babies? Toddlers? Pre-teens? Teenagers?

"Can we get some definitions here?" the Church attorney asked.

"Would you like me to start with the definition for 'is' and work my way up from there?"

"Your choice, counselor."

Nolan felt like a dead mouse being batted around by two cats.

"I suggest you move it along, counselor," the Church attorney said.

"I'll go to the next question when your client answers the first. This deposition will continue from day-to-day until it is completed."

"No," Nolan said. "I didn't abuse any children." He couldn't take it anymore. But it didn't end there.

"Where were you on June 15, 1992?"

"I have no recollection."

"Did you take several teenagers on a camp out on that date?"

"I have no recollection."

"Was there a cabin on the premises?"

"I have no recollection."

"Where did the children sleep?"

"As I've told you, I don't remember a campout so how would I know where the children slept? What children, by the way?"

Every once in a while, the Church attorney would get in an argument with the plaintiffs' attorney and they'd all take a break to go to the bathroom and smoke a cigarette, and then do it again.

After a while, Nolan began to see the frustration in the plaintiff attorneys' eyes each time he said he didn't understand. But he did understand. He understood the questions just fine, they wanted him to admit he was molesting children and that the church knew about it.

If he screwed up the deposition, the Church wouldn't protect him anymore. Or so he thought at the time, so he played dumb. Later, they threw him away when they were done with him. That wasn't fair.

As soon as he got out of this hellhole, he was going back to his small dormered room in his sister's house and he was going to write his memoir and then everyone would understand that he was the victim. He conjured his Oprah fantasy again. She'd call him on the phone, begging him to come onto her show. Well, that was silly. Her assistant would call his agent and then there would be an excited call from the agent. He would be flown to L.A., or New York, or wherever she does her show, a liveried chauffeur would meet him at the airport with a sign bearing his name and whisk him off to a luxury hotel where room service delivered two-inch steaks so tender it was like cutting through warm butter.

It was quiet in the lodge now. The only sound Nolan could hear was the incessant rain. Sheets and sheets of rain.

He reached out in the darkness and felt the cool handle of his packed roller bag next to his bed. He had bought it when the invitation to Alaska had come. The old suitcase he brought when he moved into his sister's house had fallen apart. After he brought the new bag home, he hauled the old one to the garbage can in the side yard and stuffed it in as far as it would go. He stood back, admiring the image. It was the last thing he had left of his priesthood and he had thrown it away. He felt enlivened. A whole new life ahead of him, the author.

And here he was, stuck with these miserable people who wanted to drag the whole sordid mess up again.

Maybe he should wait for the police to come. That biker woman was trying to attack him when he ran to his room. She looked like she knew how to hurt people. Francis Nolan didn't know how to defend himself. That was one thing they didn't teach in seminary. Of course, they didn't. Because boys were supposed to be safe in seminary.

How long would it take the police to get there? Now that it was all out in the open, now that he knew why they had brought him here, there was nothing stopping them. What were they going to do? Kill him. What else could they do? Would they haul him all this way just to yell at him? Would they come at him in one group? Or would someone jump him in the hallway? Knife or gun?

Staying locked in his room all night wouldn't keep him safe. It was a hotel. Someone was bound to have a master key.

Or he could escape. There must be a boat. Lester had talked about going across the bay to Seward the morning before.

Did Maeve Malloy know how to operate a boat?

***

KING KELLY COULDN'T TASTE coffee anymore. He had drunk it through the night and now his hands were jittery. He still had hours until the medical examiner would arrive from Anchorage and they could take a boat across to Fox Island Lodge.

Mud had dried on the floor from troopers coming in and out all night. King got up from his chair and stretched. He couldn't face sitting down again. So he went into the supply closet and got out the mop.

It felt good to be moving around as he swished the mop across the floor, watching the rope strands drag in its wake. The sharp scent of floor cleaner obliterated the ozone he had been smelling all night.

King washed out the mop in the kitchen sink without getting his uniform wet, returned it to the supply closet, cleaned out the sink, and made a fresh pot of coffee.

He was in the lavatory washing his hands, wondering if he'd ever get that floor cleaner smell off them, when the front door chimes sounded. When he stepped out, he found a tall, filthy man trailing dirty water across the drying floor.

The man coughed and staggered a few steps. His right hand was swollen. His shirt was torn. On his forehead was a lump the size of a bird egg. He was covered in mud, even his face and hair. His cowboy boots would be ruined. Cowboy boots. Lantern jaw.

"Tom?"

Sinclair fell into the visitor's chair. "Call Maeve."

"Can't. Cell tower's down."

King went back into the kitchen, poured the biggest mug of coffee he could find, doctored it with milk and sugar, and brought it out. He set it on the desk.

Tom picked it up with both hands, took a taste, and then chugged half the mug. "Good."

"What in God's name happened to you?"

"I tripped," Tom said. "You got a boat?"

***

"It's Seward," King said. "Everyone has a boat."

Sarcasm, that's what Tom got for being polite. "Give it to me."

"Are you crazy? You can't cross in this weather, you'll drown."

"I got here, didn't I?"

"There's no light. You can't see where you're going. You could end up out to sea."

Tom threw himself back in his chair. "Fine. First light, then. Got any clothes?"

King found an old trooper uniform hanging in the back. Tom took a shower in the locker room. Hot clean water felt good. It took a long time to get the soil out of his hair, using just one hand. His busted right hand was numb except when he bumped it. When he came out of the locker room, clean and dry, wearing the old uniform with pants and sleeves that were too short for him, rain was still pounding outside. He peeked out the window, looking for a streetlight he knew was there, and saw a dull distant yellow glow. Otherwise, gloom all around.

A half-empty box of donuts had appeared on the desk while Tom was cleaning up. He grabbed one as King stirred the computer mouse until the screen came to life.

"What do you know?" Tom asked.

"We always suspected there was a pot grow operation. They don't have a license but no big deal since we just legalized pot anyway. Thing is, they aren't selling through the normal distributors. They have that one guy that keeps coming and going, the slope worker, Roger Wadsworth. Just like clockwork every four weeks, he gets off shift, rents a car in Anchorage, takes a boat across the harbor, spends the night, and leaves again the same way he came. He's smuggling the stuff to California. You'd think they already got all the pot they need down there, being so close to Mexico but everyone knows Alaska pot is special. Maybe he has, what do you call it, a boutique market? Not that it matters. Growing pot is okay under Alaska law but transporting it across state lines is still a federal offense, so we've been watching."

Tom shoved the last half of a glazed donut in his mouth, gulped the coffee, and reached for a jelly donut. These were the best donuts he'd ever tasted in his life.

"You should have someone to look at that hand." King said.

"Later," Tom said. "You got anything else?"

"That's about it for the owners. There's an ex-cop over there, Teresa McNair. She's a nun now."

"You're shitting me."

King shrugged. "And they got an ex-priest over there, Francis Nolan."

"A nun and a priest? Sounds like a joke."

"Two nuns."

There was no such thing as coincidences.

"The priest was one of those pedophiles. You know, all those lawsuits? The church paid out millions because of him and the next thing you know, they depriested him or whatever they do."

"Read me all the names."

"Here's the funny thing. Seems like all the women are related. They were having some kind of family reunion. Sheila Wadsworth, Bernadette Parker, Sister Ignatius, and Grace Miller. Before they got married, or joined the convent, they all had the same name: McNair."

"Go back," Tom said. "Who's who?"

"We got Sheila McNair Wadsworth, the dead woman. Her husband is Roger Wadsworth. Teresa McNair is now Sister Ignatius. Margaret Monaghan is Sister Clare. Francis Nolan, the ex-priest. The lodge owners, Mary Bernadette Parker formerly McNair and her husband Lester Parker. And Grace McNair Miller who did some serious time."

"For?"

"Manslaughter."

"Who'd she kill?"

"I didn't get the charging documents, just a report of the conviction. She was just released from prison. Looks like she came straight here."

Tom mulled over the facts. "And they're family."

"Most of them anyhow."

"Except the kiddy-diddling priest and the one nun."

"And this Bernadette got a big settlement from the Church because her son was one of the victims."

"Where's the son?"

"Died before the settlement came through. Motorcycle wreck. He drove head-on into oncoming traffic."

Tom slammed his coffee cup down. "Jesus!"

"What?"

"Frontier justice. That's what. They're going to even the score." And Maeve Malloy, the love of his life, was in the way of a revenge killing.

Love of his life?

Where did that come from?

Chapter Twenty-Eight

"WAKE UP," A MAN'S voice whispered in Maeve's ear. She was in court, standing at counsel table, the judge watching her, everyone waiting. She turned to exchange that last one look with Tom before she began closing argument. He wasn't in his seat. She searched the courtroom. He wasn't hanging around the door either.

"Wake up."

Where was Tom? She couldn't start without him. Something was wrong. She could feel it, but she didn't know what it was.

"We need to get out of here." That wasn't Tom's voice.

What, leave in the middle of closing argument? The judge would have her hide.

A loud bang. Water rushing. She was dreaming. Her consciousness was being hauled to the surface. Wait, no! She needed to figure out what was wrong first.

Her eyes opened.

In the early morning twilight, Francis Nolan was standing over her, looking furtively out the window. Maeve recoiled. She took inventory. Under the bedcovers, she was fully clothed. How did she get here? Did she get drunk last night? What about her sobriety? Her AA friends? What would Tom say?

The last thing she remembered was dinner. No, it was after dinner. In the lobby with the other guests. Bernie hovering over Maeve. Hot chocolate. There was no booze in it. Maeve would have noticed. Since she got sober, she could smell alcohol from across the room. Besides, when someone, anyone, handed her something to drink, she sniffed it first just to make sure. She was certain. There was no liquor in that hot chocolate.

"What are you doing in here?" she asked.

"Your door was unlocked."

That doesn't mean he's allowed to walk in. Did she need to explain that to him, a grown man?

A second bang. It sounded like a car backfiring. There weren't any automobiles on the island.

Maeve sat upright, threw the covers off. She pushed Nolan aside and looked out the window. A birch tree on the edge of the woods had fallen, headfirst downhill, dirt-covered roots reaching out nakedly into the sky. Its crashing down would sound like...

Bang, a third one. That was no tree falling. That was a gunshot.

***

MAEVE RAN INTO THE hallway. Iggy was disappearing around the corner, dressed in a bathrobe, her short gray hair uncovered. Sister Clare was standing just inside their room door, a bathrobe pulled around her. Woman's voices were shouting from the other side of the lodge.

"Wait! Don't leave me!" she heard Nolan yell.

When she turned the corner into the dining room, she saw Bernie, Grace, and Iggy clustered near the window. Grace was restraining Bernie, who struggled to get away. Iggy disappeared into the kitchen just as someone pounded on the back door.

As Maeve came into the kitchen, Iggy swung the door open and Roger stumbled through.

He fell on the linoleum, soaked from the rain, and scrambled across the floor. "Shut it! Shut it!"

"What about Lester?"

"Bear got him."

Bernie tore out of Grace's grip. "You left him out there?"

Roger cowered. "He had the gun. He told me to run. What was I supposed to do?"

***

THE WOMEN GOT BERNIE calm enough to sit down. Bernie's two hands were wrapped around a tumbler full of whiskey. Iggy had an arm around her. Grace poured another tumbler for Roger and shoved it at him. Maeve looked on, forgotten.

"There was nothing I could do," Roger said. "Lester had the gun. We got all the way around the dead moose when the bear came at us, out of nowhere. I was ahead of Lester because I had the flashlight. He yelled at me to run and then he started shooting. Then he stopped shooting."

"And you left him," Bernie said.

"There was nothing I could do. He had the gun."

"Wait a minute," Maeve said. "Why in God's name were you out there?"

Roger looked at Bernie, apparently for permission to speak.

She shook her head. "I give up. What's it matter now?"

"We were taking down the pot grow," Roger said. "We were afraid the cops would find it."

And there you have it. Maeve knew it all the time, but she didn't have any evidence. Now she did. The alibis that didn't fit together were probably cooked up because one, or all, of them had been doing something with the grow operation the night Sheila was killed. Maeve checked the clock on the wall. Just past 4 a.m. It'd be light soon and the troopers would come.

"But he's out there. He could still be alive. He might be bleeding. He needs our help. We can't just leave him out there." With each declaration, her voice rose. Bernie lunged for the door. Iggy and Grace pulled her back and forced her back into her chair with one on each side holding her down.

***

After the Malloy woman ran down the hall, Nolan went back into her room. No one would find him there. He turned the lock, walked across the room, and took a seat at the desk, maneuvering the rolling suitcase in front of him for protection.

The banging sounds had stopped. There was pounding somewhere, then crying and yelling and then it all got quiet again.

The room door pushed open. Nolan clutched the suitcase handle.

The crazy little nun walked in, wearing only a t-shirt and underpants. Her brown hair was cut short. She had one of those faces, small and delicate, that made her look like a child even though she had to be in her twenties. Blood was streaming from slashes on her thighs.

"Brother Sun?" she asked. "Remember me? Sister Moon."

Mary, mother of God in heaven, yes. Now he remembered.

***

GRACE HAD NEVER SEEN Bernie hysterical before, gulping for air, shuddering, wailing. She must have really liked Lester. Grace poured a glass of water, put it in front of Bernie and took the whiskey away from her. The noise was getting on her nerves.

She kicked Iggy's chair leg for attention. When Iggy looked up, she jerked her head toward the swinging doors. Iggy rose to follow Grace and Maeve Malloy slipped into the chair next to Bernie.

Roger looked up. "Where are you going?"

"Be back in a minute. You stay here and keep an eye on things," Grace said. She wasn't worried Roger would trail after them. He was good at following instructions from years of being married to Sheila.

As soon as they were out of the kitchen, Grace rounded on Iggy. "Not going as you planned?"

"The plan didn't include you attacking Nolan."

"So this is my fault? Everything is always my fault. I could be a thousand miles away and still you'd blame me."

"Of course not. Get a hold of yourself."

"Nolan didn't confess. He's locked up in his room. Sheila's dead. Lester's dead. Bernie's insane. Any minute now she's going to tell the lawyer everything she knows."

"Then why did you leave them in the kitchen alone?"

"We need to talk. Look, the storm is passing over and the cops will be here soon. We didn't get what we came for."

"It's too late for that."

"Bullshit. This is why we're here. This is what kept me alive. You don't know what it's like being locked up with a bunch of crazy women year after year, waiting for the moment when you can go home to your family. And when I got out, my boy was gone. That man killed him."

"Come now, Grace. He drove his motorcycle head-on into a car. It wasn't an accident. And his blood alcohol..."

"You're saying he wrecked his bike because he took after me? Is that what you're saying? Drunk and a drugged up? So it's all my fault?"

"No one's saying—"

"My boy wasn't into drugs before Nolan got his hands on him. You should know this stuff. Abused kids get into drugs and alcohol because they can't handle what happened to them. He killed my boy. And he got away with it. It isn't right. He needs to pay for his sins."

"He will. No one escapes the Lord's divine justice."

"Is that all you can think about? What about my Danny? What about all those other kids? Is burning in hell going to fix it for them?"

Iggy gripped Grace's arm. "Focus. We have a problem. Our little sister is dead. Lester is dead. Did it occur to you that Roger was the last person to see either of them alive?"

***

Maeve was sitting beside Bernie, trying to make her feel better. She never was good at this emotion stuff. That's why she had gone to law school instead of becoming a psychologist or something where you had to understand people's emotions and respond to them. She didn't know what to do. When she patted Bernie's arm tentatively, Bernie pulled away.

The gush of tears had subsided to the occasional sob. Bernie looked at the glass in front of her and seemed to realize that it was just water, then searched the room for her whiskey.

She spotted it on the counter and crossed the room just as the door swung open. Iggy and Grace came in. Bernie stood and walked over to meet them.

With all three woman, Grace, Iggy, and Bernie, in Maeve's field of vision at one time, they all looked alike. How could that be? Her eyes were playing tricks on her. Maeve blinked. When she focused again, they were standing together, not speaking, just staring at each other. They all wore some version of a t-shirt and sweatpants. Maeve was shocked to see Iggy bareheaded, even though she had followed her to the kitchen.

The resemblance between the three women was striking. They were about the same height. Same denim-colored eyes set in square faces. The same mousy brown hair in various stages of graying.

Bernie appeared to be the oldest of the three, but not by much. She's the one always working, always getting stuff done. As kids, she would have been the responsible one. Grace the biker chick was the troublemaker and Iggy, the cop turned nun, the peacemaker. When Maeve thought of them that way, they fit together.

They were sisters. And they had kept that a secret from Maeve until after Sheila was murdered. Why? Was Nolan's paranoia based on truth? Had they lured him here? Did they murder Sheila? Was that part of the plan? Did she know something? Did a bear really get Lester or did Roger kill him? Was he in on their secret too?

Why would they kill Sheila? Bernie stood guard shooting at the bear when the body was brought inside. She was horrified when she saw what had happened. It was a surprise to her. She couldn't have faked that much emotion if she had murdered Sheila.

Grace, the biker chick, had a hard look. She could kill someone. Her alibi, Bernie and Lester, was weak. Still, she had no motive that Maeve had detected. If Grace killed Sheila, why would Bernie and Lester cover up for her? Or were they lying to cover up the pot grow?

"Why did you lie to me about the family reunion when I first came here?"

They turned to her in unison. Iggy spoke. "We didn't lie."

"You withheld a material fact. You know as well as I do, that's the same as lying."

Grace said, "You don't know anything."

Iggy continued. "We didn't intentionally deceive you. Before we came, we agreed to act as if we were strangers. Not because of you."

Iggy took a moment to compose her thoughts. In the silence, Grace spoke again. "Because of him."

"Francis Nolan?" Maeve asked.

Grace answered. "He needs to pay for what he's done."

Bernie stifled a sob. Iggy took her hand and led her back to the table.

"What's going on?" Maeve asked.

Grace was still standing by the door, her arms crossed.

"Join us," Iggy said, beckoning to her sister.

Grace stood her ground.

"Please."

Grace relented. She crossed the room, pulled a chair out, and sat down, closing the circle.

Roger spoke. "Do you need me for this?"

***

NOLAN LOOKED FOR AN escape. There were only two ways out: the window and the door. The window was high in the wall and didn't look big enough for him to get through even if he climbed on a chair. Even if he did get out, the bear was out there somewhere.

That left the door. The girl who called herself Sister Clare, he couldn't remember her real name, blocked his way. She was with the group in front of the fireplace for cocoa and recriminations earlier tonight. When she first pulled off the veil, he hadn't recognized her. He hadn't the time to figure it out before that crazy woman attacked him.

The girl was little. He could push her over and run out.

Then he saw the knife in her hand.

"Brother Sun, you have come back to me." She stepped towards him arms outstretched for an embrace.

Could this weekend possibly get worse? He needed to escape. Where were the others? What had that banging sound been and why had the Malloy woman run away? Why wasn't she back? He needed to stall for time, until something changed and he could run out of the lodge and hide in the woods until the police came. "I'm sorry," he said. "You've mistaken me for someone else."

The girl stopped. Her lower lip began to quiver. She looked confused. She spoke in a small voice. "No."

No? No one had ever said that to him before. People didn't say "no" to Francis Nolan. Even the lawyers in that last meeting when he asked to speak to the bishop personally did not say "no"; they said, "Sorry, he's not available."

Nolan needed to take command of this situation. After all, she was not much more than a school child. "Young lady..."

"No!"

Chapter Twenty-Nine

MAEVE DIDN'T WANT TO give Roger time to cook up a story. They had believed him when he said he had nothing to do with Sheila's death. Now Lester was dead too. The fact that he was the last one to see both of them alive was too much of a coincidence and Maeve didn't believe in coincidences. "If you could just remain in your seat a little bit longer, Roger, I have some questions for you."

"What kind of questions?"

"Explain to us again, if you would, what happened the night Sheila died."

"That was last night, wasn't it? Or the night before last. I've lost track of time."

The trick to questioning a suspect was to build a consensus with him. "I see your point. It's almost morning now, so the night before last. Can you tell us what happened?"

"You were all there. Why do I have to go through this again?"

"She was our sister," Iggy said. "We want to understand."

"Fine," Roger said. "Can I get something to drink?"

Grace got up and poured a tumbler full of whisky, set it in front of Roger, and then resumed her seat at the table. Roger took a sip, winced, and then took a long drink.

"The night before last," Maeve prodded.

"We were all in the conference room, supposed to see some slides, you remember, right? Then the generator quit working so there was no electricity and we couldn't see the show. Everyone went back to their rooms. After a while, Sheila started in. She'd been drinking a lot that night, more than usual. She just wanted some attention and I didn't feel like getting into it with her. So I went to sleep. The next thing I knew it was morning. I found all you guys in here." His eyes darted to the place where Sheila's body had been. "The rest you know."

"And that's it?"

"Just like I said. Like I've been telling anyone who asked. She was trying to pick a fight with me. My therapist said the best thing to do was get away from her. I couldn't, not in the lodge. So I did the next best thing. I went to sleep. I figured she'd wear herself out eventually and come to bed."

She wasn't convinced of his innocence. He drank heavily and could have easily killed Sheila in a black-out and not remembered. "You didn't know she had left the room."

"No idea. But you said there were cigarette butts. She was supposed to have quit smoking so she snuck around when she wanted one. She must have gone outside to grab a quick smoke. Used to be the last cigarette before bedtime was her favorite."

He looked like he was going to cry again. Maeve needed to redirect him before he became too emotional to talk. "Tell us about tonight."

"Lester said we had to take down the grow because the cops were coming. So we waited until dark and headed up to the cabin. There's a dead moose right in the middle of the path. Lester had shot it the first day we were here to keep the group from hiking up that way. He figured a bear would come along, or at least he could say that a bear had come along, and he could scare everyone into staying away."

"There was bear scat on the beach," Maeve said. "There was a bear. Lester had to have seen it."

"Yeah, well, as it turns out there was a bear," Roger said. "It had eaten most of the moose but the carcass was still there. So Lester took a shotgun with us. We didn't see the bear on our way up."

"Who had the gun?" Maeve asked.

"Lester did. He wouldn't let me carry it. Said he was afraid I'd trip and shoot him on accident."

"That makes sense," Bernie said.

"Thanks loads."

"And then what?" Maeve asked.

"When we were done working, we wanted to get back to the lodge before morning so no one would know we were gone. And then the bear got Lester."

"Take me back," Maeve said. "You left the cabin on your way downhill. Explain exactly what happened."

"I was in front with the flashlight. Lester was behind me with the gun. When we got to the moose, we went into the woods, going around it, just like we'd done going up to the cabin earlier, and then I heard this crashing sound."

"Did you see anything?"

"The noise was behind me."

"And then what?"

"And then Lester shot. He yelled something. 'Bear', I think. I can't be sure. And I took off running. And then I heard screaming. It was a sound like I'd never heard before. I'll never get it out of my mind for as long as I live." Roger lifted the whiskey glass to his lips and emptied it into his mouth.

Inside the room was silence. Only the howling wind and undulating rain could be heard.

She believed him.

"You're exhausted," Maeve said. "Why don't you go back to your room and I'll come and check on you in a little bit?"

"Fine with me." Roger said and dragged himself out of the kitchen.

***

"No!" Sister Clare said again, holding up one hand in a stop gesture, the other still gripping the knife. Nolan remembered when she was a child, she had that underdeveloped boyish body that fascinated him. She still had it. And she never talked much. That's why he liked her.

"Most High, all-powerful, all-good Lord," she began praying. "All praise is Yours, all glory, all honor and all blessings."

It was the Canticle of Brother Sun and Sister Moon. He remembered teaching her that prayer. It was a favorite of his and he had taught it to many young people. That first time with her, she had brought him cookies while he was working on paperwork in his office. She had come to him. It had to mean something.

When he invited her to pray with him, they knelt together, face to face, so close he could smell her shampoo. He held her small clasped hands inside of his. At first, she trembled. She seemed afraid of his touch. Then he felt a shift in her. She relaxed.

He waited until the prayer was over before he pulled her close. She opened up to him. She liked him; he could tell. She held her breath when he touched her but she didn't pull back. She let him go on. And when he asked her to do something special, she was so very eager to please him.

She was almost done with the prayer now. He felt a rushing and warmth as his little boy stiffened.

"Praised be You, my Lord through Sister Death, from whom no-one living can escape. Woe to those who die in mortal sin! Blessed are they She finds doing Your Will. No second death can do them harm. Praise and bless my Lord and give Him thanks. And serve Him with great humility."

She put the knifepoint to her upper arm and dragged it slowly across her flesh. Beads of blood oozed from the slash.

Wait! This wasn't how it was supposed to go.

**

MAEVE LOOKED ROGER OVER. He was still shaking and pale. While he told them what had happened, he hadn't shown any signs of lying, the sudden widened eyes, or laughter, or shifts in body language, but he could have been a really good liar. He could have killed Lester, for reasons unknown, and Sheila as well. Because nine times out of ten, the husband did it.

To Bernie, she asked, "Are you certain Lester would not have let Roger carry the gun."

"There's no way. Roger is a clumsy ox. Can't we go check on Lester? Maybe he's still alive."

"We don't have a gun," Grace said. "We have no way of defending ourselves."

"There's no reason you can think of why Roger would kill Lester?"

Grace barked a laugh. "Roger? Kill Lester? Roger wouldn't kill anyone. He hasn't got it in him."

"He wouldn't have killed Sheila in a drunken fight?"

"Sorry, if anyone was getting beat up, it would have been Roger. Sheila would have kicked his ass."

"I'd have to agree," Iggy said. "It wasn't Roger."

"This wasn't supposed to happen," Bernie said.

"What was supposed to happen?" Maeve asked.

Iggy rested one hand on Bernie's and spoke. "Atonement. I had hoped that if the family could share their pain with Nolan, there would be a chance for healing."

"Back up," Maeve said. "How was Nolan responsible for the family's pain?"

"I'll start at the beginning," Iggy said. "Our parents died in a car accident when we were young. Bernie was nineteen at the time, old enough to take over the family responsibilities. Sheila was just a baby and Grace had Danny already. I joined the force and left home.

Grace got into some trouble. So Bernie ended up raising them together. Several years ago, Grace was in a motorcycle accident in which a man was killed and she went to jail for vehicular manslaughter. It was decided it would be best if Bernie legally adopted Danny."

"And that's when it happened," Grace said.

"Francis Nolan was the parish priest," Bernie said. "He took an interest in Danny."

Grace shot a look at Bernie. Iggy noticed. "It wasn't Bernie's fault. It happened to a lot of innocent people. They trusted the church which allowed the priests to take advantage. It wasn't just him. It was priests all over the country, all over the world. It's been going on for centuries."

Iggy returned to the story. "Danny spun out of control. We had no idea why. When he passed away, Sheila told us what she had seen. She was just a child and didn't realize what was happening. She had caught them in the pantry together. To this day, she believes, believed, that nothing happened."

"Then we found his poetry. It all made sense. The sudden change in his behavior. Before a good, honest, hard-working boy. Afterwards, secretive and self-destructive. And then we found out t Nolan had been doing things to the other children."

Maeve had heard about the lawsuits. Millions of dollars were paid out by the church to victims and their families for abuse that had been going on for decades. The church knew. The abuse was so rampant it was part of the institution. And once complaints rolled in about a particular priest, the church covered it up by moving him to a new locale. It only started defrocking the offenders when lawsuits were filed.

"The money to buy this place?" Maeve asked.

"Came from the settlement," Iggy answered.

"And you brought Nolan here." It wasn't a family reunion. It was a reckoning.

"Because he got away with it," Grace said. "He needs to pay."

If Iggy wanted atonement, what was the gun for? It wasn't hard to guess. "The gun is yours," Maeve said to Grace. "You planned to kill him."

"You have it? Iggy stole it from me."

"It was for you own good," Iggy said.

Grace bolted up, knocking her chair over. "Who the hell are you to decide what is for my good?"

Bernie winced. "Do you have to do this now?"

Iggy stood slowly. "I'm going to check on Roger."

As Iggy walked out the room, Grace called out to her, "I'm not done with you yet."

***

IGGY HOPED THAT SHE'D have a few minutes before someone followed. It was well past time for morning prayer and Clare hadn't come looking for her. She would be concerned when she woke up and found Iggy gone. The yelling should have attracted her attention, even if the shotgun hadn't.

Last night after Nolan ran from the room, Clare became hysterical. They were still in the lounge. Grace had run for a first aid kit to treat Iggy's burns. Bernie was sitting next to Clare on the couch, an arm around her shoulders, calming her the way she had done with Danny and Sheila when they were little. Iggy had admired Bernie's ability to mother and was jealous at times when the children responded to her. It was not an emotion she wished to nurture. Jealousy, envy, and greed were poisonous. As deadly as lust.

When Grace returned, the first aid kit was tucked under an arm. In her hands were one of those little blue pills she had stolen from Nolan's room and a glass of water. She showed it to Iggy. Iggy nodded.

"Take this," Grace said, handing the pill and glass to Clare.

Clare put the pill in her mouth and took a sip of water. After Iggy's legs were covered in ointment, Grace and Bernie helped them back to their room. By then Clare seemed to be sleep-walking. So Iggy wasn't surprised when she slept through the gunshots.

Clare had been fragile as long as Iggy had known her. She had scars on her legs and arms from self-mutilation. As a social worker, Iggy knew that was a symptom of child abuse, most likely sexual abuse. She had put two and two together, remembering that when Clare was a child, she would have been accessible to Francis Nolan. He had raped her. She brought the young nun here hoping that she'd come to terms with what happened, heal and move on.

Clare had first seen Nolan again when they gathered for the slide presentation. Afterwards, she seemed lost inside her mind. The next day, Iggy noticed the blood stains on Clare's robes. She had started cutting herself again.

It had never occurred to her that Clare had taken the name of the woman who was Saint Francis' partner in life because of Nolan. Francis and Clare were such common names amongst the faithful. Now Iggy realized that Clare took that name because she believed she was Nolan's soulmate.

It had been a mistake to bring her here.

Clare needed a professional who could give her far more help than Iggy could. Hospitalization and treatment. Medication. It was grandiose for Iggy to think she could heal the sick. Pride was yet another corrosive emotion and it had snuck up on Iggy. She thought she was helping.

When she opened the door to their room, she found Clare's bed empty and unmade. The bathroom was empty too. In the sink, she saw the little blue pill Grace had given her the night before. Clare had spit it out.

"Help me!" It was a man's voice coming from another room. Iggy ran into the hallway.

"Someone please, in the name of God, help me!" Nolan yelled. The door to his room was closed. The pleas weren't coming from that direction.

"Can anyone hear me?"

Maeve Malloy's room door stood open.

Iggy found herself standing in the threshold. Clare's back was to her, wearing a boy's sleeveless T-shirt and white cotton underwear. She was so skinny, her shoulder blades protruded like angel's wings. Blood was streaming down her arms and legs.

Nolan cowered in a corner on the far side of the room, holding his suitcase like a shield. He was staring at something in Clare's hands before he noticed Iggy.

"Help me! She's insane!"

Clare turned to see who Nolan was talking to. That's when Iggy saw the knife in her hand.

Chapter Thirty

AFTER SISTER IGNATIUS LEFT the kitchen, Maeve held her tongue hoping the remaining sisters would settle down. Grace was clearly an adrenalin junkie; conflict fueled her high. She would jump on anything Maeve said to work herself up. Bernie was quiet too, apparently from years of dealing with Grace's anger.

Bernie stared into her glass of whiskey. Grace paced the room a couple of times, then pulled her chair upright and sat at the table again.

There was something missing. Something Maeve had overlooked. Last night, just before she drifted to sleep, Bernie had served cake and cocoa. Maeve was surprised at how quickly she had lost consciousness. Not even booze did that to her in the old days. Chocolate certainly never did.

"What was in that drink you gave me last night?" Maeve asked Bernie.

"Just a little something to make you sleepy."

"Why?"

"Weren't you listening?" Grace asked. "We had ourselves some restorative justice. We needed you out of the way."

Maeve had heard about restorative justice programs, where offenders and victims meet to work out restitution. She'd heard anecdotes of good results, that the meetings helped victims move on and the offenders were less likely to hurt people again. Yet she had her doubts. She suspected that people could not be taught empathy. They could fake it for a while, but if there wasn't a place in their heart or head, or wherever that trait lived, in the first place, it could not be conjured into being.

"You mean you all confronted Nolan last night?"

"Yepper," Grace said.

"And what happened?"

"The sonofabitch denied it all."

Figures. Maeve heard the word spoken in Tom's voice.

"And Grace attacked him," Bernie said.

Grace shrugged.

Maeve pictured the scene. Nolan was sitting across the room in an armchair. Iggy was sitting on the other side of the fireplace. Bernie and Grace were moving around the room And Clare was sitting next to Maeve on the couch, her hands trying to cover a red splotch on her robes.

Clare had cut herself. Self-mutilation was behavior typical of child abuse victims. It was beginning to make sense. She was part of this, not just a companion. Maeve would let them explain it to her. "Clare isn't a member of your family. Why was she here?"

"Iggy brought her," Grace said. "He got to her, too."

If Clare was cutting herself, she had a knife.

Maeve was on her feet and out the door before she had time to come up with a plan.

***

A THIRD WAVE PUSHED Tom further under water. He had just broken through to the surface and was gulping for air when it came. His mouth was full of salty sea water. His lungs, starved for oxygen, were fighting to open his throat.

He was drowning.

The last thing King Kelly did after he showed him to the skiff was to hand him a compass. Even though Tom knew these waters, he took it without argument. It'd be easy to get turned around in a storm.

Tom shoved his gun into the back of his pants and pulled the motor's chord. It coughed to life and he headed the boat into the choppy water. He kept the shore on his right until he cleared Caine's Head and then headed southeast, using the compass, towards where he knew Fox Island should be. The skies were just starting to lighten and a smudge of land was before him. He thought he could see the lodge. When he looked down to check his bearings, a big wave had come up and swamped the boat. Tom found himself in the water, struggling to figure out which way was up.

Something light-colored went by. He figured it was the boat skimming the surface. He swam to it and climbed up the inverted hull, pulling his body half out of the water. The wind was shoving the boat, and him, back towards Seward. He pushed off and started swimming towards the island. That was when a second wave pushed him down. He fought it and had just risen to the top when the third hit him.

Wasn't that how people drowned in cartoons? Their heads would bob under water as they held up one finger. They'd come up and go back under again, holding up a second finger. The last time, their arm would disappear beneath the surface with three fingers in the air.

Is this the stupid shit people think about when they're dying?

Tom always knew he was going to die someday. God knows he should have been dead by now. But he be damned if today was the day.

He clamped his finger and thumb on his nose figuring it'd send a message to his lungs to stop demanding air. At the same time he kicked and pulled with his free arm. The busted hand had quit hurting, probably because the water was so damn cold.

See? My luck is changing already.

***

"Clare, darling, put the knife down," Iggy said.

Clare cocked her head. She seemed confused.

"I'm your friend, Sister Ignatius. Remember me?"

"He came back," Clare whispered.

"Who is that, who came back?"

"Brother Sun. We're going to be together forever now. We were married. He said so. In our souls. We were joined together in holiness."

What a sick bastard. If Iggy ever prayed for him, it would be well into the distant future.

Nolan whimpered. "I have no idea what she's talking about. The girl is crazy."

"Shut up, Nolan," Iggy said.

She took a step towards Clare. If she could get close enough, she could take the knife. "This is joyous news, indeed. Let me congratulate you."

Clare was beaming like a new bride. What Nolan had done to this child's mind was criminal. He should be in jail. Punishment would have no effect on him but at least he wouldn't be able to harm any more children.

When Iggy was standing within arm's reach, she said, "Oh, gosh, you're bleeding."

Clare looked down. "It's nothing."

That was Iggy's chance. She grabbed for the knife.

Clare was faster. The swipe was so powerful, it threw Iggy across the room. She didn't feel the slash when it first happened. She felt nothing. That must be what self-cutters were looking for: that one moment right after the blade penetrates them and their mind goes blank.

***

When Tom's head broke through the surface, his only thought was air. He gulped, swallowed a mouthful of water, and choked. He had to breathe in again, he was starved for oxygen. As soon as his lungs were full, he blasted the air out clearing seawater with it. In a few breaths, the system was working as it should.

Where am I?

He treaded water, turning around slowly, looking for landmarks. The compass was gone. It had been in his hand when the boat was swamped. It was gone now. From his point-of-view, right at sea level in a storm, everything looked the same.

The sky was lighter in one direction from the sun rising behind thinning clouds. He kept moving his arms back and forth as he felt his legs sinking. Those damned cowboy boots had filled with water and were weighing him down. If he didn't get rid of them, he'd never make it to Maeve.

He pushed himself up, took in a big breath, then shoved his head under water. When he tugged on one boot, it felt like it was locked onto his foot. He stuck his hand down inside, making room for more water to rush in, then with all the strength he had, he pulled that boot off.

He came back up for air, took a couple of breaths until his body felt satisfied, then grabbed for the second boot. It was locked onto his foot. If he could have cut his leg off, he would have. Then he remembered there were killer whales in these waters. To them, he'd look like easy pickings, a big something already floundering and too tired to escape. He focused on a light inside his mind, grabbed the boot heel with his good hand, and shoved his busted hand inside, wrapping it around his ankle and pulled. The boot seemed to be stuck to his foot. He pulled again. A current of cold water washed over his toes. He pulled a third time. And he was free.

When his head was above the surface, he tried for his bearings again. This time he saw an orange glow on the horizon. There was only one thing that could make that color in the woods.

Fire.

***

Maeve was running toward the guest rooms when she heard the scream. As she rounded the corner into the hallway, it stopped. She halted, listening. If she tried a room by room search, she might not find them in time. She wouldn't need a key; the doors looked flimsy enough to kick in cop-style.

"Please Mother Mary, send someone to save me!"

It was Francis Nolan. When she last saw him, he was hiding in her room. She ran the length of the hall to her own open door.

Nolan was huddled in the far corner of the room, holding the desk chair in front of himself like a lion tamer.

Iggy was on the bed, blood pouring out of a slash on her arm. She gripped the wound with her other hand, trying to staunch the bleeding.

Clare was stepping from side-to-side, waving the knife first at Iggy then at Nolan. Blood oozed from gashes in her legs and arms.

"You cannot come between us," she said to Iggy. "Our union is holy."

Iggy saw Maeve. She frowned and shook her head. A warning.

"The girl is insane," Nolan explained to Iggy. "I don't even know her. I don't know what she's talking about."

The knife pointed at Nolan, silencing him.

"Who was that woman to you?" Clare said to him. "The one you promised to meet outside. You were going to run away with her, weren't you? I heard you."

Clare must have been eavesdropping from her room. She would have needed to open her door just a bit to hear what was being said. She had probably gotten up after Iggy had fallen asleep so she could sneak into Nolan's room.

Nolan looked at Iggy. "Help me."

"She was Sheila McNair," Iggy said. The knife swung at her now. "She was my sister. Do you remember her from catechism?"

"Sheila?"

"That's right. My little sister. You were about the same age. She was Danny Johnson's cousin. Do you remember Danny? They lived in a big house with my sister Bernie."

"Danny?"

The knife swung back at Nolan. "Danny. I saw you. Coming out of the pantry."

She waited for Nolan to answer.

"I'm sorry," he said. "I don't understand the question."

"You were going to run away with Sheila. You promised me we would be together forever." Clare jabbed the blade at him.

He screamed again and dropped the chair.

She drug the knife across her arm, hissing. "You'll enjoy it. It feels good. Let me show you. That's a good boy. Just close your eyes and pray."

The closet was within reach. Maeve could see the pistol butt sticking out from under the blanket where she had left it. She couldn't let Clare kill Nolan. He needed to stand trial for what he had done. She reached up and slipped the gun out.

When Iggy saw what Maeve had in her hand, she struggled to get off the bed. "No! She's ill. She needs help."

Maeve didn't want to shoot. "Clare, can you hear me?"

The little nun froze.

"Where did you get the knife?"

Clare turned around and looked at Maeve.

"From the kitchen. There's lots of them. Did I do something wrong?"

"Did you stab Sheila?"

"I had to. They were running away together. She stole him from me."

"You don't really want to hurt anyone..."

Maeve was shoved into the wall by someone from behind. Arms reached around her clawing for the gun.

"Give it to me!" It was Grace.

Maeve threw her weight back as hard as she could. They collided into the opposite wall, Grace taking the brunt of the impact. Her arms loosened just enough for Maeve to break free.

Maeve turned to face her. Grace came at her again and Maeve shoved her in the shoulder, sending her sprawling into the hallway. It was the least dangerous move she could think of to stop the woman.

Nolan shrieked.

When she turned back around, Nolan was holding his hands in front of him and Clare was swinging the knife back and forth, slashing his palms and fingers. He rolled into a ball. Clare raised the knife over her head.

Maeve leveled the gun. *Holy mother of God, pray for us now* passed through her mind just before she pulled the trigger.

Chapter Thirty-One

Tom crawled onto the beach and collapsed. Rocks dug into his chest and thighs. The lodge was silhouetted, black against the orange glow of whatever was burning behind it. Flames licked the roof.

People should be running out, but no one was. Were they all dead? Maeve too? Was the murderer in there holding everyone hostage at gunpoint? Was that the point of it all, to burn everyone alive?

He pushed himself up to a stand and reached for the pistol he'd stuck in the back of his pants when he boarded King's skiff. It was gone.

***

Maeve turned when she heard running in the hallway.

Bernie appeared. "What was that? Did I hear a gunshot? The generator caught fire. The lodge is burning down. Everyone out! Out now!"

Smoke roiled along the ceiling. The air smelled of burnt wood.

"Wait!" Maeve called. "We have hurt people. I need your help!"

Bernie was turning to leave but stopped when she noticed Iggy. "Oh, dear God, Iggy are you okay?"

Grace shoved Bernie out into the hall. "Bernie, you get Roger. He's probably passed out. You need to get him up and moving, make sure he gets out."

"What about you?"

"Just go, will you!" Grace slid an arm under Iggy's back and hauled her off the bed. "You should have shot him," she said to Maeve as she jerked her head towards Nolan.

The gun was still in Maeve's hand. Clare laid crumpled on the floor at Nolan's feet. He was staring at her in horror, blood splatter on his face.

"Is she still alive?" Grace asked.

Maeve crossed the room and turned Clare over. There was a hole in her shoulder, but her eyes fluttered.

"Right now, she is. Grace, you take Iggy and I'll carry Clare."

"Are you crazy? She killed Sheila."

"And she will stand trial for it. Now get moving or we're all going to die."

By the time Grace and Iggy had hobbled into the corridor, cinders were floating in the air and the ceiling was blackening. Maeve tossed the gun onto the bed and lifted Clare into her arms, as one would carry a sleeping child. She was so light, Maeve wondered how she could possibly be alive. She must have been starving herself for years.

"What about me?" Nolan whimpered.

"You have two feet. Use them."

They'd never get out the back exit. The fire roared. Flames licked the walls all the way to ceiling. Cinders spat from the furniture and mattress piled up against the door. Maeve headed towards the front door, following Grace and Iggy, when Nolan yelled, "Help me!"

A loud crack and groan ran along the ceiling overhead. Smoke stung Maeve's eyes. Heat burned her skin. The lodge was collapsing around them.

"Run!"

The run to the front door felt like being lost in a funhouse. Smoke hid her landmarks, the stairwell, the conference room, the opening to the lobby. She couldn't be sure she was running in the right direction. She could only pray.

When she made it to the massive wooden front door, she found Iggy leaning against a wall, holding her bleeding arm, her head lolled back. Grace pulled on the large iron door handle with all her might.

"Crap," she yelled over the fire's roar. "I locked it and put the keys in my office."

Maeve looked at her, incredulous. Who was she locking out? The bear?

"To make sure Nolan wouldn't run away last night."

They turned in unison to look for the back exit. All they saw was flame.

"What about the kitchen door?" Maeve asked.

"If the back hall is gone, so is the kitchen. Here, you keep an eye on my sister and I'll get the keys." With that, Grace ran in the direction of her office, disappearing into a wall of smoke.

An ax crashed through the front window. Glass splintered in every direction. Maeve thought she was hallucinating. Clare's weight felt even lighter. Maeve wondered if she had died. Iggy was sliding down the wall, unable to hold herself up any longer.

The fire roared and blasted towards them. Maeve laid Clare in Iggy's lap and covered them with her own body. She spread her arms to shield them, waiting for the flames. How long it would take to die? Had Grace been consumed in the fire already? Nolan?

A figure emerged from the smoke. Now she was certain she was seeing things. Tom was standing before her. He started slapping her head.

"What the hell?"

"Your hair's on fire. Hold still."

It was Tom. Hallucinations didn't smack you.

He brushed his hands off on his pants. "Is there anyone else?"

"Grace is in the office."

"The biker chick?"

Maeve nodded.

"Found her. I sent her out the front."

"Bernie and Roger. They left first."

"Saw them on the beach."

"And there's a man back there." She pointed into the flames. Nolan wasn't yelling anymore. A cross beam collapsed in the hallway barring anyone from going back to Maeve's room through the lodge.

Tom lifted Clare up and tossed her over his shoulder fireman-style, then pulled Iggy to a stand. "Get moving!"

"What about..."

"Too late for him," Tom said. "Help your friend."

Iggy staggered alongside Maeve as they followed Tom and Clare through the smoke, sidestepping smoking furniture and shards of glass. Once outside, they staggered towards the people standing on the beach: Grace, Bernie and Roger. The sun had risen somewhere behind the storm clouds, enough to see the three of them clustered together. The woman were clutching each other. Roger was sitting on the rocks.

The rain felt good at first, the coolness of it saturated Maeve's clothing and soothed the burning in her arms, face, and back. Then the droplets began to sting.

Tom laid Clare down on the rocks, took off his shirt, and wadded it, pressing it into her wound. Her head rocked back and forth as she tried to push him off.

"Sit still so I can hold this in place," he said.

Maeve sat Iggy down next to Clare. She stood over Tom, noticed the soaked T-shirt sticking to his ribs, and soaked trooper trousers clinging to his legs, and the trooper shirt he was using to staunch Clare's bleeding. He was barefoot. Given Tom's low opinion of cops in general, she never expected to see him in a uniform.

"Your clothes," she said.

"Mine got wet. I had to borrow some," he said.

Everyone was wet. But that didn't explain why he was wearing a drenched trooper uniform. And why he was here on this beach. "Yeah, but..."

"Yeah, but what?" Tom asked.

"What are you doing here?" Maeve said. What a stupid thing to say.

Iggy, who had been sitting, slumped onto the rocks. Maeve knelt beside her. She pulled off what was left of her hoody, as Tom had done, and held it against Iggy's arm. The bleeding slowed.

Tom said, "Where should I be when the woman I love is in danger?"

"Hey, what's going on here?" A man's voice called out.

Maeve looked up to see King Kelly and three troopers jogging towards her. A big state trooper boat was docked and more men were running up the pier.

"My husband," Bernie said, clutching at King. "He's up in the woods. A bear got him. He might still be alive."

King pointed to two troopers. "You two go with her. Find him."

"Bear?" Tom asked. "What bear?"

Maeve, Iggy, Clare, and Roger were surrounded by men carrying medical bags. Out of the corner of her eye, Maeve noticed Tom drift off with King.

As the medics separated the survivors to better evaluate them, King came back. "Tom says there's someone still in the lodge."

"Francis Nolan," Maeve answered, pointing to where the guest rooms were engulfed in flames.

"Maybe he got out the back," King said.

"No way," Maeve said. "The exit was blockaded. That's what caught fire first."

"We'll check anyway," King said as he grabbed Tom's arm. They took off trotting alongside the building.

"You got some nasty burns, there," the medic working on Maeve said. His name plate was inscribed "J. Stephens." "I don't want to touch this stuff. We need to get you to a burn unit."

Another medic leaned into the conversation. "We need to run down to the boat for the stretchers. Keep an eye on this one, will you? The bleeding's stopped."

"Sure. What about the other one?" Stephens said, indicating Clare.

"She's unconscious but she'll be okay," said the man working on Iggy. With that the two men strode away. Stephens squatted over Clare, looked her over, then spun on his heels so he could take a look at Iggy.

Maeve closed her eyes. Her bones ached. She wanted to sleep until next spring. If she laid down on her back, the burns, now searing, would hurt even worse if that was possible. She didn't want some doctor picking pebbles out of her back. So she curled up in a crossed-leg forward bend and rested her forehead on her fists.

Her mind drifted to that second when she lifted the pistol and aimed. She had a choice. She could have let Clare murder Francis Nolan. She chose to stop it instead, a decision she could live with. She had pointed the pistol at Clare's midsection, as Tom had shown her, knowing fully that she might kill the nun. He'd told her that shooting at legs and arms to wing the bad guy only worked in movies. If you pointed a gun at someone, do it with the intent to kill them and be willing to accept the consequences. It was only because of her terrible aim that Clare was not injured more seriously.

Tom had found her. How did he know? He'd said something after they escaped the building. Something that didn't register.

"Hey, where did she go?" Stephens asked.

Maeve heard rocks crunching beneath boots as he rose to his feet. She opened her eyes. It took a few seconds for her vision to clear. Iggy was laying in front of her, still unconscious. Roger and Grace were in the distance, huddled together under silver space blankets. When the medic stepped away, Maeve saw that Clare was gone.

Up at the burning lodge, a shadow flickered near the fire. "There!" Maeve pointed.

Stephens ran to catch her but he was too late. Clare passed into the flames and the roof crashed to the ground, shooting embers exploding from the impact. He halted abruptly and threw an arm up to protect his face.

Maeve felt herself go cold. Clare had just walked into the fire to find Nolan. Did she understand he should already be dead? Was she too ill to understand the difference between life and death?

King and Tom appeared, striding towards Maeve.

"Where is the girl in the underwear?" King asked.

"She just ran back in."

Stephens returned. He was crying. "I tried to stop her."

Clare had faked being asleep more than once so she could sneak off when no one was looking. "She ran in just before it collapsed," Maeve said. "No one saw her go. There was no way you could have stopped her."

There was shouting in the distance. "We need a hand! He's still alive, but pretty torn up," called out one of the two troopers who had followed Bernie into the woods. They were carrying Lester between them with Bernie trailing.

Two medics came up the pier carrying equipment. The troopers set Lester on the ground and the medics went to work on him.

That's when Tom's words registered. Did she hear him right?

"Wait a minute," Maeve said, turning to Tom. "What did you say?"

Chapter Thirty-Two

THE COFFEE WAS TOO hot to have any flavor. Maeve sipped anyway, burning her tongue. Her hands shook. She was quaking under the space blanket she clasped with one hand, cold despite her burns. She was wearing only her jock bra and jeans. A medic had cut off her hoody and t-shirt when they were still on the beach.

Everyone was crammed into the Seward trooper station. King Kelly was behind his desk, coordinating the medical evacuations from his land line. Another trooper, barely old enough to be out of high school, was passing out paper cups half full of scalding coffee.

"She's going into shock," Tom said. He was squatting beside her. He planted a thumb on her eyelid and pulled it up, staring at her nose to nose.

She tightened her grip on the blanket. "What the hell do you think you're doing?"

He dropped her eyelid and stood. "She's fine."

"I'm just cold."

The first medevac helicopter had taken Lester up to Anchorage. Bernie had begged to go along but they told her there wasn't enough room. She was now sitting with Grace at a table in the kitchen behind King's desk, each staring into the distance. As Maeve watched, Bernie took her sister's hand, neither of their expressions changing. Iggy was on a stretcher, with medics on either end, waiting for the second helicopter to land any minute. Roger was by himself across the room, sitting beneath a corkboard neatly covered with wanted posters, grasping his paper cup in two hands between his legs. His lenses were fogged but he made no attempt to clear them.

It was still drizzling outside. Soupy mud and gravel trailed from the door throughout the office. A wring mop in a bucket was propped up in the corner, its stringent disinfectant odor permeating the room. Tom had wandered to the two medics standing over Iggy. They spoke in hushed tones and looked at their watches. He then went to a window, wiped the condensation off with the blade of his hand, and peered outside. He shook his head.

King put his phone down. "It'll be here any minute," he said referring to the next helicopter. "And there's another one right behind it." After Iggy was transported, Maeve would be next. Roger, Bernie, and Grace were not injured, physically. They would be driven to Anchorage after the flooding subsided and the roads were passable.

King came around his desk and took the chair beside Maeve. "Can you tell me what happened out there?"

Maeve was suddenly aware of the burns on her back and arms and the smell of burnt hair. She put the paper cup on the floor and raised her arm to whisk her hair off her shoulder, her fingers finding only air. She must have done that move ten times since the beach, always surprised to find her hair was gone, burned off. Someone had given her a shot dulling the pain, but not quite killing it.

"They had it all planned," Maeve said. "They're all sisters, you know. Bernie, Grace, Iggy, Sheila. They lured Nolan here because of Danny, Grace's son."

"I thought he was Bernie's kid."

"Grace had him when she was a teenager. Bernie ended up raising him because Grace was in and out of jail. She raised Sheila too."

"Where were the parents?"

"Car wreck," Roger called out. He pulled of his glasses and cleaned them on the hem of his t-shirt, and then put them back on. Bernie and Grace were still sitting at the table, listening to the conversation.

"Nolan had abused Danny when Nolan was a priest. They brought him here for justice but they couldn't agree on a plan. Iggy had brought Clare along too because she had also been one of his victims. Then Clare somehow got the idea that Sheila and Nolan were running away together so she killed Sheila."

"I don't get it. What did she care what Nolan did?"

"Clare was fragile," Iggy said in a quiet voice. "She had problems before she met Nolan. In her mind, their union was holy. She joined the convent so she could be closer to him."

"I still don't get it," King said.

"It's like Stockholm Syndrome," Iggy said. "She was just a child, already saddled with emotional problems. In those days, people didn't understand psychological disorders the way they do now. She just seemed a little different. But he sensed her vulnerability and he took advantage. He paid attention to her. He made her feel special. She didn't understand it was wrong. Her mind made the suppositions it needed to in order to normalize what was going on between them. She thought it was love."

Tom turned from his vigil by the window. "Sick bastard."

"I thought if he took responsibility, it would give her a chance to heal."

Maeve picked up the thread. "So after Clare killed Sheila and I started asking questions, the sisters had to change their plan. They wanted to get him alone so he'd confess. They doped me up to get me out of their way while Lester and Roger went up to the cabin to take down the pot grow operation."

"And the bear got Lester."

"Roger had just come back to tell us when I realized the only wildcard was Clare. Sheila's death was not part of the plan the sisters had cooked up. If Roger had killed his wife, he would have planned it better. Lester had no reason to kill her. And as far as I could tell, Nolan had no connection to her. So it had to be Clare. That's when I found her and Nolan together."

"The girl in her underwear that ran back into the fire?"

"That's Clare."

"God rest her soul." Iggy crossed herself.

"Were they?" King asked. "You know."

"Because she was in her underwear? That was her doing. When I found them, she was dressed like that, threatening him with a knife and he was cowering in the corner. I can't explain it."

"He denied her," Iggy said. "When we confronted him and she took off her veil, he denied knowing her. She must have thought if she appeared to him as she had been as a child, he would recognize her."

The whomp-whomp of helicopter blades approached. "It's here," Tom said, opening the door. The medics lifted Iggy's stretcher and carried her out. Tom shut the door just as the phone rang. Kelly picked it up.

"Your chopper's circling overhead, Maeve. As soon as the last one gets off the ground, you're on your way."

The words Tom had said on the beach echoed in Maeve's mind. They had been spinning around, pushed down by the need to answer questions from the medics and from King, but then rose again when she was left alone. She looked over at Tom. He was staring out the window. He seemed to sense her watching him and turned. "What?"

Was her mind playing tricks on her? Had she heard it wrong? She prayed she hadn't. It felt right. She and Tom. All the time they had spent together. How well they worked together. He had always been there. And when he wasn't, she felt incomplete. The room suddenly grow quiet. It felt like everyone was watching her.

"What?" Tom asked again.

"I, uh, what you said on the beach. Did you really mean that?"

She heard another helicopter settling on the tarmac, the engine purring, the blades beating. Now it felt like everyone was watching Tom. "Your chariot has arrived, Counselor."

The door opened and two medics stepped inside, water dripping from their shoulders. "Where's the patient?"

"Over here," King said.

One of the medics came to her side. "Can you walk?"

Maeve pulled herself to a stand. The medic took her arm while the other stood ready to open the door. As she shuffled across the linoleum, she looked over the medic's shoulder at Tom.

"I'll see you back in Anchorage." He gave her a wink. "Real soon."

THE END

Hope You Enjoyed Hell and High Water

Help readers find their next great book by leaving a review:

https://www.amazon.com/gp/product/B0CT4V45K

Acknowledgments

It takes a village, as they say, to raise a child or to keep an author glued together. There are many people to whom thanks are owed and I pray I do not omit any of those intrepid. Without their support and input, this book could not have been possible.

A big thanks to my beta readers, ory Bryant, Jean Clarkin, Penny Cordes, Angie Garza, Jacqueline Green, Coralee Hicks, Cynthia Kuhn, Jenni Legate. Without betas, a writer is lost inside her own mind wandering around in the land of underdeveloped characters, plot holes, bad metaphors, and misplaced modifiers, a miserable place indeed. You were my lifeline.

As much as one would hope, a writer doesn't know quite everything and for this, we have experts! I wish to thank Elizabeth Amann, formerly Sister Luke, for the nun-related matters and Ron Newcome for the inside scoop on all things Seward. Your support was invaluable. Any factual inaccuracies are mine.

And a big thanks to Mila Cover for the gorgeous book cover!

Finally, to my daughter, Rory Bryant, sounding board, beta reader, copy editor, supplier of coffee, bringer of flu medications extraordinaire, thank you for your support above and beyond the call of duty.

Author's Note

I WAS SIX YEARS old in 1962 when my mother enrolled me in parochial school in Spokane, Washington. For recess, we were sent out in single-file to a black-top playground surrounded on three sides by tall brick buildings, the fourth was barricaded with a chain link fence. It looked, and felt, like a prison. A nun or lay teacher would stand in the school doorway supervising us lest the girls wander over to the boys' side or vice versa. One day, the priest appeared – on the girl's side of the playground – and a clutch of girls swarmed him. I was told that girls, not boys, could visit his office and be given wax candy lips but they had to be old enough, in third grade, because he didn't like first and second graders. At the time, I was in second grade. My mother pulled me out of that school at the end of the year for reasons unrelated to the priest.

I am now practicing law in Anchorage, Alaska. A few years ago, the Alaskan courts exploded with the cases filed by Alaska Natives who had been abused by Roman Catholic priests in rural villages. There were hundreds of victims. In some villages, virtually every child had been abused.

When the stories first started coming out about priest abusers, I was probably not alone in hoping that these were isolated incidents, a few bad apples. I was wrong. The abuse has been part and parcel of the Church institution and culture for centuries. If it were not for the very brave Jane and John Does who told their stories, it would have continued unchecked as long as the Church survives. The Church's recently adopted policies, ostensibly laudable, would not have come about if it had not been forced to account publicly.

This book, *Hell and High Water*, is my witness to the legacy of the abused. What happened to them never goes away. It can never be made right for them. The scars will be handed down, passed from generation to generation, in one way or another. The only thing that can be done is to save future generations of children.

I got off cheap when my mother pulled me out of that school. As I sat down to write this note on New Year's Day 2020, I checked the online database of credibly accused priests. A priest with the same name as the one on playground in 1962 was listed. htt p://www.bishop-accountability.org/priestdb/PriestDBbylastName-A.html.

For further reading: *Sex, Priests, and Secret Codes*, with Thomas P. Doyle, A.W.R. Sipe, and Patrick J. Wall, and *Betrayal, The Crisis in the Catholic Church* by the investigative staff of the Boston Globe, the basis for the motion picture, *Spotlight*.

About the Author

Keenan Powell is the Agatha, Lefty, and Silver Falchion nominated author of the Maeve Malloy Mystery series.

Despite being one of original Dungeons and Dragons illustrators, art seemed an impractical pursuit – not an heiress, wouldn't marry well, hated teaching – so she went to law school. The day after graduation, she moved to Alaska.

She is the author of the Maeve Malloy Mysteries, a three-book series, and numerous short stories. She belongs to Mystery Writers of America, Sisters in Crime, and International Thriller Writers. She writes a legal column, Ipso Facto, for the Guppies newsletter, First Draft, and blogs with Miss Demeanors.

When not writing or practicing law, Keenan can be found embroidering, oil painting or studying the Irish language.

Follow her at:

Amazon: https://www.amazon.com/stores/Keenan-Powell/author/B0788TKBJW

Facebook: https://www.facebook.com/keenanwrites

Goodreads: https://www.goodreads.com/author/show/17008872.Keenan_Powell

Bookbub: https://www.bookbub.com/authors/keenan-powell

Also By

Bonus: Implied Consent
Chapter One

I love the law. The law is my life.

When I stepped out of the courthouse, microphones were thrust in my face. Television cameras jockeyed for a better angle while besuited young women and men gazed up at me, cell phones cradled in hand, poised to thumb my words to the masses.

Woe befalls she who misspeaks on a hot mic. I rehearsed soundbites silently.

An old glory-hound once said to me, "Maureen, if you want to get on-camera, give reporters short phrases that can be cut up into soundbites. And if you don't, talk in long-winded, Latin-laced nonsense."

I wanted on camera.

I set my briefcase down on the cement landing, a cue to senior reporter Mickey Wong. She raised a hand. "Ms. Gould, what is your reaction to the verdict?"

"On behalf of my client, I thank the jury." Little red camera lights began to glow. "Today's verdict affirms that sexual harassment will not be tolerated."

Mickey's hand was still up. "Does your client have a statement?"

"He's happy to be vindicated, but no amount of money will compensate him for what he's endured." It's never about the money. But when criminal justice fails, money is the only way society manifests its judgment.

Anthony Paredes—"Tony," to his friends—had been a chubby-faced twelve-year-old when he enrolled in the Lafayette Academy. Tony's parents had chosen Lafayette for the chess club, tutored by a former champion who hadn't quite made it. Tony loved the game and was good at it. His parents hoped that they had another Bobby Fischer on their hands.

The chess coach, Oscar Wenderholm, took a special interest in Tony. Appealing to the parents' ambition, he easily talked them into private lessons.

Young and confused, Tony never told anyone what really went on. He was sixteen years old when the assistant principal found them together. Rather than report the crime,

Lafayette Academy gave Wenderholm a severance package and recommended that Tony be transferred to another school.

After years of therapy, Tony realized what had happened was not his fault. He reported the crime to the police. They took his statement, opened a file, and swiftly concluded they had insufficient evidence to prosecute. Too much time had passed. Evidence disappeared. Memories faded. Case closed.

So he'd called me, the hotshot former prosecutor, now champion for the abused.

A delivery truck rumbled by, earning frustrated glances from the reporters. One young man shouted, "Is it true that Lifetime is planning a movie about your case?"

Lifetime? Good God, no. This wasn't a romance. Netflix, maybe. By the time I got back to my office, I should have messages from *Dateline*, *60 Minutes*, and prospective clients. Splashy wins always lit up my phone lines. I gave the boy reporter a frown and scanned the crowd for another question.

Another reporter raised her hand. "The jury awarded a little over fifty million dollars, the second largest verdict of its kind. Are large awards the trend in alleged sexual harassment cases?"

Here was the trap. Something I said could be cut into a soundbite that made me sound greedy.

"Not alleged. Proven." I was shouting, ostensibly to be heard over the truck's clamor, but, in truth, infuriated by the word "alleged." Juries decided what the truth was.

"Our case was proven. We—meaning the judge, opposing counsel, and I—carefully selected a jury that was committed to fairness to both sides. The jurors worked diligently, and we have complete faith in their verdict."

With that, I hiked my briefcase onto my shoulder and pushed my way through the reporters. Yolanda Martinez, my secretary/paralegal/office mom, was waiting for me on the sidewalk, a red patent leather tote hanging in the crook of her arm. We headed across the street to the parking lot where I had left my BMW. When I saw the yellow fender peeking out from behind a sedan, I pushed the remote start button. She rumbled to life.

"That's my girl," I said, patting my Beemer on the hood.

In the privacy of the coupe, we pulled out our cell phones. A text popped up from my soon-to-be ex-husband. "Answer your goddam calls!" I deleted the message and tossed the phone back into my briefcase.

"Have you heard from Jake?" Yolanda asked.

I spiked her a look.

"He's a good man, and you deserve to be happy. That's all I'm saying."

I jammed Sunny into gear and pulled out onto the street.

"You won, girlfriend."

The case had dragged on for two and one-half years. Reams of motions. Countless hearings. At trial, psychologists explained how a child's mind works, that Tony was not capable of consent, and that his delicate mental state was not pre-existing or faked. It was real, caused by repeated rapes.

Today's verdict was the largest, the most significant case anyone in my family had litigated, earning my place in the Gould mythology alongside my venerated grandfather, the Supreme Court Justice, and my father, the senior partner in the most respected law firm in the state.

I reached for the pearl necklace I always wore to court for luck, checking that it was still there. It had belonged to my maternal great grandmother, Elizabeth Shaughnessy. "You're as smart as any of them and smarter than most," Granny Shaughnessy used to say. She would have been proud of me. The Goulds? Not so much. To them, I was damaged goods. Just like Tony Paredes.

Yolanda took a hard look at me. "So how are *you*?"

Before I could answer, a Gene Krupa drum solo erupted from the cell phone in her hand. A man's voice rumbled from the other side—that of my investigator, Eli Conroy.

"It's for you," she said.

"Put it on speaker."

Eli shouted over my engine roar. "Chief, when are you coming back to the office? We have a situation."

"Tony?" My throat tightened. He had seemed stronger in the past few weeks, but he was still a fragile young man.

"Nah. I dropped him off at his place. Hold on." He spoke to someone, assuring that he would be back in a moment. A door closed. "New client. Found her standing in the hallway outside the office when I got back. Been waiting a couple hours. Has a suitcase. Looks like she's been crying."

"What's her story?"

"Won't tell me. She'll only talk to you. Says Mickey Wong sent her, says you're the only one who can help."

Learn more about Implied Consent: https://www.amazon.com/Implied-Consent-Maureen-Gould-Thriller-ebook/dp/B0BKYMP37V